Generation Mars: Blood Red Dust

By

Stuart Aken

Generation Mars: Blood Red Dust

By

Stuart Aken

FIRST EDITION

First Published by Fantastic Books Publishing 2016

Cover design by Gabi
ISBN (ebook): 978-1-909163-50-8
ISBN (paperback): 978-1-909163-63-8

Acknowledgements

Creating a novel isn't a one person task. For this book, I requested suggestions for additional character names, having already decided on most. Ideas came from readers and some of those I used. So, my thanks to Liliana Negoi (summaryofmysoul) for Daiyu and Akash; to Dr Meg Sorick (drmegsorick) for Katniss; to Doren (dreamingd247) for Jiang (river) and Ying (intelligent, clever); to Jennifer Giradin (morristonhousebooks) for Sarm (a clever reversal of Mars); and to Trike for Brigitte (actress who played Maria the robot in Fritz Lang's Metropolis) and Rakesh (first Indian in space, as a cosmonaut on Soyuz).

I also sought suggestions for appropriate expletives for a largely atheistic community unlikely to use the more common ones in use at present. Glen Donaldson (Glenavailable) from Brisbane, Australia, came up with 'For the love of iron oxide!' and Roger Lawrence (threehoodies) suggested using Phobos and Deimos! There were others I liked but couldn't use!

A huge amount of research was needed to get the science 'right' in this novel and I used so many sources it would take another book to name them all. However, I can name and thank NASA and authors Robert Zubrin (The Case for Mars) and Stephen Petranek (How We'll Live on Mars) for much source material.

The team at Fantastic Books Publishing deserve my sincere thanks for their tireless work in getting this book from manuscript to publication.

Finally, an enormous 'thank you!' to my wonderful wife, Valerie Allison, who, in spite of the fact that she doesn't really like science fiction, read the entire manuscript and identified authorial passages, typos, repetitions and inconsistencies. She also kept me fed, watered and clothed for the entire time it took to complete this book.

Intro: 24:13-135.03.49 Acacia Peake.

(If you must know what I look like, follow this *Hololink*. Yeah, cute, aren't I?) Final Year History Student at MU.

Okay, you don't do intros: boring, superfluous. Your loss. Don't blame me when you're confused by aspects of this presentation. This intro's under four hundred words. For an average reader that's less than a minute and a half. Seventy seconds to really enhance your enjoyment. Try it!

Early attempts at colonising Mars were clean, as no native population was displaced, but they weren't straightforward. In those chaotic years, business and political leaders wanted their own selfish ways. Some groups hoped to create Utopia. Others wished an end to all human life. Fortunately, such aims are self-defeating, or we wouldn't be sharing this! Still, some campaigns of hatred and violence did succeed. People died. Bases and their settlers were destroyed. But for the actions of a small, dedicated group of brave people, we wouldn't be here.

This account's compiled from sources on Earth, the Moon, Mars, the Asteroid Belt and space. I've found narratives previously kept secret. I've overcome bias, prejudice, and privacy barriers placed by profit-driven moguls. It's a tale of endeavour, courage, heartbreak and persistence.

As required by the University of Mars in students' work, this is in textual form. Boring! Those we call Generation Mars used technology now fully developed as PanSensory (PaSe). But we have to make do with text! Their reports were given individually or as spontaneous conversations. Annotations show links to further info. Accounts from others might've been recorded voluntarily by participants, or made by spy technology without their knowledge. Each record's headed with its date and time, using the Generation Mars Calendar, or the

1

Gregorian Calendar. They're presented in strict chronological order. And I've generally introduced the individuals making the reports.

Some contain grammatical and spelling errors as found.

Records made by The Chosen form the bulk. They wanted to educate later generations in the history of the planet, so give most info. Their accounts show unusual frankness: Reppod's recording suite purposely had no editing functions, and members could access all reports, so their inbred honesty was encouraged by peer awareness.

I had a bit of help from my grandfather, who guided me to some of these reports.

This is how I compiled the account. Enjoy the read!

Record 01: 14:17-055.01.01 Zaphod.

In the Reporting Pod (Reppod), Zaphod, one of The Chosen, stands in front of a short row of input points complete with 3Dee displays and ergonomic keyboards. Clad in short boxers made from smartfab showing a 360 degree moving panorama of a Mars horizon, he sits at the bench. A young man, with kind blue eyes, blond hair cut short, and a fit and strong body, he keys in the following title before talking.

'These are the Accounts of the First Days of The Chosen on Mars. Experience and Learn; for Here is Your History.'

We were supposed to start this process when we first landed, and continue it daily. But we talked it over on the flight and agreed we'd start once we actually begin the breeding program. So, why am I reporting now, when we aren't even trying to produce the children this account is for? I've been struggling with an issue that would've caused us to abandon the whole idea of colonising Mars.

I've solved it! Had to tell you.

At last, I've established there are no human affective pathogens or toxins in the multiple bacteria we discovered in the underground reservoir. It's not only safe for us to shower, but to consume in any amount we like! We can live and, more importantly, breed here after all, which is just as well, considering the terrible things happening on the home planet. Earth's in a very bad way. Terminal, we think. Well, the planet's okay, but chances of human survival are pretty slim and getting worse by the day. Glad we're on Mars, safe from that insanity.

Record 02: 17:35 – 02/07/2074 WorldWideNewsCorp.com

Televised news report:

An overview of an unidentified submerged city seen from a drone. Isolated tops of former skyscrapers emerge from a turbulent sea. The camera slides by one building as it collapses. A brief but powerful spurt of water and foam momentarily drowns out the sound of the motors. The drone continues over what appears to be an endless, wildly restless ocean, dotted sparsely with small icebergs. No signs of human activity.

A ship finally comes into view, and the drone descends. A small multi-ethnic group of people await its arrival and it lands a short distance from them.

A distant cry of alarm is heard.

The picture scans from the group out to sea again. A waterspout, under dark heavy clouds, approaches. A short period of shaken and tossed images concludes in a deluge of dark water.

We switch to a studio. News presenters, a black man and white woman, both clearly chosen for their appearance, smile at the camera from behind a glass-topped desk. He is bare-chested but wears a brightly coloured bandanna loosely round his neck. She wears a plain red cropped top that exposes her abdomen.

The man speaks. 'Well, folks, I guess that's the last we'll hear from Ocean Explorer 3. Shame those climate scientists were lost, eh?' He turns to his co-presenter; grins at her. 'Don't know about you, Noreen, but I'd never go to sea.'

She smiles back. 'Me, neither, Mo. Still, that's scientists for you.'

He takes a tissue from a small pile on the desk between them and wipes his shining forehead. 'By the fires of Texan oil, it's hot in here today! But not as hot as you! Any other news, Noreen?'

She takes a tissue and wipes her throat, smiles at Mo and then the camera, as she reads text from the autocue. 'Looks like that there war over the water in Arabia's finally over. Their Royal Family escaped by hydrofoil and are making for El Obeid, now Mecca's been destroyed. Long as they keep clear of pirates, they should make it over the submerged sands. Oh, and here's a great sequence by Princess Amani, showing off her latest fashion range. That sheer fabric's threaded with pure nine carat gold, you know. Still, she's got the body for it, so why not?'

Mo, transfixed by the images, fails to realise he's back on camera. Noreen pokes his arm and he awakes to reality. 'Oops! Can't blame a man for watching the bitch, yeah? To other news.

The President has authorised use of maximum force to eradca … eradcat … yeah, that's it, eradicate the packs of dogs on city streets. There's a seventy-dollar bounty for every head you get to your local sheriff. So go hunt those pesky hounds down and make the streets safe to walk again!'

Noreen returns on camera. She's wiping a tissue across her abdomen and looks up, as if caught doing wrong. 'Y'all thought you in for a treat. Not before the watershed, fans o'mine. Anyways, before we take a commercial break, I should let you know the storm over the Carolina's reached them there Appalachians an' there's gonna be some pretty bad flash floods arrivin'. So you folks as clings to those foothills better get your boats ready or you'll all be drownded by mornin'. She laughs at her joke and the commercial break cuts in.

Record 03: 21:01-02/07/2074 High Command Under Sacred Protection of Almighty. (CUSP)

Order sent by CUSP command centre:

Take nucular weapons from them and take them in spacecraft. The World dies already soon, so no waste on that piece shit. On Moon are men and women to be done. And Mars. If convert they become us. All others kill or make slaves till we find proper sacred end.

Record 04: 13:03-06/07/2074 NUKTV

Televised news broadcast:

A man in a dark suit with short trousers, untied garish-patterned yellow and red tie, and unbuttoned striped shirt in purple and fluorescent green, sits against the edge of a desk in a TV studio. Behind him, dark clouds race across a landscape of small hills surrounded by rough seas. He holds a thin tablet and looks up as the camera closes on him.

'It's with great regret, and all that stuff, that I've to report radiation levels around the coasts have now reached critical. No fish are to be caught within seventy kilometres of the shore. Infringement will result in death by drowning when the Sea Police arrest offenders. No joke! Sounds sensible. Don't want folk eating contaminated fish, do we?'

A young woman, in bellbottom clinging hipster pants and bikini top, slides along the desk to rest beside him. He makes a show of gazing at her and she moves a little away before taking the tablet from him and gazing at the camera, adopting a pseudo-serious expression.

'News just in: the war between Pakafghanistan and India is reportedly over, now nuclear weapons are ...' She squints at the autocue. '... exhaustipated on both sides. All communication between forces in

5

Pakafghanistan stopped after the last explosions. Satellite images show all life in the region's either extinct or maybe reduced to mere survival. Still, that's what you get when you fire atom bombs at each other. I mean, like, what did they think would happen?

'And, would you believe, the Indian space rescue mission to their Mars colony has been hijacked? Apparently insurgents from that there CUSP are headed for the Moon bases on the spacecraft. Don't know exactly, 'cos they've cut all coms from the module.'

The pair move out of vision as the broadcast focuses on the large screen in the background, which switches to sequenced images of severe war damage accompanied by martial music.

Record 05: 10:28-061.01.01 Zaphod.

Zaphod, clad in the same boxers, but showing a picture of the Earth slowly revolving against the blackness of space, sits. He speaks with a steady voice in an attractive baritone. He introduces himself as the nominal doctor for the group and explains he's making the first agreed instalment of a projected series of reports. Others will add to it. He explains that the group may soon be entirely cut off from their commanders on Earth. They've decided to record life in the colony before events overtake them.

An ancient pop song, Imagine, by some guy called John Lennon, plays in full before he speaks. He's obviously moved by it. (It's a pretty interesting song, but hardly revolutionary.)

Zaphod's report:

That piece of inspirational popular music has served as a sort of anthem, a musical statement of our philosophy and beliefs. You'd do well to listen and learn.

Looks as though things on Earth have taken another serious turn for the worse. My old home country, the New United Kingdom, which ought to be called the Scattered Island Kingdom, after rising seas divided it into numerous small independent islands, has suffered another setback. Decades ago, authorities were warned against siting nuclear power stations on the coast because of the danger of inundation. Guess what? Typical of Big Business and political leaders, they took no notice and went with the cheapest option, or perhaps the one that put most bribe money in their pockets. Now, all those power plants are completely or partially submerged. Latest outcome: all fishing within seventy kilometres of the coast has been banned due to radiation levels. The entire Irish Sea's included because decades of nuclear waste were stored at Sellafield, on its coast.

But that's a minor issue for Earth. The more worrying concern is burgeoning nuclear war. Again, those who actually cared about the future tried to ban those weapons and get stockpiles reduced to nil. But did the nations' leaders listen? Of course not. Idiots!

Newly-merged Pakafghanistan has been sparring with neighbouring India over a country called Kashmir for years. Pakafghanistan, ruled by a group of multi-faith extremists, a partial offshoot of a slightly less extreme group called the Taliban, declared war. Calling themselves the Command Under Sacred Protection, Cusp for short, their declared aim is to rid the world, in fact the whole known universe, of all human life.

The Cusp, or as we call the moronic fools, the Cult, used atomic bombs against India. Both states now effectively cease to exist. No doubt this local war will escalate and those weapons of last resort, so-called deterrents, will be launched from all over the world. Radiation will destroy most sentient life on the planet. So it looks as though the Cult will get their wish, on Earth at any rate!

I've family, albeit estranged, still living in NUK. They'll probably all be dead within weeks. I tried to raise them before I came in here, but there's too much radio interference to get through.

Sorry to load this on to you who'll one day be exposed to these records. But, if you're to form a realistic picture of your parents, you need to know what we're dealing with in these early days on Mars. We're safe here. But it won't be long before those of us who've left Earth are the only viable representatives of the human race. That makes it all the more vital we succeed in our breeding program.

Record 06: 14:00-07/07/2074 WorldWideNewsCorp.com

Televised live news event:

Outside New United Nations' headquarters in Denver, a gang of camera operators, reporters and onlookers are gathered as the Secretary General slips through the sliding doors. She's surrounded by heavily armed and armoured guards. But she's unshielded; wearing a light business suit with a knee-length skirt. She approaches the ranks of microphones and reporters, leaving her escort to watch her rear, the hem of her skirt flapping wildly in the gusting wind.

'Good afternoon. With sincere regret I must inform the world that atmospheric turbulence has finally grounded all aircraft. No further air travel is possible until the atmosphere returns to normality. It is uncertain when, or indeed if, that will occur. Also, all space travel from the surface of the planet is suspended indefinitely. No nation has the right to risk untold lives by launching a rocket under current climatic conditions. Any such breach of this World Law will result in immediate retaliatory action from the remaining states of the N.U.N.

'It is now universally accepted that runaway climate change is the result of irresponsible activity by various states and industries. Punitive action will be taken over the coming months and years to attempt some redress from those who failed to accept the reality described by the scientific community. It may now be too late to prevent events likely to result in the effective extinction of our species. The planet will continue to exist without us. In fact, it is almost certain to do better than it has with our presence.

'We accept that belief in myth and faith, as promoted worldwide,

8

encouraged people to believe in divine intervention. This was irrational and criminally insane. All those who instruct, preach and otherwise oversee religious institutions are subject to instant execution. The killing of such individuals is hereby sanctioned by the New United Nations. Be it known and understood that a person who executes any priest, imam, cleric, rabbi or any other similar evangelist will be considered a social hero: no crime is involved. There will be no bounty on the heads of these leaders, but their removal should be seen as the absolute duty of rational people everywhere. We have tolerated fictitious deities far too long. It is clear no God exists, and those who encourage such juvenile beliefs must pay for their crimes against humanity. Regretfully, we lack the resources and means to place each of these antisocial creatures before judge and jury and it is for that reason we empower all rational people to rid the world of them.

'Our small group of member nations no longer has the means to subdue those rogue nations led by dictators and despots. We recognise global war is now inevitable as vital resources become increasingly scarce. Our only real hope is that the very atmospheric turmoil that now prevents all flight will adversely affect the use of missiles against neighbours. But be it understood all such attacks will be defended in like manner, regardless of loss of life or other consequences. We will not allow the world to be left to those who place no value on life and use their power to maintain their own self-interested and extravagant lifestyles.

'That is all I have to say to you. I end this brief statement by advising people in all lands to go home, spend the remaining time with families and friends. Life will rapidly become, if not impossible, then very difficult for the foreseeable future. I wish you all the best. But I have no wish to exist in the world we have now created. Goodbye.'

With that final word, she parts her jacket, withdraws a small pistol from within, places the barrel in her mouth, and pulls the trigger.

Record 07: 23:35-061.01.01 Annika

Annika, another of The Chosen, is in Reppod seated at the consoles. Her loose top, in brief bolero style, depicts a scene from a tropical jungle, with bright birds and monkeys moving in the trees. A stunning blonde, she gazes into the camera through penetrating blue eyes that shine with purpose and determination.

She speaks with a hint of a Scandinavian accent, detectable only in odd words as her steady voice relays what she has to say in pleasant tones. There's confidence and strength in her delivery.

Annika's report:

Since Zaphod's started this programme, and I have to be up through the night, tending hourly to my small collection of bird's eggs about to hatch, I've decided to add something to the record.

Introduction first, I think. Annika. Known by all and sundry as Anni; my choice, though not that of my overly conservative parents. As one of The Chosen, I'm supposed to have special qualities. Personally, I think the claims of The Guardian are exaggerated. We're really not that different from everybody else. Clever, skilled, physically well formed. But those attributes result from genetic enhancement, not natural gifts. My own cause for small personal pride lies in my sculpture and painting. Not that I get much time to do either at present. But when I look at the pioneer women who've joined us here, I have to express my admiration for their skills, intelligence, tolerance and, to be absolutely honest, their appearance. Okay, so looks are considered superficial by many. But we're hard-wired for appearance, so it impacts on our decisions and judgments.

The Chosen are made up of just four women and four men. We were supposed to have been more, but politics and the idiocy of world leaders messed that up. Our prime purpose on Mars is to breed a new,

10

supposedly perfect, breed of human. I prefer our term, abliform, for its non-gender stance.

We're all equal. Men and women without the added burdens of status that so bedevil those left on Earth. Here, we live without the false imposition of classification. We are, first and foremost, people. None of us is subject to the demands of any other, regardless of gender or role.

Let's get something clear from the start. There's a misconception on Earth that men are superior to women. But men just produce the seed, it's women who …'

Zaphod enters Reppod. He's dressed as before, but the moving pattern now shows a band performing at a concert, fortunately without accompanying soundtrack. Anni turns as he enters. She rises, and they greet each other with a brief kiss before sitting side by side to talk.

'Decided to have a go, then?'

'Time to kill between checks on the eggs. You?'

'Couldn't settle. Hoshiko's fast asleep. Sorry, I think I interrupted you in mid flow, Anni.'

She nods. 'Doesn't mean your company's unwelcome. I was going to tell them why we're more women than men and got side-tracked into explaining the reasons for historical gender inequalities.'

He smiles. 'That old chestnut … What is a chestnut?' (*Hololink of Sweet Chestnut tree and its fruits*) 'Ah. Interesting. So, how far had you got?'

'Barely started. Just stating the idea of male supremacy is a misconception.'

'Misconception, wench? On your knees before your all powerful and potent master!'

She leans forward, cups his scrotum. 'Potent? I could demand you prove it …'

11

He gathers her to him.

'Maybe later, Zaphod. I'm determined to finish this report. Any case, I'm still basking in the aftereffects of my last session with Jai.'

'Love him, don't you?'

She nods. 'Like you and Hoshiko.'

He sighs a contented smile. 'Thank Deimos we ditched that male supremacy crap.'

She stands and stretches out her tiredness. 'Have to be more women if we're to succeed in a reasonable time frame.'

'Could've opted for more in vitro.'

'Breeding a better person depends on mother and child bonding. Vital for well-balanced individuals. We need fewer seed planters and more crop sustainers. Means you men get more sex, of course. But for rational biological reasons.'

'You mean it's nothing to do with our ownership or superiority? But, Anni, how can I develop a proper harem if the women don't …?'

Anni grabs and tweaks his nose. 'I will, you know.'

He detaches her hand and leans forward, kisses her. She kisses him back and they relax in their seats.

Zaphod's hand lingers on her upper arm. 'But you can see how early man could be corrupted by the idea of ownership of women. Brutality and sheer strength ruled the world, so those qualities protected the tribe. Leaders gained prowess by having many women. And once they knew about sperm, they'd want many sons, so their power would increase.'

A droid enters, carrying a tray with a jug of amber liquid and two small tumblers. It places these on the bench and pours each of them a drink.

'Thanks, Zaphod. Good idea.'

They clink glasses and down the liquor. The droid refills their glasses. 'Excuse my question, but I believe you were discussing the ancient roles of men and women in society?'

'Certainly were.'

'I am droid 159. It would increase my functionality on a social level if I could learn more of such matters. May I ask you questions on this topic?'

'Fire away, 159.'

The droid acknowledges Zaphod's permission with a slight bow. 'I heard your earlier comments. Is the false idea of male supremacy the reason tradition requires more sons than daughters in certain cultures?'

Anni nods. 'Women were reduced to the role of child bearers. Tribal fights often ended with the men killed or enslaved and the women raped and stolen as concubines.' She moves closer to him. 'Then religion came along. It saw women as physically weaker.'

159 considers this. 'And as property, they were easily controlled and blamed for everything that went wrong.'

'Too right. No leader's going to let his sons be thought wanting. Much easier to accuse women.'

'Eve, the wicked witch, gets Adam chucked out of Eden.' Zaphod drains his glass again. 'But men usually caused the problems and women were just trying to break free.'

Anni looks up at the droid, standing behind her. 'And repressed men, who couldn't attract women, took the blame game further. Made us responsible for everything that happened to us, blaming women for being raped ...'

'Instead of curbing male behaviour?' The droid appears surprised.

'Can't halt male urges. We're all ruled by our cock and balls. No room for the brain. No need for restraint. Women are always available to men, regardless of the woman's wishes.'

'I detect satire, Zaphod.'

'Well done, 159. Keep women in check, or they might show they're better than the men who own them. Imagine if the system broke down. Men would have to accept responsibility for their actions. That'd never do!'

Anni laughs and shakes her head. 'Then, by some irrational

extension, female inferiority leads to the totally mad idea women aren't interested in sex. It's really odd how religion dwells on sexual conflicts, but worshippers never notice the hypocrisy.'

159 looks pensive. 'All humans are sexual creatures, aren't they? And inclination seems to be nothing to do with gender.'

'That's right. And birth control lets us all accept sex as just another pleasure. Not the binding act it was when it often resulted in pregnancy. Thank Deimos for contraception.' Anni slips her hand up his leg.

159 nods slowly. 'No wonder Catholic and Muslim leaders want nothing to do with it. Imagine what would happen to their dogma if women were permitted to enjoy sex without the burden of children! Their whole order would collapse.'

Anni takes Zaphod's hand and pulls him to his feet. 'And, thank Deimos, that's what's happened.'

The droid smiles and bows. 'Thank you for this insight.' It leaves.

'Come on; let's exercise our freedom. Have to be quicker than I prefer, because of the eggs, but I want more practice so I'm expert at making babies.'

'Sorry, Anni, I've got a headache.'

They both laugh and leave Reppod, hand in hand.

Record 08: 20:46-062.01.01 Zaphod.

Zaphod's seated at the bench in Reppod. Before he starts to record, he rises and paces the small room, the cameras and sensors following his progress and showing the changing background as he passes the consoles, 3Dee displays, a large sofa, a row of three soft adjustable chairs, and the wall with its closed door and glass panel.

Zaphod's report:

Rumours. I hate rumours. No reliance, no actual knowledge: they remind me of my early days on Earth, when everything we heard, read, or witnessed had to be filtered through a sieve of utter cynicism, and truth was either absent or hidden. How is a person supposed to live under such circumstances?

We recently received intel that the Secretary General of the N.U.N. killed herself after announcing the effective end of life on Earth. There's no doubt the situation there is rapidly deteriorating, but it's difficult to believe someone in authority would do that in a live broadcast.

I tried again to reach my family. Managed to contact my younger brother, Adam. He told me the rumour's true; saw it happen live on screen. And she's not alone. Seems a whole load of prominent people in various world organisations have done the same. Suicide's reached the status of a pandemic, especially among people in positions of authority or influence. That tells me Earth's in a perilous state. If the rich and powerful have lost hope to that degree, the rest of humanity has no chance!

Adam says there are riots everywhere. Even the staid town he lives in, high on the hills of the Pennines, is rife with violence and lawlessness. Murder, rape, gang warfare and theft stalk the streets. He's terrified of leaving the house.

My parents were both lifelong devout Christians even in light of all the evidence against such beliefs. I've been estranged from them since the day they sold me to The Guardian: I thank them daily for that betrayal of parental responsibility. Adam found them in bed with their throats cut, apparently by each other. Poor sod. Jeez! To do that. And why? Their short note said their god had abandoned them. They couldn't bear to exist in a world so full of destruction and wickedness, where no divinity existed! A little late in the day to come to terms with reality.

He says signs of imminent nuclear war over the whole globe are so clear it's only a matter of time … In fact, his last words were cut off by what sounded like a large explosion, and I can no longer reach him. The others have tried their families, but atmospheric disruption on Earth is now so great it's virtually impossible to make any contact. So, I must assume I'm an orphan with no siblings. Such waste! Thank providence for The Guardian!

I need some solace. Perhaps one of the women …

Record 09: 22:16-08/07/2074 High Command Under Sacred Protection of Almighty.

The final command from the CUSP authorities to their soldiers in the field:

Show no mercy to heathens! Strip of cover and put outside. See they learn science and reason not saves from might and wrath of Almighty. Unworthy perish in pain. Their fate and rightful end. Take women. Uncover. Use them. Instruct in right ways so are obedient and serve as duty.

Record 10: 21:45-09/07/2074 Abdul-Aziz: Terrorist Leader in Space.

The first report gleaned from encrypted records made by a leader of the space terrorists:

Despite the promises of High Command, we found only one small neutron bomb and three armour-piercing missiles in the stores of the Pakafghanistan traitors. And the spacecraft. We fitted it with standard weapons from the armoury and ensured there was enough living space for our loyal troops on the flight. The launch was undertaken from the last space elevator, which we destroyed immediately after take off, with remote explosive charges placed during the ascent. This means no more space flights are possible from Earth. The atmosphere is too unstable to risk ground-based launches.

Any of the Cusp remaining on Earth can therefore concentrate on their duties there. They will continue the sacred work we have been engaged in for centuries. Soon that task will reach its glorious conclusion. And we, those of us entrusted with the dangerous and glorious mission in space, will conclude the whole divine purpose.

We, martyrs for the Sacred Cause, will stand with the Almighty as he judges all souls to determine whether they should be consigned to the eternal delights and pleasures of Paradise or to the fire pits of Hell as they deserve.

Record 11: 23:56-11/07/2074 Buzz, MB2

Buzz is an Astrophysicist and computer expert based at MoonBase2; this is his first report.

No warning. None. Earth must've known. Can't believe everyone down there was in the dark. But facts speak for themselves. MoonBase3 is a ruin. No one survived, far as we know. Rumours are, some leisure women were offsite and captured as sex slaves. It might be their normal job, but I pity them; they'd be better off dead.

Going in when we've modified our suits to protect against residual radiation.

They hit with armour-piercing missiles first. Talk is they stole them. Cult's good at stealing. Been doing it for decades. They kill everyone who gets in the way. Destroy all historical artefacts that might prove they're liars.

Had a bit of damage here, being close to MB3. But it's reparable and we're onto it. No help likely from Earth now. At each other's throats down there. Fighting for water and food now the climate's gotten so chaotic. Typical: years of warning about excess CO_2 and only now they start to take action that would of meant something back then. Way too late to stop the runaway effect now.

Brigitte's on Mars, so well out of trouble. Aldrin knows when I'll see her again. I miss that gorgeous woman. Get my share here on the

Moon; loads of willing female flesh. I bet Brigitte's getting hers on Mars. We agreed. It's the only way when we're so far apart. But I'd rather be having sex with my wife.

Based at MB2, I'm on the computing side of the astrophysics department. Maintaining servers and equipment, writing programs for calculation of data and observational results. Making sure the telescopes work.

This attack on MB3's devastating. Waste of human life; some of them people were my friends. Colleagues trying to make life better for them on Earth. It's a real worry when our link with Earth's getting worse every day. Only a matter of time before they abandon us. Aldrin knows what we'll do then. We depend on regular flights from Earth. If they stop … well, it don't bear thinking about.

Record 12: 20:46-066.01.01 Zaphod.

A short report taken from his private journal:

They told us, promised us, war on Earth could never spill over to Mars. All was peace here and so it would remain. They lied. It's hard to accept The Guardian could treat us this way. They've been our sponsors, our mentors, our guides and our providers since the days they took us from our families and formed us into The Chosen. But now it appears our new home may be under threat from those insane extremists made up of individuals with a death wish and an unshakable belief in a totally fictitious afterlife. How in the name of all that's logical do you defeat a group of people whose only desire is their own death? Impossible. Unless you can get to them before they get to you. At present, it's no more than a potential threat. But it's deeply unsettling to know it exists, and means we must delay the breeding programme until we can be certain we actually have a future for our proposed children.

Record 13: 10:47 12/07/2074 Buzz, MB2

I'm leading Systems Analyst here. Top Secret message from the N.U.N. came into my inbox. Tells me government servers are housed deep underground at MB3. Must be desperate to entrust such info to a lowly worker like me. Say there's a hidden tunnel from there to our underground server centre. I'm to go down and back-up all data from the servers at MB3 to ours. An 'At All Costs' priority, which means I'm to do it no matter what it takes. Once the data's secure, I've to destroy the servers under MB3. And – get this – record everything on removable media so we can take it to Mars. Got to transfer it to another set of Top Secret servers at the base where Brigitte works. Another priority! It's like they know exactly what's gonna happen here. So, what is gonna happen? No answer to that. And, no surprise, I've to keep all this to myself.

What's my reward for this dangerous job? Everlasting gratitude of the future human race when they can access files on history in some unspecified future. I was gonna tell the bastards to frack off. Then I thought, well, when Brigitte and I have kids, I'd like them to know about the past. Makes sense to preserve our history for the future. Who knows? We never learnt from mistakes before, but we might, I suppose. So I'm gonna do it.

Record 14: 03:19 14/07/2074 Abdul-Aziz: Terrorist Leader in Space.

This report was held in an archive hidden deep in servers that most people don't even realise exist:

First operational report, to be lodged in the eternal archive constructed for that purpose alone, since our aim is the death of all human life. My superiors, however, insist I keep a record of all that we do. They have given me no reason for this. But I am an obedient

19

servant of those who know the truth, so I comply.

My name is Abdul-Aziz, which means 'Servant of the Almighty' and is the name I chose when I saw the light and converted to the CUSP. I lead troops of the Enlightened Resurrection that the heathens have named the Cult. Let them call us what they will; their insults are of no significance. They will all die anyway. We are engaged in the sacred destruction of all remaining human life outside of Earth. Our brethren, confined to that evil planet without hope of joining us on this glorious mission, will end all remaining life there, leaving that degenerate place scorched and clean. To them goes that particular glory. Peace and victory be with them!

We may be few but we are strong in will and passion. And we have right and Almighty God on our side. We cannot lose. For who can defeat the Almighty? No one. That is the absolute truth!

We took the Moon Base numbered 2 and eliminated the heathen crew. Some women who were employed as providers of pleasure escaped the blast of the neutron bomb. They were sheltering underground in a safe place. We took them and they now serve us, as is their purpose and destiny. A few disobeyed so we made examples of those, and the rest quickly understood their proper situation and now comply with our demands. We keep them naked, as advised by High Command. But they distract the men as they work. I may wrap their skins against visibility so we can work with women in attendance but without being always excited by their pleasure parts.

Once our objective was accomplished at the Moon base, we captured the unmanned ore carrier as planned. It was tethered to the space elevator and undefended. We transferred our portable living quarters and supplies to the hollow interior of the first storage unit in the long train of such containers.

It would have been good to complete the eradication of life on the Moon, but we have insufficient numbers of men and weapons for that, so we will continue the crusade on Mars. There we will convert more to our Holy Cause. When we have completed the Sacred Duty on

Mars, and killed all the heathens in that place, we will travel to the Asteroid Belt and bring an end to their wickedness. Afterwards, we will all return to the Moon, in numbers swollen by our recruitment of right thinking men, and there complete the final part of the cleansing process. Then will come our reward, as we go to Paradise and spend eternity in pleasure unending.

We leave for Mars in one day. I will report later on progress and again on our arrival at the target.

Record 15: 06:13-068.01.01 Hoshiko

Hoshiko, The Chosen, a scientist from Japan, is in Reppod making her first report. She is dressed, as all the women in their base, in clothes she has designed. The outfit consists of a simple, loose, bolero top and a skirt. Made of smartfab modified by Hoshiko, these outfits have the ability to carry moving designs chosen by their wearers. On this day, hers carries a moving depiction of a Japanese formal garden with water features and a couple wandering the paths. She has also built into the control systems of all their clothes, for both men and women, a device that senses certain signals from the brain and body of the wearer. This allows the pictures to fade completely, leaving the fabric sheer. The intention is to use this as an unambiguous sign that the individual is eager for sex with the person before them. They decided on this to avoid misinterpretation of body language and the sometimes ambiguous messages conveyed in conversation. In this way, both men and women can be certain that the partner is definitely desirous of sexual activity.

Hoshiko's report:

Time for me to add words to the accounts already begun. In common with those who've gone before, I'll begin with an introduction.

21

Hoshiko here: Japanese. Born and raised in the city of Matsumoto on the island of Honshu, sometimes called the gateway to the Japanese Alps. Our house was in sight of the famous castle, Matsumotojo. I spent my early childhood drawing and painting that magnificent building. But that's all in the past. Since I was Chosen, I've never returned home. I don't even know if people still live in those beautiful mountains, or if floods and bad weather have made the old city uninhabitable.

As for my particular skills and gifts; I'm a nanoscientist with other skills relating to smart fabrics and associated areas of engineering. Also, I'm an astrophysicist and the group's navigator when needed. My main creative outlet is drawing and painting; skills not easily managed yet due to our very small supplies of paper and pigments. We'll develop such things as time passes. Anni's even growing some trees and a small crop of papyrus reed so we can try to make paper.

I enjoy our sexual and social freedoms, so different from my old homeland's strict traditions and customs. I'm glad Zaphod, our excellent physician, has the hots for me. I find making love with him most satisfying and enjoy many other aspects of his personality.

What do I miss about Earth? Surprisingly little. Rice, and the Saki that comes from it. But it'd be wonderful to run free instead of being confined to underground chambers. Not that I'm claustrophobic, but I love being in the open and having sun and wind and even rain on my skin, as I did when a child.

Enough of me. To the matter in hand.

We're getting rumours of an invasion by the Cult. For the men, it would mean painful death unless they feign conversion until we can retake control. Our fate's much worse. They use us as objects to pleasure themselves with no regard for the feelings of the women. We're considered less than human and reduced to the status of objects they can use and discard as they wish. Their complex, self-contradictory faith's a mix of Islam, Judaism, types of Christianity and some Hindu beliefs, rites and rituals. Those religions, especially the

Abrahamic cults, arose during paternalistic times in misogynist cultures, so their beliefs and traditions are very bad for women.

At the moment, invasion's only a rumour. They've destroyed a base on the Moon. Poor Brigitte's desperate for news of her husband, Buzz, who works there. We've only hearsay reports. Last we heard was they'd left the Moon and are on their way here. But we've no info re their trajectory and so don't know their destination. Their intentions on arrival will be very bad for all of us, however.

I hope they never arrive and that some who find this account in the future will be offspring created from the love between Zaphod and me. And I greet you in that expectation. Welcome!

Record 16: 20:25 14/07/2074 Buzz, MB2

Just after the attack on MB3, we got an announcement off of all support bases on Earth. Unique. They've always contacted us separately. Reason for their combined message is clear. See no way to continue supply flights! Atmosphere down there's so unstable ground launches are too risky. And those morons, the Cult, destroyed all three space elevators on Earth. They used them to pump ice melt water into tanks they sent here. What happened to security?

So we're stuck, without enough resources to feed and water ourselves. Okay, so we're pumping water from the polar ice. But it's slow, and the purification plant needs work to get it to produce the full amount we need. There'll be no more from Earth, so that's a priority for our engineers.

Food'll be a problem in a year. We've stockpiles till then, but we'll miss the fresh food we've been getting. The loss of MB3 and its personnel means stocks'll last the rest of us a bit longer. Sound brutal? In serious trouble here. It's sheer survival now we're cut off from Earth. We'll all die from poor nutrition if we can't leave the Moon and get to the food security on Mars.

Record 17: 23:49 069.01.01 Jannine from MMMB1O

Jannine was one of large number of female and male sex workers contracted as freelancers at the mining consortium's processing base, MMMB1O.

She kept a private journal for reasons of her own. Although it is sometimes rambling and often irrelevant, it does provide insight into the lives of such individuals whilst giving some historical info relating to the base and events there.

Jannine's report:

Look, that time's right at the top up there. But that calendar's just stupid. Them there lot over at Marion said we 'ave to use it. No idea how it works, but this terminal fills it in anyhow.

And the music you can hear playing? That's Endurin Einstein singin Clover's Lover. One of my favourites.

So, been here a few months now and decided to keep a journal, like. Might make it public, like a blog. Might keep it jus for me. Earnin good money. Mostly the blokes is okay, but some think they're better'n they are. Gavin, a line supervisor who hails from the old state of Texas come up to me yesterday and put his hand up me skirt.

'Lips 'ere as fat and welcomin as them on your face, Babe?'

So I asked him, 'Prick in your pants as small as the nose on your ugly mug?'

He showed me, and it wasn't. Decided it were worth a go, specially when he offered more'n the goin rate, like. Turns out he knows what to do with it an'all. Good fuck. I'll do 'im again.

Workin 'ere to get me that Lamborghini. You know, the one what does two-fifty. A red one. There's a good lot of us 'ere at the minin base. We serve all the needs for the men, and the women. Keeps them from rebellin so the boss says. I mean, workin conditions is 'orrible for them. So good job we're 'ere.

We live in special units next to the processin plant. Get daylight through the walls. Well, what passes for daylight on this godforsaken planet anyway. But life's okay. There's a gym for us to keep fit in. No man wants a fat woman or one who's always tired. So we do our dailies. Up to me how many men I take each day: don't generally do women, but I will if they're willin to pay a bit more. Jus don't do it for me, you know? I usually have about five or six. It's easy work an' the boss makes sure there's no violence from them. Anyone hurts us and they're put in solitary for a week, wages docked, and the woman what he's hurt can take a strap to his skin. So we don't get no bother now.

It's okay fuckin in low gravity. Keeps your tits nice and bouncy an'all. No droopy boobs 'ere! And you can bounce all you like on the blokes. Gets them really goin. Get's me goin an'all!

Anyway, there's a bloke at me door, so it's off with the lot and give the bugger what he wants, eh? Back later to chat a bit more.

Record 18: 12:16 16/07/74 Buzz, MB2

The Cult cut our coms. Planted timed explosive devices on the ground-based dishes and set them off when they left. Thank frack they didn't come here!

And our only space elevator's damaged beyond repair. Worse, it's a radioactive ruin.

Missed one satellite. But that's in an orbit that takes it over us only every twenty-eight hours. Coms with Earth, Mars and the Asteroid Belt are completely fracked. We've done a rota, to communicate with all of them in stages. But we can't act as the hub we once were. That's a major concern. Still, we got messages off to Mars and the Asteroid Belt.

The morons from the Cult have set off into space on some other murderous mission. Trouble is, we can't say where they're going. Best guess is they're off to Mars. Taken an ore carrier, modified with life support systems. Looks like they're gonna destroy or capture the metal processing base, MMMB1O. Manager's sent a warning and I've sent one to Marion, where Brigitte works. Hope the Cult don't even know about that one.

Nothing we can do from here about it, but we've got a party working on evacuation from the Moon. Some weirdly want to go back to Earth. Most want to go to Mars. That's a more likely prospect. So, the working party's looking at two ventures. Earth'll be easier, as we've a couple of EVACs here and numbers are small enough to take them all. But Aldrin knows why anyone wants to risk re-entry into an atmosphere that's now so unstable. Or go to a planet where life's almost impossible. Still; their choice. I'm off to Mars asap. Not what Brigitte and I planned. But looks like the best option. And it'll be so great to be with her again.

Record 19: 12:40-070.01.01 Zaphod.

Zaphod is seated at the consoles. Alone and looking serious.

Zaphod's report:

The Cult's already attacked the Moon bases and they're now headed our way to deal in death and destruction. At present, that threat's speculation, since no one really knows their actual destination. It's also some time away, so I'll return to it later. However, it is the reason for me doing this record. We discussed our situation and concluded we should do our best to compile as much info as we can about our time here. It should form a sound basis for your understanding of your place on Mars. So, we'll all be contributing to these records. So far, I've done the most here in Reppod, but the others see it as their duty as well.

For now, though, I'm going to give you some factual info to help you understand how things are in this fast-developing colony. I hope my music won't be too distracting, but I like background sounds

26

when I'm doing this for any length of time. That track's Transgender Chicken playing Tomorrow I May Dream. Great number. Want to see them? Here's a (*Hololink to Transgender Chicken*). Chill band, eh?

There's much to tell you, much you need to know if you're going to grow up to become the rightful heirs to our new planet. On Earth, history was distorted, damaged, made incomplete and dishonest because those who recorded it were biased or deluded. They wished to hide their misdemeanours and enhance their victories, such as they were. Here, in our new world, with new laws and standards, we'll let those who come after us experience the whole truth, warts and all (whatever that might mean: I've no idea what a wart is).

(*Hololink to Wart: definitions and images pasted to record from Centrarch.*) Oh, now I know! Yuck!

Anyway, we address this to you, our children. You'll first experience this record in full when you reach puberty, so you'll understand how you came to be here on Mars, why, and what's expected of you.

You'll have noted this record doesn't start at the beginning of our domicile here, but on the fifty-fifth day of the first quarter of our first year. To start at the beginning, or somewhere near it: as I make this report, Earth date is, what?

Zaphod consults a calendar he brings up on the console before him.

It's 16.07.2074. We quickly decided there's no point sticking to Earth dates, and the Sol Day system espoused by NASA and other space agencies is fine for space travel but too generic and clumsy for our home. We live here on Mars and move at a different rate from Earth. Mars has different day lengths, different length years, different seasonal lengths. Makes more sense to develop our own calendar, re-gardless of what Earth might want. So, today's date, from our point of view, is 070.01.01, calculated from the date The Chosen landed on the planet.

Okay, there were landings before ours. Lots of them. But those early occupants lived with Earth dates or sol days. We're more sophisticated, more intelligent and more likely to produce viable progeny, so we're in charge of this new world. We're 70 days into the first quarter of our first year. We've ditched old concepts of weeks and months, since they've no practical purpose. Our year naturally divides into four quarters of 167 days, Marsdays, that is. And we'll need a leap year, to add a day once every ten years, to compensate for the fact our years last 668.1 Marsdays, near enough.

For those who may read this not as our children, but as students of history from the future, we'll explain aspects of life on Mars that'll be self-evident to those born here. Be patient of things you already know, for there'll be others without your advantages who need to understand the reality of our joint history. We want this to be a lasting record of proper use to future academics.

As I record this, I can't actually know whether any human – sorry – abliform, will ever read it. To clarify; we're trying to avoid the term 'human' with its ancient gender bias, and have developed the term 'abliform', aboriginal life form, as an alternative non-gender term for our species.

Who are The Chosen? We're special. All selected at an early age for the mission, kept free of certain influences and the traditional indoctrination that robbed so many of their freedom to think without bias. We were shielded from bad ideas when young, and made to understand we were destined to spend our adult lives here on a world far distant from our mother planet. We arrived here after a pretty straightforward launch from CisLunar orbit. The flight was also normal, but for an unfortunate incident involving Georgiy.

I'd love to claim to be a real pioneer; one of the first colonists on Mars. But the truth is that a whole gang of people, droids, and bots of various kinds were here long before any of us Chosen kicked up the blood red dust of this outpost.

So far, my only claim to fame is establishing that the water in our underground reservoir is safe. Filters take out the actual life forms, which we recycle as part of our organic resource to help feed the various crops we're growing inside and on ...

A dark-skinned young woman enters the chamber. Zaphod is clearly pleased to see her and rises from his seat. Her top and skirt carry pictures of spacecraft moving against a backdrop of the cosmos.

'Hi Amber.'

She stretches up and kisses his cheek. 'Time for lunch, Zaphod.'

The record continues briefly but contains only irrelevant intimate activity before the pair leave.

Record 20: 14:18 071.01.01 Jannine from MMMB1O

Shit! They're sayin them terrorists called the Cult is on the way! Why?

I mean, what they want with us? We're not a threat to their weird culture nor nothin. The boss says we've got to be prepared for them takin command if they come 'ere. But no one seems to know nothin about if they will. What's he want to go and tell us if he don't know for? I mean, it's not like we can do nothin about it, is it? Jus a worry now.

Me, I'm a good Catholic girl. Don't want no truck with them there extremists. They say their faith's the only one. But that's crap, innit? I mean, we Catholics've been around a lot longer than them. We started the God thing. They should respect us and join our church, I say. My mate Mary says they believe in the same God as us. But not jus Jesus. I told 'er, they put all the prophets, even that there Mohammed fella, in together. Even that there Buddha and t'other one with a funny name. Confucius, Mary says. And even some of them sort of not real Gods like what they have in India. The Hindus, Mary says. Them what worship cows and loads of other things what's not holy.

My Pastor says they're not at all sacred, like. Says they're a death cult, whatever that means. They believe the afterlife's the most important thing ever and do everythin to get to Heaven. Like those Mormons, they make everyone change to their faith before they kill them. Not that the Mormons killed, like. But they want us all to be like them. That's what the Pastor says, anyway. I don't understand it to be honest. I jus do my prayers and confession and do the penance what the Pastor sets.

If they come, I don't know what I'll do. I'm not dyin for no one. If they want to fuck me, let them. Even free, if that's what they want. I got a life to enjoy and a fast car to get and drive all over the NUSA soon as I get back to Earth. So I'm not gonna do nothin to spoil that.

Oh! Knock on the door. Time for a fuck, I guess.

Record 21: 18/07/2074 Originating source unidentifiable, but almost certainly from Earth.

Garnered from fragments of signals received on the Moon, this series of short moving and still images, with accompanying sound-tracks overlaid by static making them incomprehensible, shows destruction at every place where the cameras point. Some images appear to be from individuals, some from close-circuit TV systems, some from dedicated news teams. Someone compiled them into a form of documentation of the decline of humankind, though who that was is lost in history. Not a single image gives hope. The sequence is short and violent.

Record 22: 19:13-073.01.01. Zaphod.

Zaphod, wearing his boxers, with a repeating display of a rock band at a live concert, without soundtrack, is at the recording console.

Zaphod's report:

What are we? Who are The Chosen? We're the hope for the future of what's left of the human race, no more, no less.

Seventeen manned missions landed here before The Guardian allowed us to really begin our life's work. Seventeen successful missions. And two ill-fated ventures that failed to reach fulfilment. But I'll come to those later. As I will to the irresponsible commercially and politically driven attempts at ecopoiesis: just because some of that activity resulted in accidental benefits, it doesn't mean they were right to try it! Those early gambles over terraforming may have been effective in some ways, but they delayed colonisation by decades.

The Chosen should've been twelve, but war between India and China reduced us to the bare minimum. And for what? Time on a planet that's daily growing more inhospitable for humanity, sorry, I'll get used to it eventually: inhospitable for abliforms. What a pointless waste of lives, resources and opportunity.

Turns out Stephen Petranek was right all those years ago about the need to use Mars as a human ... abliform, insurance policy. (*Hololink to Petranek's book, How We'll Live on Mars.*) Earth's dangerous slide into climate chaos seems destined to cause the extinction of abliforms on the home planet. But I'm getting ahead of myself.

Who am I? Zaphod. And before you ask, yes, I was named after Zaphod Beeblebrox by parents who were avid fans of that ancient comedy, the Hitchhiker's Guide to the Galaxy series. (*Hololink to Hitchhiker's Guide to the Galaxy*) Better Zaphod than the pathetic Arthur Dent! I'm 31 Earth years old, which translates to 16.49 Mars years: still a kid! I'm single, a multidisciplinary scientist and lead physician here on what started out as MaB12 for reasons best ignored. MarsBase12 was too impersonal as the name for our new home, so we found something more colourful, something with reference to our roots. It's logical to name the first real residential area, what will become the capital of Mars, after the first person to step on the surface of the planet. Here, in this location, almost blood red dust because its specific mineral content reacts with new gasses being pumped into the atmosphere through continuing ecopoiesis.

So, I live, and you'll be living, in the first proper town on Mars, the town called Marion. Marion Armstrong that is; who you'll know as a distant descendent of Neil Armstrong, the first man to step on the Moon. She wasn't supposed to be first to step on Mars, of course. In those still patriarchal days, that was supposed to be a man. He failed. But we avoid mention of that, and his name. Suffice to say, Marion took the reins and saved the day. Shame she didn't live long enough to benefit from her amazing courage.

My land of origin is on Earth, of course, so I was born a human; an Earthman. See how the male gender bled so easily into language? Anyway, we're veering toward calling our new race, Marspers, short for Mars Persons. We don't use 'Martians' with its threatening connotations of 'little green men' and aliens. And you know why we use the term abliforms. Our terms will be second nature to you, having been educated here. But, for us there's still a tendency to refer to our race as 'humans' and to us as Martians. The new terms are novel at present, but we'll get used to them over time.

I'm the only Brit amongst The Chosen, though plenty of the pioneer corps came from my homeland. Let's get to stuff you need to know to begin with. What'll be ancient history for you can wait for now.

We Chosen come from different nations. Madonna's (*Hololink to Madonna*) an engineer and robotics specialist and the sexiest Australian redhead you'd ever hope to meet. Hopefully, you'll have met her in the flesh by the time you get to this, but she'll be older by then, and we still don't really know what effects reduced gravity and high levels of radiation will have on any of us. Our genetic make-up's designed to make us more or less impervious to such things, but only time will prove the efficacy of the gene editing.

Amber (*Hololink to Amber*), from the NUSA (New United States of America; a forced fiscal-political alliance of the old USA with Canada, Mexico, the small states from Central America, and the remaining islands of the Caribbean) is as hot as you can imagine. Well, I guess you saw her with me in an earlier report, didn't you?

She's our clever rocket propulsion specialist, a gifted photographer and our second pilot.

Tu (*Hololink to Tu*) is a Chinese atmospheric engineer born and raised in the ancient province of Italy, part of USNEu. He's a bit cool for some, but gets no complaints from the women. After all, he's as buff as the rest of us. Tu's particularly busy with constant work on developing the atmosphere.

Georgiy (*Hololink to Georgiy*), our most experienced cosmonaut from what's left of ancient Russia, was nominal mission leader for our flight. He's a flight engineer and the oldest member of our party but probably the fittest, and definitely the best space pilot ever. All the women have the hots for the horny bugger, which is just as well since he's as eager as they are.

Annika (*Hololink to Annika*) is every man's dream: a blonde from Sweden, also part of USNEu, with all that generous friendliness they're so good at. She's the genius in charge of food production, water technology and also an ecopoiesis expert. She and Jai are doing wonders growing plants in the regolith.

Jai (*Hololink to Jai*) works a lot with Annika. He's our other gut bacteria expert, a plant specialist and our resident arts virtuoso as well as being an engineer and general scientist. Indian by birth, he was brought up in Canada around the time the USA bullied the fragmented continent into uniting.

Then there's our oriental beauty, Hoshiko (*Hololink to Hoshiko*), from the small part of Japan that escaped the ravages of nuclear fallout and earthquakes. She's truly gorgeous, isn't she? A brilliant navigator, nanotechnician, and talented visual artist, she blends kindness with her sensuous nature. It's her we have to thank for the few clothes we choose to wear, since she's fantastically clever with smart fabrics.

We all know each other well, and I do mean very well, since we lived and trained together for years on Earth. The Guardian had us spend our time on the island mostly naked so we'd get used to one another's bodies and not be embarrassed by Earthly hang-ups over nudity. Our final phase was spent in the Aldrin Training Centre at Lunar Base 7 to give us a proper taste of micro gravity and life in isolation from Earth's facilities and resources. We've all been frequent partners with our opposite numbers. Each of us has our favourites, of course, but there's no jealousy and none of that stupid possessive stuff that ruined so many relationships, lives even, on Earth. We disagree with a lot of what they did on the old planet. But, as our children, you'll already know that. History scholars may not, however.

If you're second generation, you'll be living in Marion. Later readers will be spread all over Mars as the population grows; that's the intention. So, I'd better place us geographically. We're in the western equatorial sector of the planet, north of the dividing line between the hemispheres. Still not sure whether we'll settle for 'equator' for that divider yet. More specifically, we're in the Tharsis Quadrangle, at a location originally labelled Ulysses Fossae. Not on the mound itself, of course, but close to it. Why here? It's where pioneers discovered a large aquifer deep underground but accessible for pumping, together with hollow lava tubes big enough to accommodate our initial living quarters and growing halls. It's in the region where Mars is warmest during the long spring and summer seasons. We're currently working on new names for the whole world. Latin labels are archaic and anachronistic. Let's face it, Latin's a dead language, for all its use in scientific labelling.

So, that should give you enough detail to be going on with.

All of The Chosen are wise and mature enough to understand we have different viewpoints on all manner of things. We know we each have our irritating habits, so there's unlikely to be embarrassment or resentment at anything any of us records. Mind you, bearing in mind the way the human brain works, we'll no doubt portray certain events in different ways, according to our own perceptions and emotional responses. But we'll definitely stick to the truth.

Now, should I explain the hows and whys of our journey here at this point, tell you about our progress, such as it is, in dealing with less savoury commercial elements fighting for a profit base on Mars, or in working out a defence strategy against the Cult? If anyone's reading this, it shows we succeeded, so there's no excitement in that tale. Oh, except, you might not be one of our children. Maybe we'll never reach that stage. I can't tell from my place here in the year 0001. Maybe you're a space archaeologist from some other place in the solar system decades, even centuries, after our experiment failed through the actions of a group of criminal religious fanatics! Maybe you're not even our species! Who knows?

But let's stay optimistic. If you're a student, we'll be competing for your attention and time. You'll have essential duties to perform, there'll be boys or girls, maybe both, who'll capture your concentration, games and sports you want to play, books you want to read, movies you want to watch. But you'll also have been brought up in a disciplined environment designed to help you concentrate on the task in hand, so your propensity for distraction should be less than it would've been back on Earth. Excluding, of course, the attraction of the opposite sex, which, given that you won't have access to this record until you've reached puberty, is likely to be your most pressing concern right now. If, on the other hand, you're a space archaeologist, you'll have the patience and discipline to wade through all the matter here to get at the truths you seek.

So, let's start with a very recent event: how Georgiy came to be shut outside during a dust storm and couldn't open the air lock. Imagine it from his point of view. The temperature out there gets close to minus sixty, in spite of the infant warming effects of terraforming. At the time of writing, the atmosphere's increased to around four percent of the density of Earth's, so the wind's more powerful than it was originally, by a factor of four. Still means Earth's hurricane force winds are only equivalent to a strong breeze, but it chucks plenty of dust and light debris around. Gravity's your only friend out there, since you weigh less than forty percent of what you did on Earth and you still have most of the strength you had then. You've gone out to collect equipment for a specific defence weapon because, well, there may not be much time before the extremist idiots come to attack us.

We've tried droids for the work. Their skin's impermeable to the dust, but their visuals don't function brilliantly in storms. The pioneer corps are used to working in these conditions, of course, but the few we allowed to stay here after our familiarisation period are all women, for obvious reasons. All engineers of one sort or another, and very gifted technically, but no experts on laser technology. Anyway, you're out there, alone, trying to get essential equipment and now you've reached the end of your safe period and can't get back inside the base because the airlock won't open.

Scary, eh?

I'll try to record it exactly as I recall …

Amber, her top and skirt displaying a moving panorama of a rain forest, enters the reporting suite and interrupts Zaphod.

'Pointless. You weren't there at the start. Let me tell them about it. Okay?'

Amber has a point. And what man could resist a body and brain like hers? Not this one. 'Fire away, Amber.'

'Zaphod's promised the story, so I'll tell it as I remember. Just not now.

'I only stopped by as I'm cooking tonight, Zaphod. You okay with chickenburger and sweetfries?'

'Fine. Wear a pinny this time, or you'll damage that lovely skin with hot oil.'

'Will do. Maybe you should describe the incident that caused Georgiy to make the stupid trip out there in the first place?'

'On the flight?'

'Yeah. Needs recording, as an explanation, if nothing else. And he's never going to do it, is he? Neither am I.'

'Still hoping, eh?'

'Mind your own business, Limey.'

Amber gives him a mischievous grin. She turns and leaves.

Zaphod continues his report:

So: Georgiy and his moment of madness. (You know it has to be recorded, Georgiy). None of you will have been in space at this point: too young. So you'll have no concept of the stresses and strains of a long space flight. In any case, by the time you come across this, who knows where technological advances might have got us? Maybe we've developed faster-than-light transport in the intervening years. Wow! That would be something.

We launched from Cis-lunar space, taking the LB2 space elevator to the docking station, as Luna Base Two is closest to ATC. They were getting a bit nearer to self-sufficiency when we left; still reliant on Earth for some water and fresh foodstuffs, though. The Moon's only able to support hydroponics and it's impossible to grow stuff on the surface. But, with luck, there's a chance they'll continue to escape the madness overtaking Earth. We hear from them, but only at need. Coms there was essentially set up for Earth/Moon traffic but they installed new sat2sat arrays for Mars when the pioneers prepared their first expeditions here. And the commercial lot have set up their own network. But we have as little to do with that bunch of money-grabbers as we can. Profit, their entire reason for existence, is a dirty word to us.

Launch didn't go as we'd intended. We'd been working to a window when distance and gravitational pulls would be optimum, but events on Earth meant we were ordered to escape earlier. There was a strong possibility of another total collapse in the financial markets and, for reasons The Guardian never divulged, that could've pulled the plug on our venture. We all thought the whole scheme had already been paid for. I mean, the spacecraft was built, supplies already either here at the base or on their way, so we couldn't see any way financial constraints would stop our launch. But business isn't our forte: we find that whole area of operation alien and unattractive. As it happened, the markets apparently recovered again after we'd left. Of course, they've completely collapsed now and are unlikely ever to recover. But the panic then to get us underway buggered up our preparations and meant our flight to Mars took a little longer than planned. We were in space for 159 days. It was supposed to be 138. Doesn't sound a terribly long time, does it? But when eight of you are cooped up in a very small space, albeit designed for twelve, and knowing things back home are deteriorating fast, life can get a bit fraught.

We'd all had familiarisation training, EVA experience, psychological profiling and all the other standard training and tests every astronaut goes through. But, because of the unusual nature of our mission – a one-way trip with no intention of a return to Earth – we'd also had pretty intense personality testing and mutual bonding experience. After all, we were selected and raised to be breeders. That was, and remains, our prime function. It'll be yours, too.

They say the viable population for a species to survive and flourish for any reasonable length of time is around 3,000. As I write this, we've increased the initial eight Chosen by thirteen female pioneers who you'll learn about later, but no infants. Still too soon and uncertain to bring new life into our developing world. Frustrating, but a necessary delay until we get a grip on the war and ensure those idiots from the Cult are out of commission. Preferably dead, since they have no concept of compromise.

Anyway, I digress. The flight to Mars. A sort of claustrophobia infects those on long space flights. You deal with it in your own way. Me? I took to partnering the women as often as possible. They're all very happy to indulge. It passed the time as well as taking minds off the confinement. Pretty good physical exercise as well! Mind you, our private quarters were pretty cramped, so you had to be a bit inventive. But we managed; living in half Earth gravity on board helped a little.

Hell, we were all selected for our initial drives and appetites in that area and then we were enhanced by GE.

I had no favourite among the women at first, but confess I started to take a particular liking to Hoshiko. There's something about her looks, something about her style and the way she's strong without trying to dominate. And I love her brain. Yes, I know what you're thinking; you've seen her: of course I love her body. That goes without saying. I mean, look at her. (*New Hololink of Hoshiko*) She's gorgeous.

Sorry, there I go again; getting off the point. Georgiy. Thing is, I don't fancy him at all. We were all tested for sexual orientation. Let's face it, you're not going to get much actual breeding activity between gays of either gender, are you? No doubt, somewhere along the line, as we increase in numbers, we'll gain a few gay, bisexual, asexual or even hypersexual individuals as infants and they'll bring their own unique viewpoints and preferences to the growing community. But, to begin with, we need sex to produce babies: lots of them!

Georgiy's the only real pessimist amongst us. Balance, to prevent the rest of us optimists becoming too idealistic, I suppose. Of course, he considers himself a pragmatist, a realist. But the fact is, he's a pessimistic personality and I had worries about him on that score from the start; they can be so negative. Command noted my concerns and dismissed them. So much for ensuring we were all happy with each other. In every other regard, Georgiy's ideal. And, as the most experienced astronaut, he was nominal leader on the flight. I say nominal because rational experience of the dangers of leaders in general was accepted by our mentors. Our group set out with the intention that we'd have no leaders on Mars; every important decision is made jointly. As we expand in numbers, we'll elect committees to do the decision making, but we'll never have any individual in charge. Disaster, that; since it encourages sociopaths, with all their personality hang-ups. But you do need a commander, a decision maker, on a space flight, there's no doubt about that: things can happen so fast, and you need someone able to make split second judgments.

Things were going as well as we could expect. Mechanically, there were occasional problems. Let's face it, our ship was pretty complex and the biggest craft ever to fly in space. I should say, the biggest occupied craft. Some of the trains that carried supplies here in the early days were whoppers, as are the cargo trains used by the mining conglomerates. But they're occupied only by droids, so living space is no issue.

We had a central core where the cryopens with the most sensitive occupants were well protected from radiation. Moving out from that, corridors linked our individual quarters, and the main living pod, where radiation protection was still pretty effective but rotation gave us fifty percent gravity. Beyond that were the store tubes, stationary and devoid of gravity. If we wanted to get an actual view of the stars around us, we had to don protective suits and go up top to the Hubble Bubble, which we still use as an observatory here on the ground, now we've dismantled the rocket. Other spaces were various labs and workspaces, biodomes full of growing or dormant life of various less sensitive sorts, massive storage holds forward and aft, and the leisure pod where twelve at a time could watch movies, and live news from Earth. I suggested that Georgiy avoid the news. It really got him down at times. But he's a stubborn Ruskie and, let's face it you can't get more stubborn than a Ruskie!

We had this problem with a solar sail. Part had become detached and it was no longer giving us max speed. It had to be fixed. The sensible thing would've been to send a droid out. I mean, Madonna's talent and expertise with those things is legend. She'd have had no trouble guiding and commanding one to do the work. But Georgiy insisted on doing the spacewalk himself. Said it was his responsibility as leader. In reality, he felt he needed to prove himself 'as a man'. One more instance of the problems caused by leaders.

He suited up and went out. By this time, we're travelling in excess of 67,000kph. Should be doing 73,000kph, but the loose sail's causing 'drag'. Of course, in space, you've no sensation of movement and, outside, you're doing the same speed as the ship. So, Georgiy's out there, tooled up and ready. And what does he do? We've had months of training on EVAs. He knows to always have two tethers. Always. It's fundamental. So, it's not a mistake. Can't be. He's done this so often it's second nature. But he makes a move with only one tether. And he 'slips'. Garbage! It was deliberate. Subconsciously so, but deliberate all the same. Had to be. There's no way an experienced astronaut like Georgiy would make a rookie mistake like that. He did it on purpose.

They called me from my quarters, where I was engaged in a pretty hot time with Hoshiko. I wasn't best pleased. Neither was she. Amber was on coms and transferred me. I spoke to him; cameras showed him floating above the ship on a single line. He was making no effort to reel himself in to return and I could see the real danger that he'd detach the tether. No going back from that. I signalled Madonna but she was already on it, so I concentrated on Georgiy. Talked to him, reasoned with him, listened to his issues.

It was Earth, of course. His family, such as it was by then, was in real danger from the inundation caused by 'unexpected' slippage of mainland ice on Wilkes Land in Antarctica. Unexpected, my arse! Everyone knew it was inevitable, but the authorities had tried to keep a lid on it because the resulting tsunami, along with the sudden rise in sea levels, was bound to have catastrophic effects around the globe. His family were stuck in a location where they were at severe risk but the slip was sudden and there was nowhere they could escape to in the time frame available. (*Hololink to Geosat15AST live recording of global tsunami*) In effect, the whole region was abandoned as unsustainable by the leaders in Moscow. They were more concerned to keep their own living spaces safe and viable. The peasants in the north were dispensable. No wonder Georgiy was worried. I mean, let's be brutally honest: that region of old Russia is now under the waves and unlikely to resurface for millennia, if ever.

I kept him talking. And Madonna did her magic with the droids. I had to keep him distracted so he'd remain unaware of their presence as long as possible. Last thing we needed was for him to see them coming, and detach his tether. It was pretty tense. We had a protocol for this situation, of course. I'll say that about the guys who engineered and designed this project: they thought of just about everything. One of the droids inserted the coupler into Georgiy's air line and injected the necessary dose. The other attached a second tether from behind. Once he was under, the droids reeled him back in and got him to the airlock, where Hoshiko and I unsuited him before he came round. Madonna had the droids fix the sail whilst they were out there and we continued on our flight, picking up speed more or less straight away.

By the time Georgiy was fully conscious, Navigation had recalculated our course and we were back on target for our landing. That was now 67 days off, but we knew we'd land safely, even if a little late. I kept Georgiy on a mild dose of antidepressants and we made sure he was never alone for the rest of the trip. Space depression isn't common, but neither is it unheard of. And, given the circumstances, it's no surprise he'd had a bout. But it was that incident that caused him to do the second macho thing, this time here at Marion. I'll let Amber tell that tale. For now, I'm off to eat, since Amber flashed me a few seconds ago, and it doesn't do to keep that lady waiting when she's on cooking duty!

But, just before I go, I should let you know we've had intel that the Cult is now known to be on a trajectory that will take them to MMMB1O. Those frickin' corporate lot are megalomaniacs; what a pretentious name for what's essentially a shitload of ore processing capacity with residential and leisure inflatable add-ons! The mining base is essentially a commercial operation licensed from Earth by a multinational corporation, so defence was never considered an issue. Though there are rumours that management there is equipped with hand weapons to quell any potential riot among the workers.

Problem is, we're also meant to avoid weaponry and were never provided with any mechanical means to defend our base against attack. But we're probably next on the list for the Cult. And that's something we must prevent at all costs. They see us as the ultimate in genetic design; one of their most hated scientific developments. In short, we represent the work of their frickin' devil. But that's another story. And I really must go and eat.

Record 23: 22:09 20/07/74 Buzz, MB2

Finally got to visit the location they gave me. How the hell we never knew about it is a mystery. Mind you, it's behind a small hatch that looks like there's nothing there but rock. Labelled with a sign that says, 'Danger to Life! Extreme radiation beyond this point.' Then there's a digital lock. No wonder no one's bothered with it. It's way down the end of what I thought was a tunnel built for new storage but never used.

Anyhow, I opened it up, found the board hidden behind a false cover and checked connections to MB3. They work, and everything seems okay after the explosions. The depth under the surface must of been enough to protect it. Linked it to our servers with spare cable and I'm downloading everything to our spare capacity. Take a while; most of the data stored on Earth is on those servers! Won't leave us with much capacity for new observation results, but we'll be away from here soon anyway. Once the download's done, I'll copy to portable media from our servers. We've got a megastore of that at any rate!

Hidden behind the distribution board I found something unexpected. It's a connection to a beta device that can intercept intel from anywhere in the solar system. How the hell it works is a mystery. The device itself must be buried in the servers at MB3. It'll collect the intel and transmit it to their HQ on Earth. What I'd found was really nothing but a card reader linked to the unit. Be there to let agents test the system, or maybe access it. There was talk that NUSA's CIA installed listening devices everywhere. I found the link to the central processing unit for those bugs.

The stuff I downloaded to a memory card was just noise, I thought. But when I went back to my terminal a few hours later the data was all there as text translated from thousands of different sources. Trawled through some of it, all with coded annotations of the source. Came across one of myself, singing in the shower! Bastards obviously bugged our accommodation. CIA always was a suspicious bunch. Wonder if there's anywhere they didn't bug? The man-hours needed to review all that data! Probably had algorithms to detect suspicious activity. Much good it'll do them now.

Didn't find much of interest. Boring, sad, and sometimes weird conversations between people I've never met. A few interesting snippets from colleagues: never knew those two had the hots for me! A couple from Marion having a pretty steamy time. And a man at the mining centre who's a bit too frank when he's with customers. Really didn't want to hear that stuff!

Left another memory card and I'll go back for it later. CIA must of had a direct link to the MB3 servers; with the reader as back-up. Wouldn't make sense otherwise. Won't be getting the direct stuff now. Never know, I might learn something of interest. And it'd be handy to know if those two ladies really were talking about me.

Next thing, though, is to see if I can find their transceiver. Must be on the surface. Got to be well hidden, or that load of shits from Cusp would of destroyed it with the rest. Might be able to rig up a better transmission system for coms with Mars and the Asteroid Belt. Even if I can't discover it, I might be able to redirect the signals. Have to go into the server centre at MB3 for that, and I'm not gonna risk that. Told me to destroy those servers after backup, but it could still be lethal down there. Maybe that's what the N.U.N want.

Record 24: 19:26-074.01.01 – Amber

Amber is at the consoles, bare feet up on the bench supporting the equipment, ankles crossed. Images of dancing men and women caper around her top and skirt, their light costumes a contrast against her dark skin.

Amber's report:

Zaphod's insisting I tell you the story of Georgiy's moment of idiocy. Which one? That's my question. Okay, so I know which one. And, Georgiy, I know you're not an idiot: far from it.

Georgiy may be many things, but a fool isn't one of them. He's a Ruskie, so you have to consider his history and background. It's only in the past forty years they've really understood what democracy means. Not that the rest of the world was any better in real terms. But they finally gave the Ukrainians back their rightful lands and opened up their borders to the Baltic Three again about 35 years ago. That was after Putin's vile descendants were ousted from the throne and the new democratic leadership was recognised. But that's all for later, when we educate you about the history of the planet that gave us birth and you the chance of your new life here on Mars.

I suppose I ought to start by saying who I am and why I'm here, telling this story.

Amber's the name. Though Ma and Pa had me christened Ruth. Christened! Can you imagine, in this day and age? Sorry, of course you can't. Until you learn your social history, you won't even know what it means. Enough to tell you it was an ancient ritual designed to stop your soul being taken over by Satan, another name for the Devil of the Cult, and consigned to a mythical place called Hell. The fact that none of these things has ever actually existed wasn't important to those who believed, of course. But, hey, I'm doing what Zaphod did, diverging from the story.

I'll describe myself in brief, then tell you all about what happened to Georgiy, yesterday. You need to know this, because you need to understand where all your character traits come from, and Georgiy may well turn out to be your dad. And maybe I'm your mum; who knows?

45

So. I'm 26 Earthyears old as I write this. My parents were still of the old Christian faith when I left Earth. Much good it'll do them. But I was fortunate to be brought up properly, without brainwashing, initially in a good state school in a large city called Tallahassee, which has the good fortune to be just enough above sea level to avoid the Great Inundation. It was never on the coast, of course, but it was getting close when I left. The city's in the state of Florida in a country once called the United States of America.

Believe it or not, the USA used an old system of measurement that wasn't base ten. Weird. Can you imagine calculating distances with a system that has twelve inches to a foot, three feet in a yard and seventeen hundred and sixty yards to a mile? (*Hololink to imperial measurement system*) Madness. And their calendar: don't get me started on that. Anyone would believe computers hadn't been invented!

Enough of that.

Georgiy and his stupid, dangerous and unnecessary mission outside: I'll tell it as I recall it, but you have to know I was in love with Georgiy. Still am. Damn! He'll read this and know now. Thing is, we've been brought up and educated to tell only the truth. Back on Earth, myths turned into religions and faith systems and caused no end of conflict and violence and backward thinking. Tell the truth, the commercial base here on Mars allows that, in spite of our efforts to outlaw it. And rumours are the failed Chinese and aborted Indian missions were faith based. That's where the war's coming from, too. Centuries of fighting between different interpretations of so-called sacred texts has resulted in some extremists coming together to form the Cult. Looks like we could become embroiled with them, whether we like it or not.

All of their shit is lies dressed up as religious truths. Incredible, I know, but that's the way it is. So it was decided we'd have none of it here. Only the truth.

Okay. The story. As it happened is probably best.

I was on coms and starting to worry Georgiy wouldn't make it back. The dust storm had been raging for many days. He'd gone out to gather parts he believes to be crucial to the defence we're organising, and the weapons we're having to make. The idea is we'll act once our radar spots incoming threats from those murderous frackin' Cult morons. They captured neutron warheads and combined them with armour-piercing missiles to make holes in their targets before they explode the bombs and wipe out all life. I mean, what sort of mind even thinks of such things?

Georgiy decided to go out and get this equipment. 'One of us has to. The effin' droid's responding badly to the dust and we need those parts. Someone has to go. And that one's me.'

I told him it's a joint responsibility, and if anyone goes it should be me, since I'm the rocket expert. Well, rocket propulsion's one of my specialities, but I was trying to get him to see he's not really responsible. Trouble was, he was overcompensating for his space depression on the flight. None of us blamed him. None of us thought him less a man; least of all me. Even though I've shown him how I feel, that stupid Ruskie macho pride sent him out.

On coms I could've contacted him and asked again how he was doing. But we have protocols. Wasted energy and time on needless chat might delay work and put him in danger. Still, I desperately wanted to know.

Hoshiko passed Comspod on her way to Washpod; we all go for showers without clothes, as the humidity in there makes everything damp and clothes stick to you afterwards. It's easier to dress in your quarters.

'Enjoy, Hoshiko.'

'Georgiy not back yet?'

I started to explain, but he came online, his voice muffled and indistinct at first. Then he came over loud and clear. 'Frickin' airlock's not responding. Been here five minutes trying to get the fricker open.'

Hoshiko loped up the tunnel to the airlock, gravity letting her dancer's skill elongate her steps into three metre floating leaps.

'Hoshiko's on her way to check interior controls. Copy, Georgiy?'

47

'Copy. No reason it should be stuck.'

'Stop talking. You're wasting air. Send me the signal every ten.'

'Autolocation's on, Amber. And there's half an hour in my tanks.'

I smiled at his use of the old term; something we all did from time to time, but I knew what he meant. I consciously relaxed before speaking again. 'Listen you Ruskie moron, I can see autolocation's on. I know where you are. But I need a live feed from you, so I know you're still actually there. Now shut the frick up and do it every ten.'

'Don't talk to me like that! I'll have you …'

'You can have me any which way you want, Georgiy: upside-down, backwards, on all fours, dangling from the ceiling, anything. But not until you're back inside. Now, cap it and await further instructions. Copy?'

'Copy. And I didn't mean like that.'

I knew what he meant, more's the pity; still in his old command mode. But I waited, and got the first short beep after eleven. A smile. It was good he was still able to play the fool.

Hoshiko's gentle tones called from the end of the tunnel. 'Some idiot's set the lock on timed. Tell Georgiy I'll release it in seven. Copy?'

'Copy, Hoshiko.' I re-ordered the multiple screens and found him; a hunched figure at the entrance with thin dust and odd bits of waste swirling round him, shouldering a droid. Darker red clouds blurred more distant shapes. 'Try again now, Georgiy. Copy?'

'Copy, Amber.'

I watched as he turned the mechanical lock. He left the edge of one screen and re-emerged on the next, inside the airlock, dragging the droid behind him. The scrubbers and vacs went to work as soon as the hatch was shut.

'Inside. Copy, Amber?'

'Copy, Georgiy. I'll join Hoshiko and wait for you.'

'Two of you? Maybe I'll go back out if that's the prize. Mebbie Annika might be persuaded too, eh?'

'Behave yourself, or I'll deny privileges.' As if!

His snort of disbelief had me smiling. I passed Anni's workpod on the way along the tunnel. She was relieved to know Georgiy was back inside.

'He should never have gone. It's a joint problem.' She stroked a hand through her long blonde hair and rose from the bench. Her current experiment, to increase the nutritional value of the maize, evident in samples scattered over the graphalloy sheen of her bench top.

She joined me, glanced at my body. 'On Earth, those wouldn't still be that pert, they'd already be showing signs of gravitational sag.'

'Mars does as Mars is.' I cupped one and then the other. 'Anyway, you can talk, with that pair! Has to be some benefit to livin' in a hole in the ground; we're not frickin' Hobbits, after all.'

We reached the airlock, where Hoshiko had her face glued to the small porthole.

'He started unsuiting yet?'

She jumped at my question, concentration on the view holding her mind. 'Started. Took a while for the vacuums to get rid of the dust. He insisted they clean the droid thoroughly. Pressures equalised now.'

I opened the hatch and stepped through to help him shed the rest of the suit: always easier with two.

Hoshiko peeked through and watched. 'Be twelve minutes before he's ready.' She pulled back. 'Time for my shower.'

We watched the pale skinned woman skip lightly down the tunnel to Washpod. 'Don't forget to leave that there for water reclamation.'

Once showered, we could turn the unit into a water reclamation plant to suck the moisture out of everything, so always left our drying cloths in there afterwards. We have a good supply of water here, but it's still a finite resource and we've been trained to waste nothing.

Hoshiko turned, posed, and waved at Georgiy before she entered the cubicle.

'Exhibitionist!'

She stepped back out, a grin of mischief warming her perfect features.

Annika sighed. She was the only one who still felt shy at times. Didn't stop her, but she felt uncomfortable. 'I wish I could completely ditch the traditions and beliefs of two millennia. I know you're right, Amber, but it's hard to get completely shot of those ties.'

Thoughts about my own fundamentalist parents surfaced. I even found my hands covering my breasts. Damn them with their brainwashing. I needed to do something. I started a short programme of exercise to deflect unwelcome thoughts while Georgiy stood in the final booth and let the soft brushes and suction pump tease off the last of the dust he'd collected. Annika watched me for a while. Finally, she nodded as though she'd come to a decision and joined in. To conclude the routine, we used each other to oppose muscles less easily exercised alone. As we were doing this, Georgiy exited, dragging the failed droid behind him.

'Nice, girls. Couldn't wait for me?'

Anni detached herself from me and planted a firm palm across his buttocks. More than I dare! The sound echoed along the alum walls, joined by his brief grunt of surprised protest. Hoshiko returned, floral and fresh, and smiled at the tableau.

But Anni was serious. 'You deserve a good spanking! What makes you think you can go out there without consulting us, Georgiy?'

Sufficiently attuned to her real concerns to avoid encouraging her threat of further personal discipline with a suitable quip, Georgiy nodded. 'Had to do something, Anni. We've been trapped by this frickin' dust storm too long and time's counting by. As colony leader, the risk was mine.'

'Colony leader? Leader, Georgiy? No one's leader here. And don't you forget it. We're all equals. And I don't give a fried frack about your macho need to demonstrate your courage. None of us ever doubts you on that score. But you should've spoken to us.' She allowed him to respond with a nod of penitent agreement. 'Get the parts?'

He leant the damaged droid against the curved wall and hugged Annika. I watched her slowly relax into an embrace I envied and saw her echo the movement of his hands as he stroked her in comfort. 'Sorry, you're right. The droid had nearly done it, to be honest. Dust defeated it; clogged lenses. We need to do something about that. But I got the parts.'

'We should get Maddie to look into it. You'd have thought by now they'd have solved the problem.'

Georgiy nodded. 'Exactly.' Conscious of the growing effect of their prolonged hug, he parted from Anni and turned to a more pressing matter. 'But what I want to know right now, is who took the frickin' airlock off manual after I'd gone out. That's either criminally stupid or a deliberate attempt to put me in danger.'

We all need to know. That one of us could have acted so stupidly, or worse, dangerously, is a serious concern. Our very existence relies on total trust. It's hard to believe any of the group could do something so irresponsible.

I should finish this report, really. But I'll indulge in a bit of history for you. Probably best you learn it in short bursts so it doesn't get too boring. I know I found a lot of the history they taught us at school irrelevant and dry. Only later did I see how vital it is to know what happened before you were born. I mean what really happened, not the stories made up by those with their own agenda.

A personal story? Maybe tell you how I was selected as one of The Chosen? Yeah, that might do.

It started way back when I was six years old; Earthyears. Yeah, six. It was like that for most of us. Already, secret powers, the ones who'd been running the world, knew Earth was getting more and more perilous for humanity. They formed a Power Action Group, which they called The Guardian; shorthand for their aims. The Guardian had agents on the lookout for the right sort of kids. This mission to Mars was already in the planning stages even then. Scary to think those minds were aware of the coming dangers on Earth but even such powerful people couldn't stop it. Gone too far by that time.

Vested interest made it impossible for right thinking people to get their voices heard for decades. Commerce, Multinationals they called them, had taken over the running of the world in all but name. And the people who formed The Guardian were all financially independent through inheritance or active at the top of Big Business. There wasn't a government anywhere with the freedom to do what its people wanted, even if politicians were minded to take such action. Most were in the pockets of business moguls anyway. The likelihood of positive action against industry and exploitation was highly improbable. The Guardian told us they were an elite group who'd concluded, rather too late in the day, that their rape of the planet had caused the damage. Creating The Chosen, was their way of trying to repay their debt to humanity. Money had ruled them all, like a drug: addicts, the lot of them. Addicted to wealth. Mind, you won't know about money, or leisure drugs, since we don't use either. I won't go into detail: you'll learn about that folly in your education sessions. (*Hololinks to posts on money, wealth, leisure drugs*)

Then there were the various god squads. Again, I won't go into detail: you'll be taught about the various legends that ruled people's lives. (*Hololink to world religions*) My parents were active in what they called the Church. Good people, but brainwashed by their own parents and the schooling they'd had. People used by these organisations to raise funds and keep people of power in positions of influence.

We lived in a world where it was actually considered good, laudable even, to believe in something there was no evidence for. 'Faith' they called it, and it was something those who held it were very protective over; proud, even. So much so, it was even difficult to discuss it rationally. They seemed unaware that encouraging people to believe in something without evidence was the same as pressing people into believing lies. Hard to credit, but it's true. I was lucky my parents were also right wing; a political term describing people who think money's more important than society. (*Hololink to political parties*) The coincidence of their religious and political beliefs persuaded them to let me go to The Guardian in exchange for a large sum of money. That let my parents raise my brothers and sisters in traditions and beliefs they'd been raised in themselves. Sad. I've had almost nothing to do with them since they sold me. They appeased their consciences by allowing themselves to believe they were doing the best for me, too. The reality is they didn't care; could've been selling me into slavery for all they knew! But it turned out to be the best thing they could've done.

Anyway, all these vested interests made it hard for common sense and rational thought to have any sort of say in what was happening in the world. Mixed philosophies let a third of the world exist in starvation when there was food to feed everyone, and some to spare. They let a small number of individuals accrue vast wealth on the spurious grounds they were worth more than other people. That combination of religious faith and commercial distortions of reality let people truly believe they'd made fortunes entirely unaided. You'll know, living here, we're all utterly interdependent. None of us could manage even everyday tasks without the input of others. That was equally true back on Earth, but it wasn't valued. It wasn't understood the way we embrace it.

So, these agents of The Guardian were looking for kids who showed a basic sense of justice and fairness. We had to be well into genius levels of intelligence. Had to show we accepted nothing without question. Had to be physically fit and active. We all had some sort of creative ability, even as kids. For me that was, still is, a love of inventing dance and music. I love to move, and music moves me.

Once we came to the attention of those who were looking for us, we were separated from our families. Teachers, child carers, medics, social workers, (*Hololink to social work*) all the people with close connections to young children, were paid to look out for the qualities required for The Chosen.

Thousands of kids made it past the first hurdle, but only a dozen of us made it all the way. A dozen! There's a term you won't come across often. It means twelve and was a commonly used measure back on Earth. Stems from their weird distance measures, the ones I've already mentioned. And those strange measures started off for reasons mostly lost in time. But, according to some sources, a foot, which was twelve inches, was based on the length of the actual foot of the King in power in England at the time. And twelve was the base figure because one of the many prophets worshipped by the early primitives was believed to have had twelve followers. (*Hololink to Christianity*) Too much info. You'll gradually learn what all that means as time goes on.

So, we were placed in special units and kept away from godbotherers so we wouldn't be brainwashed. We were also kept free of money-lust by sharing things that interested us all. So, if a lot of us wanted to play a certain game, the necessary equipment was provided. Some children who hadn't been sold were removed from the units early because their parents were convinced they had to have a certain type of education. I felt sorry for those kids; they lost a real chance to move forward and become something special, just because their parents had no vision.

Once we reached puberty, we were taken out of the units in our States and put in a special international school where we lived and worked together. By this time, we'd been whittled down to a few hundred, and our families had little more to do with us. It must have been hard for those who actually cared, as we lived in a place considered the most neutral and unlikely to be affected by environmental or political upheaval. The international school was on a small island in the South Pacific Ocean, about two thousand kilometres from an island nation called New Zealand. One of the Cook Islands, its population was completely wiped out by the Great Inundation (*Hololink to Great Inundation*) that swamped the coast and drowned all the tiny villages there. Our school was built on the hills that remained. It was well away from influences The Guardian felt we should be spared …

Annika enters the space and stands behind Amber.

54

'Telling them about our induction and education, Amber?'

'Oh, hello, Anni. You going to have a go at the record thing again?'

'Not just now. Busy with the newly hatched butterflies.'

'And the hatchlings, I suppose?'

'It's so time-consuming, trying to keep them fit and well at this stage, Amber.'

'Vital to the ecology once we expand production, though.'

'I just came in to let you know we'll be eating soon. And there's the meeting about Georgiy's misfortune after that. Maybe time to draw to a close for now?'

Anni's gone off again. You'll find this record interrupted like that now and again. Reppod's the only place in Marion isolated from coms. It's made that way to stop unwanted announcements intruding into reports. We can be flashed a pre-arranged signal, but that's all. Anyone who wants to talk to you has to come in and catch your attention.

She's right. I'll break here. I'm glad we're having the meeting, though. I want to know which idiot put Georgiy in danger.

Record 25: 24:21-144.01.01 Georgiy

Georgiy is seated at the consoles. His hairy chest is broad and he's a muscular man with his head hair cut too short.

Georgiy's report:

Okay, so I'm a Ruskie. It don't make me a bad man. Don't mean I'm a gangster or a shmuck. Yeah, our leaders in the past were despots or gangsters, or, in the case of that Putin clan, both. But we're a stubborn people. And we don't want others telling us what's right, even when we know it's true. Takes us a while to come to the right conclusion, but we get there. Proud? Yeah, we're proud. With reason.

Hadn't been for us, this enterprise would never have got off the ground. We put as much into this as the Yanks, Brits and Neuropeans. More'n the Aussies and Japs.

I'm the only Russian. We could only afford a small number for a project like this. I'm lucky to be here. Good folks in this group. Brilliant hot women, talented men. Everyone's a genius, except those pioneer ladies we took on. Still they've got engineering and other science skills and we've all got our specialist areas to keep things going and develop new ideas.

Before I fill you in about myself, history, that stuff, I'd best let you know about that incident with the airlock. It's caused a deal of fuss.

Yeah. It's right I did it because of the stupid thing I did on the space walk. But, hey, like Zaphod says, I wasn't in my right head. Been a long trip and the delay caused by that frickin' sail dysfunction tipped me over. I was responsible on the trip here and it was like I'd let them down. I see now that was crap. But, like I say, my head was a mess. And the gender equality thing's still in its early days; The Guardian said some of us men (meaning me) might have problems adjusting. I do; I know I shouldn't, but, hey, I'm Russian. They, well some of them, think I'm old school. I'm not. I know it's a privilege, not a right. And I treat every one of them that way: an honour to share her body. But you have to give the impression you're in charge as the man, even when she's on top. Enough on that.

We held the meeting in the Mess, since that's the only space with enough seats for all of us. Some to spare, in fact; ready for the new-borns. People like you reading this account. Not the most comfortable room, but the place we can all meet without stepping on each other. Anyhow, we had to find out who'd locked me outside.

No one admitted it. That was a problem, since we all tell the truth. It's in our bones now; the way we were all raised together and how we really all know each other better than even if we were brothers and sisters, we can't lie.

'So,' I said, 'if it wasn't one of us, who was it?'

The pioneer women looked uncomfortable. They never had our intensive training or the GE, so they can tell lies. They're all pretty good women; nice bodies and useful skills, but they ain't The Chosen. It's natural we'd suspect them.

Sarm, the skinny sexy Brit with skin like silk, spoke first. (*Hololink to Sarm*) 'I know you all think it was one of us. I can only tell you it wasn't me. For a start I'd have no reason to put you in danger, Georgiy. You know how much I love fucking you and I'd never want to lose that. I can't see why any of us here in this room would want to endanger anyone.'

'Jealousy?' Tu suggested.

Katniss, she's the boobiful American, looked guilty at that. (*Hololink to Katniss*) 'Okay, it's true I fancy the hell out of that Ruskie brute, but I get my turn. And the other men turn me on, too. I'd never let jealousy make me do anything so stupid. If anything, I'd be finding ways to lose the other women, wouldn't I? That way there'd be less competition for the few cocks around here.'

I love the way Katniss talks. She's named for some movie heroine from the past: her grandparents were fans, apparently. And she's got balls, which I like in a woman. A good screw. I give her what she wants when I can. But, like she says, with four cocks to pleasure fourteen fannies, there's bound to be some dissatisfaction.

'Wasn't me. If it's not robotics, I'm a dummkopf. You all know that. Hell, you tell me often enough.' Brigitte, with a jucilicious body fit for one of The Chosen, is a German married to an astrophysicist or something still on the Moon. (*Hololink to Brigitte*) She's a genius with heavy robots but hasn't a clue about much else. Phobos! To look at her you wouldn't think she'd have the strength to deal with all that heavy metal. But she's strong. And when she gets over her guilt about havin' some fun while her husband plays at science on the Moon, she's a good screw.

Jai glanced around the room, black eyes squinting with speculation. 'Could it have been a droid?'

It's a thought. Disturbing and unlikely as it is, there's just the faintest possibility.

'I'll run checks. Make sure none of them are malfunctioning. I'll start after the meeting.' Madonna nodded at me.

'Thanks, Maddie.'

'The only alternative's one of us. Can't see that, though.' Amber's observation had everyone shaking their heads in agreement.

'A mystery, then. Let's assume it's a droid until Maddie's checked the frickers, eh?' I was dissatisfied but closed the debate, for now. 'Need any help with that?'

'Maybe I can help?' Brigitte looked keen and Maddie nodded. The pair went off together to her workpod to find out what they could from the twenty-three droids we've got in the colony.

I came in here to get this off my chest before sleep. That's where I'm off to now.

Record 26: 03:33-21/07/2074 Abdul-Aziz: Terrorist Leader in Space.

This report was intercepted at the time by automated spyware fitted to all spacecraft by a NUSA agency called CIA. They must've been a very suspicious lot to fit equipment to cargo carriers that were never intended for live occupants!

Message from the terrorist leader in flight to the head man of CUSP on Earth:

Babak, most respected and worthy leader of the Sacred mission. We have commandeered the necessary transport facility to permit our onward journey. As agreed, we are destined for the minor stars, where the heathens will fall from power and we will cut off their source of income as easily as we cut off their unworthy heads! They will wail at our audacity. After we clean those rocks of their pollution, we will take the return and undo all they have achieved on the place of war. Nothing will remain then of their existence and we will come back to the shining night sphere and there conclude our mission in space. Our final act will be to plunge our craft into the turmoil of the air around the world and thus join you, our brothers, as we burn with the righteous heat of sacred passion on our most final journey.

This is the last message from Abdul-Aziz, your most humble servant, leading the good men into final battles against the evil. Peace and Glory be to the Almighty!

Record 27: 23:14 22/07/2074 Buzz, MB2

Rocket scientists at Aldrin TC are looking at ways to modify ore carriers. Those things are just automated containers for ore and refined metal brought from Mars for onward launch to Earth. We've lost that connection, so the local workers for MegaMetalCorp say there's no need for them to continue the traffic. No point, in fact.

If we can modify enough containers, we can get everyone off the Moon to Mars. Brigitte's lot won't want us, but we've got enough equipment to house and support us on the planet till Marion or MMMB10 take us in. It's not what we wanted, but we've got no choice. They've got plenty of water and their food production's meant to support a growing population, so they should be able to manage.

Looking at how I might help them at Marion, so they'll be more welcoming when we tell them we're on our way.

Record 28: 02:49-077:01:01 Georgiy

Georgiy is pacing up and down in Reppod. His boxers show scenes from past Russian space missions. He seems agitated but he finally sits down.

Georgiy's report:

Tension's been a bit high since the meeting. Maddie checked all the droids and they're operating right. So there's a bit of suspicion in the air. Not good for morale. We had another brief meeting in the mess, but it didn't solve anything and we all went off to do our own things.

Sarm (*Hololink to Sarm*) had been eying me with undisguised lust at the meeting. I felt like a bit of uncomplicated action so I beckoned her over and she came right away. As a pioneer, she doesn't have private quarters yet. They all share till there's time to build more individual rooms, so I took her to mine.

I say, 'took her', but she's been on Mars for months, preparing for our arrival, so she's got the walk down to an art. And what an art!

It's always twenty-four Celsius underground so we're always warm. What with limited fabric and only basic laundry facilities we decided on the bare minimum. The Chosen ditched the idiot false modesty about our bodies long before we set out for the planet. Sarm, like the rest of the pioneer corps, used to wear a uniform of grey sleeveless top and black knee-length pants. But she took advantage of our dress code right away. Wears that short skirt and the usual bolero top the women tie over their boobs. No need for bras on Mars (hey, I'm a poet!) Low gravity stops their boobs drooping. Some wear a thong underneath, men and women, but only a couple. Some use them for exercise. Personal choice. The way Sarm moves; well, in spite of her skinny frame, I was glad to get her into my quarters, I can tell you.

Afterwards, I held her shoulder as she rested her head on my chest. 'Georgiy, will we pioneers really have to make babies with you men?'

'When we're settled: that was the agreement. Accom's sorted for that already. It's why we're here, Sarm. The future of the human race is with us.'

'What about the Lunar Bases?'

Good question. 'They're not set up for growth or permanence. Any case, The Chosen are superior breeding stock and we all want the best kids we can make, don't we?'

She lifted her head and brushed blonde strands from eyes the colour of a winter Russian sky (see, said I was a poet, didn't I?). 'I'm not Chosen. Won't I dilute the quality?'

I wasn't sure she was serious; that twinkle in those eyes ... 'Long as half the genes come from one of The Chosen, the kids'll be fine.'

'So, no one from the Moon, then?'

'The Moon colony's only for telescopes, a transit camp and a staging post for equipment and people to get to Mars. And the commercial mining stuff for the Asteroid Belt. It's no place humanity can survive for long without support from Earth or Mars.'

'Will they be able to get here, do you think?'

'Someone you fancy there, Sarm?'

'Brigitte's husband's on the Moon.'

Her chances of seeing him again aren't good, but you can't tell women that. Any case, I had other things on my mind.

'First, we gotta stop those Cult morons destroying us.'

'Can we do that? I mean, it's pretty advanced tech for a small base.'

'If we don't, we're history. So is the human race.'

Right then, the power died. Anyone superstitious might've taken that as a sign. I know better: coincidence is a lot more common than people think.

Underground, it's about as dark as can be. No way we'd find our clothes. But I knew my pod as well as a man knows anywhere. I took her hand and helped her into the corridor. The sounds told me others were there, too. Not a light anywhere. Without power, we'd all be dead in a pretty short time. But auxiliary cut in within the five minute window. I checked later; took exactly three minutes and two seconds for the emergency lights to come on.

That was a scene. Anni and Jai were holding hands a little way up the corridor. Maddie was still half asleep and Tu wasn't much more awake, but they were wrapped round each other. Amber came out of her pod just as the lights came on, followed by Zaphod. In the dim green light from the emergency LEDs down the middle of the corridors, nothing looked real and detail was unclear.

Amber saw it first. She stared into the depths of the main corridor and then nonchalantly turned her back to the spot she'd been looking at. Her finger went to her lips very deliberately and we all waited. Everything about her pose and look kept us quiet. Our training kicked in; possible unknown danger.

Amber leant forward and whispered to Zaphod. He stiffened briefly, then relaxed as he took her hand and they moved forward together.

'It's probably nothing. Auto'll fix it. We're off for some fun in Rec. See you all in the morning.' She let Zaphod lead her down the corridor towards whatever she'd been staring at; nowhere near Recroom.

They walked purposefully but in no hurry, hands lightly clasped and looking like they were after some fun. The rest of us moved back into the nearest spaces, waiting for the result of their investigation without being too far to help.

Two paces from the door leading to Plantcon, Amber let go Zaphod's hand and reached forward quickly. There was a gasp and Zaphod moved to the other side of whatever she'd grabbed.

'Everyone here, now!' Zaphod's voice echoed down the corridor and we all ran toward them.

What we saw didn't make sense. They were wrestling something that moved unseen between them. They carried on struggling as we approached. The change from mystery to solution was sudden. Amber moved purposefully to something we couldn't see. There, between them, struggled an intruder in a full-body skin-tight that shimmered and made his features difficult to see. Amber found where the top half of the suit joined the bottom. She pulled it up. Pale, yellowish skin showed, but the man continued to struggle, making it hard for her to take his suit off. But we all now knew we were dealing with a man and not some unknown life form.

'Stay still or I'll disable you!' Zaphod's warning worked.

The man stopped struggling. Amber stripped the top off over his head. There stood a stranger, a Chinese man about her age and height.

'Who the frick are you?' I was certain he was the bastard who'd locked me outside.

He was terrified but didn't talk. Just shook his head.

'Listen, Chink, tell me your name. Now. Or I'll strip the rest of your suit off and put you outside.'

The man couldn't move with Zaphod and Amber holding him. My threat terrified him and he looked like he might collapse.

'Now! Last warning.'

He nodded. 'I Chang. I from Chinese mission.'

Impossible. The Chinese Mars mission had famously crashed on landing. Everyone knew that. Their own control centre had said the mission was a failure. Anyway, how the frick had the bastard got here and inside our complex without being detected? The whole thing stunk. Working in the way our training as a team dictated, we all moved along the corridor into Recroom.

'Someone get systems back up and running.'

Chang spoke again. 'I turn off main switch.'

Simple as that!

Only my training stopped me giving the bastard a frickin' good beating. Jai left, and the lighting went back to normal. The rest of us found seats in the room we use for relaxation and recuperation. Jai came back with a pair of restraints. He secured Chang's arms at his back and attached him to a support strut. With the invader secured, we began to relax a bit.

Chang couldn't look at the women and kept his gaze to the floor, like he was scared of them. Mind you, his gens reacted in an entirely different way! I stood in front of him and reached to raise his chin but he jerked his head up and scanned us all. He settled on my face. 'Why you all ... naked?'

We'd all been in bed. 'Was it you changed the airlock settings?'

He looked down again. 'You go outside. Might see … see signs I come here.'

'So you locked me outside? You were happy to kill me to keep me quiet?'

He mumbled.

'That's stupid, anyway. There won't be any footprints or any visible signs in this wind. And we'd spot your rover straight away.' Anni's tone was reasonable and Chang glanced at her for an instant. 'Unless you hid it, of course.'

'Look, Chang, you've come here in secret, you say from the Chinese mission, and you've risked the life of one of us. What did you come for?'

He glanced at Amber but seemed unable, or more like unwilling, to explain. I'd had enough. 'If he's not going to talk, let the bugger stew. Amber, Madonna, strip him to make sure he's unarmed.'

They looked puzzled, but I had my reasons. Gently, they peeled away the lower half of his suit, in spite of his struggles. He was wearing patterned cotton briefs, bursting with undisguised desire. Madonna tried to take them off, but he wriggled and squirmed in protest.

'Everything. His suit made him invisible. We can't trust he's no other tech hidden. I want him secured for the night.'

Zaphod held him still as the women stripped him completely. There was no more tech to be seen. Chang grumbled loudly in his own language, threatening and noisy. He was embarrassed and tried to curl up to hide his sex from us.

Hoshiko left and returned with a handheld scanner. She signalled Tu and he helped Zaphod hold the prisoner upright as she checked for internal electronics. It showed a fairly standard chip planted under the skin above his left ear. It was likely a com-enhancer: he jerked into stillness when she used her own to send him a translation of her command to be still.

'Okay. If the fricker won't talk now, let's leave him to think about

64

it. He's secure here. But someone should be on guard. The rest of us should sleep. We'll try again in the morning. Any volunteers?'

'The women make him uncomfortable. I'll stay with him.' Tu's offer surprised me. His Chinese heritage was something he never talked about and we'd never heard him speak the language, though he spoke Italian fluently alongside English, Russian and a couple of other European tongues.

We accepted his offer and the rest of us shuffled off to our beds, together or alone. I gently rejected Amber's offer of company: of all the women, she distracts me most. I needed to be alone to think about the problem of Chang.

'Two minds, Georgiy …'

'Maybe, Amber. But two bodies …?'

She shrugged and went alone to her own quarters.

I lay awake, wondering what we should do about the intruder. He'd been willing to let me die out there. That showed he didn't care about human life or else he'd been desperate not to be found. But, if he didn't want us to know he was here, why had he come to the base? How the hell had he found us anyway? How had he got here from the Chinese mission? That had failed. Word was all the crew had died on landing, or a short time after. In spite of the Chinks' attempts at secrecy, the failure was common knowledge. No surprise, given their lack of proper funding and the way they relied on the pseudo-Christian god they'd made their leader since the end of communism. Except it wasn't a deity in charge. It was priests as front men and the rest of the hierarchy as it always had been; just hidden. Same men in control; different titles.

What did he want? He'd gone to the trouble of wearing one of the more reliable invisibility suits; technology rumoured to be well-advanced in China. But it must've made the experience really uncomfortable. Those things have to cover the whole body and face to be effective. I couldn't imagine walking far in a space suit with one of those underneath. It would've made the journey horrible. But,

Chang must've put the suit on in his pressurised rover and walked from wherever he'd hidden it. And how the frick did he get in? Where's his space suit? Why didn't our security systems discover him? There are cameras everywhere for frack's sake!

He couldn't have walked all the way from the Chinese base. Their camp was a hundred and fifty odd kilometres away, so we gathered. Too far to walk. He must have transport. Where the frack was it?

The questions kept me awake, so I came in here to write this.

Record 29: 03:37-23/07/2074 Original source possibly WWNC

The final, broken and distorted images are received on the Moon. Lacking any meaningful soundtrack, they show a part of the world shattered beyond identification. Ruined buildings, blackened tree stumps and pools of filthy water in craters all crouch beneath a sky in deepest turmoil, its dark clouds rent by incessant lightning strikes. The clip lasts only seconds and nothing further can be retrieved from the home planet after this short insight.

Record 30: 04:57-077.01.01 Tu

Tu, a muscular man who clearly works out, is bending over the consoles in Reppod. His chest is devoid of hair and his boxers display scientific symbols of various types, some of which are in construction as they move over the surface. He brushes a hand through his dark hair and then sits.

Tu's report:

Tu. Chinese by parentage. Italian by birth. Marsper by choice. 27 Earthyears old. No siblings. No special female partner. Like the others, a multi-functioning scientist. My speciality's atmosphere and, in particular, the ongoing terraforming project.

We're still working out how to building a weapons grade laser, which is likely to be our best long distance defence against the brutal Cult. You'll know about war on Earth, using missiles, aircraft and other fast moving devices to deliver death and troops to the enemy. But Mars can't yet support flight in that way. So weaponry's limited to strikes from outside the atmosphere by rockets, which we don't have, or ground deployment, which is slow and ponderous. Fortunately, those conditions apply to both sides. And we know the Cult came here in a single stolen spacecraft. We're certain, through intel from all sources, they've no access to other spacecraft, so they'll have to invade overland when they arrive. That gives us the benefit of knowing when they set out and when they come into range. Once we master the techniques needed to build the laser and find a way to deploy it over long distance, we should have an advantage. It was never expected we'd be involved in conflict, so The Guardian, rather idealistically, missed that element from our supplies and training. We were supposed to occupy a world of peace and tranquillity with the only challenges coming from the environment and our pioneering status. A nice dream, but unrealistic.

So, that's the latest on the Cult. Let's get to our present situation. In particular, the sudden problem of Chang. I speak five languages and get by in another seven. One's Mandarin so it made sense for me to talk to him. (*Hololink to Chang*)

Let's try to understand that man. You'll not know many Chinese and those you do meet here won't be anything like those living on Earth at present. China was ruled for decades by a hard-line communist elite who, like all leaders, had one set of rules for themselves and another for the people. Guess what? Their rules allowed them to live in luxury and privilege while the people they ruled often lived in poverty. No surprises there. Just one of many reasons we abandoned the idea of leaders.

When capitalism started to fall apart, or to be more precise, when the inevitable cracks in that unjust system started to widen to chasms, the Chinese hybrid structure became untenable. Their brand of communism was a sort of slave-based socialism for most of the population. Selected individuals were allowed to operate as capitalists, as long as part of their profits went into the pockets of the ruling elite. It depended on trade with the rest of the world and was utterly reliant on the success of other economies. The world economy was fractured and broken by the rich and powerful who let greed overcome common sense.

Anyway, cut a long story short, Chinese leaders saw they were in the shit with Communism. But they knew the power of superstition over the gullible and needy: Communism's just a different type of religion. So they designed a new one. They concocted a faith based loosely on the Abrahamic myth of Jesus, merged it with the philosophy of Buddha and chucked in a few bits of home-grown Confucius to make the population comfortable. All three are traditionally paternalistic and give women a subservient role, so the new faith, which they called the Complete Church of China, was a poor deal for females. Typical of Chinese isolationism, which grew tighter after they merged with North Korea, they kept their people ignorant of the rest of the world and much of the rest of the world ignorant about internal happenings in China.

Computer technology was already global and the internet, in spite of attempts by the rich and powerful to constrain it, was a widespread source of info. The Chinese put barriers in place to stop international traffic for their people. But there are always individuals who'll break such restrictions, in both directions. So some Chinese got to know the reality of the outside world and some of the outside world got to know truths about China.

What I'm trying to get over to you is Chang's a child of that society. He's been raised in a world of faith based on fear of a demonic afterlife for those who disobey, where women are objects to serve men. Not just raised that way, but indoctrinated: brainwashed. And this is the man I had to try to reason with. It's almost impossible to get a man of faith to understand a rational point of view. But that's what I had to try. First, I had to win him over, get him to trust me, so I could discover as much truth as possible.

He's scared and embarrassed by nakedness and his immediate and obvious physical reaction to our uninhibited way of going about. Whether that's due to the women, the men, or both, being naked from our beds, I can't tell. On Earth, people generally concealed their bodies in public, except when they were taking part in certain sports.

We accept casual nudity. We've lived together for years. All had sex with all the opposite gender on many occasions, so nothing needs to be hidden and none of us has any shame about our bodies. We're comfortable in our skins and sometimes walk about in them.

So, first thing I had to do was get Chang's confidence. He wasn't going to open up tied naked to a strut. I unshipped a couple of the emergency foil wraps we have for cases of exposure to cold. Thin, almost weightless, and made of grapholene merged with aluminium, they're soft and relatively concealing. I released his restraints and gave him one to wrap round himself and, though I dislike the restriction, wrapped myself so he wouldn't be embarrassed.

'Time to talk, Chang. I'm Tu and speak Mandarin, if that's easier for you. But I'd rather we converse in English, since it's the universal language.'

'Chinese spoken by more people.'

I nodded. 'Might've been once. But not now and not here.'

He screwed up his eyes, examining me. I gave him time to consider his situation and his future. Once he seemed a little less anxious, I started questioning.

'First, how did you get here?'

He bit his top lip, pulling the teeth over the flesh a few times before settling. 'I come in rover. Your Comtower and space elevators guide me.'

Those tall structures could be seen for many kilometres, but not all the way from the Chinese base. 'GPS?'

He nodded.

'Alone?'

69

He nodded again.

'How many at your base?'

'Twenty-one of you here. Thirty-three of us at Glorious Chinese Complex.' (*Hololink to GCC*)

'Thirty-three? That's quite a number. How many men, women?'

I swear I could see his mind at work, counting.

'Three men, rest women.'

I wonder what the truth is. 'So, the stories about your crew dying on crash-landing are just rumours?'

He bristled. 'Chinese technology superior to all other. We landed our glorious craft exactly as planned and our base is the supreme …' He became aware he was no longer speaking in the pidgin English he'd adopted to begin with, and turned away from me.

'It's okay. I see why you were pretending you couldn't speak perfect English. But the reality's easier for both of us, isn't it?'

He mumbled something inaudible in Mandarin, then straightened up and looked at me, his dark eyes full of challenge. 'Mandarin is the supreme language. But the rest of the world's too ignorant to understand the wonder of our tongue, so we use our greater intelligence to learn English.'

'Good. And, of course, none of the many Chinese languages and dialects are ideal for digital purposes, are they?' I became aware I sounded hostile. Something about his manner got to me. But I was supposed to be winning his trust. 'So long as we can communicate easily, it'll suit both of us, eh?'

He nodded at that.

'Where's your rover, and your spacesuit, Chang?'

He glanced at the floor, then raised his head and thrust his chest out. 'I hid them. I hid the rover beyond the horizon, walked the rest of the way, and made one of your androids hide my spacesuit after I entered the airlock.'

That explained some of the mysteries. 'How did you evade our detectors and cameras?'

A cunning look swept across his face before he had the resolve to prevent it. I think he's pretty near exhausted after his trip and the effort of staying hidden.

'I'm the best coder ever. I can hack anything. Anything. It's easy to fool autos once you know the basics. Simple.'

He'd blanked the system so he would be unseen. Clever to make it specific to him. And a little worrying he'd found it so simple to bypass our security.

'Three men and thirty women living at your base, Chang? What made them send you here alone?'

He stared at his feet. 'My decision. I'm their leader. Their Prime and Holy Pastor. They expect such action from me. The women are weak and unsuited to danger. The other men are brilliant scientists and technicians but know nothing of personal risk. I'm the only one with survival experience. It had to be me.'

'I have to ask, then, since your base is so perfect and without problems, why you came here in secret?'

He raised his face and stared into my eyes. Superiority? Arrogance? Difficult to tell, until he spoke again. 'I come to offer our services and give you help. Why else would I come?'

I was growing tired of his obvious lies. 'Because your base is in serious trouble and you're desperate for help but you'd rather play the part of supreme leader and pretend all's well, even if that means putting the rest of your party in danger.'

To my amazement, that seemed to completely deflate him. He sort of shrunk into himself and sighed long and deep; a sound that carried all the worries of his world.

'You're right. We did crash land and much equipment was destroyed. Some was only damaged. Some crew died. We'll run out of water in sixteen days. The aquifer we use is smaller than our pioneer team claimed. Our energy source is compromised. Our food stocks are dwindling. I came here for help.'

'It might've been simpler if you'd just called us and asked.'

'We're a proud race. We know how degenerate are the heathen peoples of the West. We know about the rape of strangers, the en-slavement of foreign women, the torture of all men not from your lands ...'

'Rumours put about by your government to keep you from freedoms we represent. Rape's been almost unknown in our society for three decades. Men and women are equal beings. Torture's anathema to us. You've been lied to, Chang. No wonder you wanted to remain hidden. You must've been terrified.'

'I've seen evidence! Videos, documents, news reports. Our defensive barriers in China didn't stop us learning what happens in the outside world.'

I should've noticed the zeal in his eyes, but I ploughed on. 'What you've seen is what you were allowed to see; fiction, not reality. Your government spent decades restricting the people's access to truth and filling the gaps with manufactured images and stories. But that's all they were: tales to frighten the children and keep them in line. You must know this. You're a brilliant computer coder: you know how easily data can be altered or created, Chang.'

I hit the real truth with that. He looked at me with utter dread, as if I'd uncovered a secret he'd desperately tried to keep hidden. But he shook his head, denied everything I said. In the end, I had to resort to pure logic. 'If you don't believe me, stay with us and see how we live. For now, I've more important and immediate concerns than the false beliefs of an intruder who refuses to help himself.' I rose and moved towards him to re-attach the restraints to the strut, so he wouldn't be free to wander the base while I caught up on sleep.

He made no move to struggle, but his demeanour changed. 'What problem concerns you all so much here? What threat makes you anxious?'

If that was insight, it was pretty impressive. 'You've been threatened by the Cult who destroyed the base on the Moon? Had intel about suicide bombers?'

His eyes widened with alarm. He nodded. 'It's another reason I'm here. Not threatened directly, but heard rumours. We don't have a proper way to defend our base from such wickedness. We heard you were a group of highly intelligent scientists and engineers and thought you'd have weapons to defend yourselves. At GCC we are closer to MMMB1O than you.'

The truth at last. It's true GCC is just a little to the west of a line direct from MMMB1O to us. The Cult would almost certainly attack there before they reach us.

'The man you locked outside was gathering essential pieces of equipment to allow us to construct the means for our defence. Your foolish act of self-preservation might have resulted in this base being destroyed. Perhaps you'll understand why we didn't welcome you with open arms, Chang. You could've increased our danger. Think on that while I sleep. We'll discuss your future in the morning.'

I left him to it; now he's visible he can't wander unseen even if he manages to free himself, and that's unlikely. Came in here to do my first report, since Zaphod seems to think it's important to continue this process. Tired as I am, I see the value of a contemporaneous account of our early days.

Record 31: 07:43 24/07/2074 Buzz, MB2

Bugger me! Don't believe it: that CIA thing bloody works! Caught a message from the terrorist leader on the spacecraft to his moronic boss on Earth. Fool will never get it anyway. Pure gold! Read it a few times to make sense of it. Got to mean only one thing. Moron tried to send it in a sort of code to put anyone listening off the scent. Obvious what it means. Send it to MMMB1O first, or Marion? Both; they'll be acting on false assumptions. And this could be my ticket to Marion and life back with Brigitte!

Thought the buggers were on their way to Mars. But this message says they're off to the Asteroid Belt first. Be years before they get back to Mars. Plenty of time to prepare for the shits. If there's any left after they tackle that lot on the asteroids. Never mess with that gang. Tough as old boots and hard as nails. They'll kill them terrorists. Fucking good job, too!

Can't wait to let everyone know.

Have to break my oath of secrecy to the N.U.N. Jeez, what am I saying? The N.U.N. don't exist. Nothing exists back on Earth. I'm free to say what I like!

Record 32: 17:33-079.01.01 Madonna

Madonna, a red-haired siren, leans over the consoles, her long hair drifting across her shoulders. She moves awkwardly and a small dressing covers part of her lower abdomen, partially concealed by her skirt. Her clothes depict fast cars racing around a track in competition. Slowly, she sits and faces the displays.

Madonna's report:

I really can't believe they put me to work with that Chinese creep! Okay, so he's an expert with droids, but the man's a moron with women. I bet I got him because I was late to the meeting. I generally am; late, that is. Poor sense of time, especially if I'm working on a project: I get a bit obsessed. This morning, I was due to sort that droid Georgiy brought in after his adventure out there in the dust. So that was on my mind, but it wasn't the reason I was late.

Sorry; haven't introduced myself. Madonna, known as Maddie. Hottest Ozzie you'll ever meet. Redhead. Boobs to kill for, they tell me. And I do have a thing for men, so probably every man's dream in that way. I'm another of The Chosen. Sky high I.Q., several skills; mostly mechanical but specialising in robotics at the more subtle end. I can handle the big machines, but I have a thing for near human droids; almost an empathy with them. Love their rational intelligence and lack of self-awareness. Makes them ideal companions for many tasks. Not much use socially, but great for getting work done.

So, this morning, the meeting was scheduled for after breakfast and, as usual, I was late to the meal, having spent the last half of the night with my favourite stag. Georgiy's a man of few words in bed, but long-lasting and skilful application to a woman's needs, so sexili-cious! Left me utterly satiated this morning and I took a while to come round to the realities of the day, if you must know.

When I arrived in the mess, the rest of them had eaten and were already assembling in Recroom. I fixed myself a coffee, well, what passes for coffee here till Anni's got a proper handle on growing the beans. And a slab of the stuff we call bread, spread with something approximating marmalade. Deimos and Phobos, I'll be glad when we've got proper food on the menu. Anyway, I joined the gang. Chang was wrapped in the shiny sheet Tu had given him. It was obvious they'd already had several words about what to do with our intruder.

'Maddie. Nice of you to come aboard.'

I stuck out my tongue at Georgiy. 'Your fault. A woman needs time to recover after such a thorough seeing-to.'

Amber gave me a look to freeze my heart. We all know she has the hots for Georgiy but he doesn't favour anyone, doing each of us in turn.

'Got any further with Chang, here?'

Tu nodded. He filled us all in on what he'd learned. Some was sur-prising, some not so much and some obviously a pack of porkies.

'What will we do with him?' Hoshiko always asks the most pertinent questions. I noticed she'd chosen a sunrise for her top today; arranged so it just hid her norks from sight through the sheer fabric. Her wraparound was in blues, shading from dark at her hips to almost colourless at the hem and masking her puds. Zaphod couldn't take his eyes off her. I liked his boxers with the dark spaceship floating against the brightness of a spiral galaxy so the ship covered his ample gens.

'Task in hand please, Maddie.' Deimos! Zaphod can read me like a book.

'We need to get this meeting over with so we can concentrate on building the means to defend ourselves. The question's simple: does GCC and its population have anything to offer in our defence or is it simply a matter of rescuing their people from imminent disaster?'

I gave Jai a look that had him squirming. 'Simple?'

'We all know what Jai means. Can we afford the time and effort to run a rescue mission if there's no gain for us?'

Trust Hoshiko to put it bluntly. Chang looked from one to the other of us and went through a spectrum of emotions before he settled on determination. That was good. I like to see a man who's decisive.

'We have many advanced technologies. Powerful lasers, surveillance satellites that look into space as well as to the surface, advanced androids and mechbots, and people with multiple skills. What we don't have is enough water or food. That's why I'm here.'

'We obviously can't leave the poor buggers to starve or die of thirst, anyway. So we have to do something to get them here. That's a priority. We've got the capacity. The first thing we must do is get them safe. We don't have to send a big group. The rest of us can get on with the defensive task.' Zaphod looked at Georgiy, who's in overall charge of the defence project.

'Time's short. We don't have the means to complete what we've started making. We'll solve those problems. This rescue's a distraction. But, like sailors of old on Earth, we can't leave fellow travellers in danger when we're able to rescue them. Let's concentrate on how we do that, so we can get back to saving our base.'

Anni stood, her peach flowered wraparound barely long enough to cover her puds. She brushed long blonde tresses over her left shoulder and consulted her smartwatch. 'Metsats show the storm's waning from the east. Forecast is we'll be completely clear in two days. Gives us time to put together a rescue mission with the necessary supplies, and organise a temporary rota here to replace the duty rosters of those in the party.'

Tu stood, his green forest boxers misting his gens with the swaying motion of trees in a gentle breeze, and took the floor. 'I'm obvious for the mission. Heritage and language skills, along with my understanding of their culture, as far as that's possible, make me the most sensible choice. I think two of us should go with Chang, taking his rover and one of ours, both with trailers. We should have a couple of droids with us and, although we don't hold with them, I think we need some form of personal armament. Chang's shown how desperate they can be and we'll be a small party approaching a pretty large gang. His info's been unreliable at best. I don't think we can trust him to have told us the truth in full. We don't want to be walking into an ambush.'

'We don't have personal weapons.' Chang stood, rising awkwardly because of the tether and blanket. 'Our only defences are inbuilt devices to protect against invasion.' He looked down. 'We were warned you'd attack, rape us, and eat our flesh.'

I knew I'd have difficulty working with a man brought up in such a restricted and backward society.

'Chang's a robotics specialist, Maddie. Maybe he can help solve the issue of dust clogging the vision of our droids?'

I gave Georgiy a look I hoped showed my annoyance.

'The whole future of our race depends on cooperation and best use of what's available to us. We can't allow personal differences to …'

I knew where he was going and turned to Chang. 'Hopefully, you've seen we're civilised and intelligent and not at all warlike. I agree with Tu. And we should get started on the rescue mission straight away. Planning and organising, that is.' I glanced across at Tu. 'Once you've got all the info you need from Chang, send him to me. Like Georgiy says, he can help me prepare the droids for the rescue mission.'

I grinned at Georgiy's look of surprise. It's good I can do that. Keeps a man interested if you're not predictable.

The rest of the meeting saw us deciding who'd do what, what we'd need to prepare, and who'd go with Tu and Chang. Obviously one of the women, but which one? In the end, Amber and Hoshiko both volunteered but it was Amber we chose.

'She drives the rover like she was born to it.' Zaphod reminded us.

'Any case, the spare headset's configured for my brain pattern already. It'd take too many tests to prepare another as well as the one for Tu. I'll get on to that as soon as you've got a free couple of hours, Tu.'

Back on Earth, in the wild time before they started to take things a little more seriously, Amber would've been a dead cert for world champion rally driver. Oh, you won't know what that is. It's a contest involving multiple vehicles driven as fast as possible, usually through environmentally sensitive areas with crowds watching from the sidelines. Burned up fuel like there was no tomorrow, which turned out to be pretty accurate, and wasted precious resources in events designed to encourage consumption of even more. I know: totally incomprehensible. But so much of what they did in those days on Earth was utterly stupid. Still, they've made their bed, as they say, and now they've got to sleep in it. At best it looks like the only survivors will be those lucky enough to live on high fertile ground, and tough enough to deal with the extreme climate conditions, and the radioactive fallout. I'd hate to be forever wondering whether the next tornado or super-hurricane was going to hit my home.

So, the decisions about the rescue were sorted. I went back to my lab. Chang was still wearing his blanket when I left, still with an erection poking a generous peak in the material. Tu and he were deep in conversation, but he looked again at me and there was something in his eyes that made me anxious. I wasn't happy about that Chinky. Not happy at all. But I knew none of the men would let him roam free unless they considered him safe. Just shows how wrong you can be.

I'd been working on the droid Georgiy had brought in, cleaning out the last of the dust from the orifices, and making it more comfortable. Comfortable! Get me; I can't see them as just machines. They're so human in their looks and movements. In fact, I'd bet most people can't tell the difference at two metres. Ours are sexless, of course. Who needs sex toys when all the real people are both sexy and willing? Androgynous; so they're also naked, except their 'skin' is coated to make it look like an outfit. No real fabric to get tangled when they're working. The one I was servicing was MA137, a droid that's been on Mars for around 4 years. It's learned a good deal about the place and the various areas it services and is a good worker. Reliable most of the time. But the dust does have a tendency to get everywhere. Often the worst thing is the mouth and the eyes. The dust creates a barrier to proper vision, and their eyelids are generally only needed a few times a day to keep the lenses clean, so they're not really built for the extremes of dust storms. Then, their mouths are used for speech and, though they don't take in air or breathe like we do, they do open and close them to make it look as though they're speaking like us and that allows them to get full of dust.

I'd finally got the offending stuff out of everywhere when Tu arrived with Chang in tow.

'There's not much more Chang can usefully contribute to the mission planning just now, so I've brought him to help you, Maddie. If his knowledge of droids is anything like he claims, he could be quite an asset.'

Chang's erection had died at last, either satisfied or just grown tired of waiting, I suppose. He'd been released from the restraints and given spare boxers that were simply opaque black. Soon as he set eyes on me it was back! I made a point of dragging my top and wraparound back on. I prefer to work free. Why put up with restrictions?

'Am I going to be safe with him?'

Chang looked offended. 'I am a civilised man. I would never take advantage of a lady. I am Christian: we respect our women.'

So I'd heard. Respected them enough to treat them as second class citizens, the way it always had been on Earth. Respected them enough to believe their only value was for sex, breeding and domestic tasks. I wasn't convinced and turned to Tu. 'What do you think?'

'I don't think you need concern yourself over your safety, Maddie. Apart from your excellent self-defence skills, I'm convinced Chang's a gentleman when it comes to women. Okay if I leave him with you while I go about organising the mission and getting the rover's headset attuned to my brain patterns?'

I could've made a joke about that but resisted, nodded and watched him depart.

'Okay, Chang. Let's see what you know and whether you can help us solve some of the problems here.'

He tore his gaze from me and looked at the droid, frowned at it. 'It has no sex. Does it function fully in other respects?'

'It functions excellently in all its roles and duties. Dust is the problem.' I explained the issues.

He was stiff and awkward in his moves. He woke it as if it was one of his own and told it to stand and revolve so he could examine it. I had the uncomfortable feeling he was assessing it as a partner. Creepy. He got it to open its mouth and stuck his fingers in, feeling around inside before he made it close it again. 'We use a graphene shield internally. It's almost invisible, soft enough to conform to any movements made by the mouth, and fine enough to prevent the intrusion of dust. You have graphene?'

Obviously. With its almost inexhaustible range of applications, in its many forms it's fundamental to our survival. I showed him the store. He examined several different rolls and then clipped a small piece from one and took it back to the droid and opened its mouth again. The fixgun was lying on a bench and he used it with great skill. Once he'd finished, he turned the droid to me. The shield was almost invisible. I poked gently into the open mouth and felt the resistance. It seemed a serviceable solution, so I nodded my approval.

'MA137 report on your comfort.'

'I'm content with the modification, Maddie. It will improve my performance.'

Great.

'The eyes? They get covered in dust.'

He examined the droid's eyes, coloured green and as bright with interest as you could hope for. He got it to flex the lids several times and then nodded.

'Wrong grade of grapholene. The best mix is the finest grade inside with a heavier covering to make it hardwearing.' Again, he went to the stock of rolls and selected a couple from the wide variety on hand. I watched him cut, combine and then replace the standard lids with those he'd made by hand. The change was unnoticeable. Only a test would determine how reliable and effective it would be. He must've read my mind. He picked up the vacuum pump I'd used to remove the dust, emptied the container on to the bench top and took some dust on to his palm. He blew the dust into the droid's eyes, right then left. By the time he'd attacked the left eye, the right was bright and clear again. He did this several times and each time the result was the same. His modification clearly worked very well.

'You can see well, MA137?'

'Vision is fine. The new covers protect and clean in a single pass. My performance outside will improve greatly as a result. I thank you, Chang.'

'Great. Thanks, Chang. We'll do the same to another couple and they can accompany you on the journey.' I summoned one of the standby droids from its storage point against the wall. It moved over and I watched as Chang made the same modifications. The third droid was stored in a bay that had suffered slight damage in transit. It was a minor fault I'd meant to deal with every time I'd used the bay, but it hadn't caused me any real problems, so I'd let it be. Typical; on this occasion, the jagged metal edge of the opening snagged my top and stopped me moving. Without thinking, I slipped out of the top rather than risk tearing it, intending to remove it gently later: we're pretty low on fabric for comfortable clothing. I activated the droid and ordered it out for Chang to do his magic.

He had other ideas. His response to my bare breasts was immediate. Never seen it in any other man. Like he was programmed to respond instantly to bare female skin. He took my accidental exposure as an invitation and peeled my wraparound off in one move, his other hand pulling down his boxers.

'Fuck off, Chang! I don't want you.'

He pressed me against the bench and pushed a hand between my thighs. Don't get me wrong, I love sex. Love men. But I like finesse, a bit of priming before the coupling. And I make the decisions whether and when. But Chang was urgent to the point of insistence. I wasn't having that and pushed him away.

'Patience, man. A bit of preparation and ...'

But he was frantic. Picked up a starblade driver from the bench and pointed it at me. 'You open for me. Now!'

It was a command, not a request.

'Bugger off!'

He came at me with the starblade and I was too astounded to move quickly enough. I felt the point against my skin. I think I screamed before I blacked out.

Record 33: 21:09-079.01.01 Zaphod

Anni rushed me out of my surgery and dragged me down to Maddie's workpod. Chang was on his front, arms behind him bound too tight with a restraint strip. Tu had his foot in the middle of the man's back. At first, I thought it was a bit weird, as I assumed I was attending Chang. Then I saw Maddie lying against the other side of the lab, flat out against the side of the bench, blood pumping from a small wound to her abdomen.

I opened the medipak, found a dressing, applied it to staunch the bleeding and then examined her. She was coming round from a faint and I raised her feet gently to help the blood flow to her head. At once, she struggled to rise. I settled her down.

'Calm, Maddie. Could be internal bleeding. Tell me what happened and what stabbed you.'

She took a deep breath, winced with pain, and explained how Chang had attacked her. I found the tool he'd used. A pointed star shape at the end of the driver, but no sharp sides along the shaft to cut. So, it was a puncture wound only. But I didn't like the way the blood had been pumping.

I gave Chang a short term shot to take him out until we could deal with him. That left Anni and Tu free to help me get Maddie to the surgery. Fortunately, I'd been using it for inserting the pregnancy inhibitors for the pioneer women, so it was out of its sterile wraps and ready.

Once she was sedated, I examined her more thoroughly. The scan showed the wound was deep but had missed vital organs. It had, though, punctured the common iliac artery. So far, I hadn't needed much of the surgical training I'd had. There'd been no violence and no serious accidents. My surgical laser was unused. I threaded it through the laparoscope, loaded the nanobots, and found the tear in the artery wall. It was sealed in moments and there seemed little spillage, but I replaced the laser with the suction pump and drained excess blood from the cavity, giving the nanobots time and space to clean up anything I'd missed. I left them to work for an hour or so and then called them back out through the small wound.

A follow-up examination showed no other damage: the bots healed muscle tissue as they returned to the surface of her skin. The final repair, to the external skin layer, had to be done carefully to avoid the risk of a scar. In spite of the small entry wound, I knew Maddie would want to be restored to her near perfect condition. It was tricky, but the nanobots managed to hide it well. Once the skin's recovered its normal condition, I doubt the wound will be evident.

Maddie came round quickly and I eased her upright. 'Two days without. And your first time with me, so I can be sure you're properly healed. Okay?'

She nodded. 'Did that bastard …?'

'I don't know, Maddie. I was more concerned to stop you bleeding to death. Want me to check?'

She thought for a moment before positioning herself for the probe. The samples showed evidence only of The Chosen; no unknown DNA. She nodded her relief.

'You should be fine to walk. Slowly. Let's go find out what we can, shall we?'

Chang was in Recroom, tied to the upright. Sporting a dark patch around his right eye destined to become a real shiner. I could've seen to it, but it'll serve as a reminder to him, as well as us. The whole crew was present, including the pioneers, making the space crowded. But there was room enough.

'You know, if we're to have the others from the Chinese mission here, we're going to need a bigger Recroom.' I was trying to lighten the mood, without reducing the seriousness of the situation.

Maddie did me the favour of nodding her agreement. 'A lot bigger.' That lowered the tension a little.

'So, exactly what happened? Maddie first.'

She explained from her point of view. We recorded the info in her earlier report for Reppod.

Anni chipped in with her account. 'I heard a scream and rushed to Maddie's lab. Chang was holding her down. I kicked him from behind and he fell on top of her. Tu arrived and we got the vile bastard's hands behind his back and lifted him off her. That's when I saw the blood and came for you.' She looked at Chang with utter contempt. It was all she could do not to hit the bugger.

She wasn't alone in that sentiment. Tu corroborated her account.

'At least he didn't penetrate her.' I turned to Chang. 'What the frack were you about? Women aren't objects for your gratification. Attacking someone with a lethal weapon's unheard of here. Explain yourself.'

He kept his face pointing to the floor. Maddie, still fresh from the operating table, stood in front of him and jerked his face up with a hand under his chin. 'Talk, you savage bastard.'

Chang glanced down her length. His response was immediate and obvious. It seemed so utterly inappropriate. As if he had no control over his reaction to women. Had he been brainwashed? Programmed? I thought Maddie was going to attack the offending organ but she pulled back, shook her head in utter scorn and walked away from him.

He had the grace to appear ashamed. 'I cannot help it. I must connect if a woman is naked. I have no choice. It's what I'm for: why I'm on Mars. I'm to impregnate all women so the human race continues and the glorious Chinese peoples continue to reign supreme.'

I couldn't tell whether he was ashamed because he was made this way or because he'd failed on this occasion. But it was clear he was telling the truth as he understood it. His physical reaction leant veracity to his claim. And what we knew about Chinese culture, since the Complete Church of China had taken control, tended to make some of us accept he might be the victim of their twisted ambitions.

'You're biologically compelled to fuck any naked woman?'

He nodded at Georgiy's incredulous question. That's a major issue. We've no inhibitions; were raised to be confident and happy in our natural state and enjoy the resultant freedom.

'You can't expect us to cover up all the time just because he's got no control.' Sarm spoke for all the women.

'Agreed. We have to do something to protect you all from what amounts to rape. Any ideas?' Jai looked around the room.

'I've chemical means to reduce sexual arousal. But I'm not sure it's powerful enough to work against the sort of programming Chang's gone through.'

'Try it, Zaphod.' Jai's suggestion was sensible and I returned to the surgery to seek out the drug. When I went back with the shot, Chang was on his knees, begging forgiveness of Maddie, who'd slipped into clothes Anni had collected for her. He was also addressing his apology to the other women. He seemed sincere.

'It's supposed to be effective within half an hour. I must ask Chang if he's willing to try it. I really can't impose it, in all conscience.' Their glares said it all. 'Look, I've taken an oath as a doctor.' I shrugged my lack of choice in the matter.

'You sedated him when he attacked Maddie.'

I nodded at Anni's remark. 'An emergency. This is different.'

'He tries it. Or goes back to his own base without our help.' Hoshiko was so definite. Coercion wasn't her normal way and I shot her a questioning glance.

'Logic, Zaphod. Your thinking's mushy. He's a threat to all women as he is at present. He's one, we're many. We have to be sure he can be controlled, or none of us will be safe, now or in future. Your oath doesn't require you to sacrifice us for his sake. I know, I've read it.'

I couldn't argue with that. I looked at Chang for his reaction. He nodded. We had to wait to see whether the shot had been effective. General indications suggested it should last up to seventy-two hours but I had a limited supply. Let's face it, such a drug's hardly the sort of thing we're likely to need under normal circumstances. It had been included in case I needed to perform minor surgery on that area of any of the men.

There are more important pharmaceuticals to be manufactured to keep us all healthy in reduced gravity, but I can switch the program and allow the system to produce more inhibitor if necessary.

'Are all your men the same, Chang?'

He looked up. 'Only me. I'm the most fertile, so they modified me to act this way.'

That, at least, was a relief. 'It's only a temporary solution. Assuming it actually works. We're going to have to do something more permanent for the future.'

'Suggestions?'

'They had chastity belts to stop women having affairs during those crusade thingies, didn't they? Maybe we could make one for Chang?' Brigitte's contribution was off mark, but started the discussion.

I explained. 'The myth's untrue, like so many. They were actually designed in England in the days before Queen Victoria's reign as devices to stop children masturbating. I know: bloody insane. Anyway, I'm not sure it's possible to design something similar for a man.'

'Anyone else got any ideas?' Amber's question brought quiet contemplation for a few moments.

'Actually, I think it's possible. It would have to be flexible, to accommodate his programmed response without injury. And be fitted with a lock to release it at need. But could he be trusted to control it, or should the women hold the key?' Jai looked around for responses.

'Jai's right. I can't think of an alternative for the longer run. I can make something from one of the tough smart fabrics and apply a lock that responds to the female voices. He'd have to ask one of us when he needs to pee, but it would protect us and stop him having to take the drug. How about it, Chang?'

He frowned at Hoshiko's suggestion and put on a sullen face, reminding me of a child sulking because he was unable to get his own way.

'It's the belt or the drug until we run out, Chang. Assuming it lasts the predicted time, I've enough to treat you for thirty days. I won't be able to produce a new supply before the rescue mission, not without disrupting essential treatments for bone density and muscle tone.'

'Okay. Make the belt. I'll wear it until the trip, but I must use the drug for the journey.'

I frowned at him.

'For practical reasons.'

He was right. It's difficult enough accommodating human needs inside a spacesuit without the added complication of a chastity belt!

'How long before the shot takes effect, Zaphod?'

I consulted the medrec on my watch. 'Another fifteen minutes. Let's take a break and then expose him to one of you and see how he responds.'

'It's us who'll be exposed, Zaphod.'

I was pleased Katniss used humour. Our comfort with our bodies was a major reason for her staying behind when other pioneers left. Although not one of us, she has a splendid body and a healthy sexual appetite. I happily installed the pregnancy inhibitor for her and she's been a willing partner with us all.

After a brief lunch, she stripped in front of Chang. His response was pretty normal, with just the hint of excitement expected from a mature male. Certainly, he was no longer driven to pounce. The others were content he was safe whilst under the influence of the drug.

That allowed us to get on with crucial work without having to permanently monitor him. I checked Maddie again and she shows no further signs of damage. Readings indicate she's healing well. She's gone back to work. To her credit, she's taken Chang with her to continue work on the droids. I've always admired her courage and determination but never as much as now.

I returned to the surgery and checked the stock of the inhibiting drug again. Enough to cover thirty days, assuming he's an average subject. We won't know how long it'll last with him until he's been under its influence for a while. I told Maddie to keep an eye on his undercarriage and made Chang work uncovered. He objected, but we gave him no choice. Maddie regularly works free, so she's acting as a stimulus to test efficacy. He started to object to that as well, but she pointed out the problem's his, not ours. And now she's aware of the depth of his drive, she's ensuring she isn't at risk of another attack.

I'll have to devise something more permanent when they return from the Chinese Base. I can't medicate him for the rest of his life, and the chastity belt's a temporary solution at best. Maybe I can re-program him, but psychotherapeutics isn't one of my specialities. I'll have to do some serious research. I could do without it, especially now we believe the Cult's preparing to invade.

That trip to the Chinese base is an unknown. Could take longer than planned. More of the inhibitor's needed as insurance. I set the pharmolab going. One or two of the more complex constituents take a while to manufacture but it'll be ready in time. It means I've interrupted the production of pharms that keep us healthy. But I've a good stock, so it's not vital at present.

I left the lab running and went to find Brigitte. She was sorting duties for the heavy mechbots that are expanding our accommodation for the newcomers. I thought I'd give her a hand. She was in Recroom with two of the bulky machines standing one either side of her. Looked so tiny and fragile between those mechanical giants. Droids were busy stripping furniture and fittings out of the space and carrying them to temporary storage. Another mechbot was putting the mobile dust and blast screen in place to protect the rest of the area from pollution and damage. I've never fully understood how it works, but they can move in and out with their tools and materials while the screen does its job.

'Anything I can help with, Brigitte?'

She finished her instructions to the lead mechbot and turned to smile at me. 'I'm nearly finished, Zaphod. Making space to take fifty. That should do, shouldn't it?'

'More than big enough. How long will they take?'

'The lead bot estimates forty-seven hours without breaks. Might be the odd interruption of our sleep when they use explosives, but they'll do the noisy work in normal daylight hours and use the rest of the time to clear and finish.'

'We need to get this room done and then start them on accommodation for the new lot. Any reason we shouldn't expand enough to get you, Katniss, Sarm and the other pioneers private quarters whilst we're at it, Brigitte?'

'That'd be great. Tu says the geology's fine and Jai says we've capacity on the atmosphere generators, so they'll manage pressure and oxygen content. Georgiy has no specific plans for the mechbots for defensive work at present, so they shouldn't be needed elsewhere. Good idea, Zaphod. Let's take a look at the area and see what we can organise, shall we?'

I still have to concentrate on moving in low gravity, but Brigitte's lived here for months and got the walk down to an art. More of a loping dance, really. I watched her. 'When we're done here, eh?'

She gave me that look. She wants to, but misses her husband.

The corridor leading to the accommodation sector is still under construction and the end is unclad. The bare bedrock's prepared and smoothed to take the metal lining, but it lends a sort of savage beauty to the place as it is.

We're planning a further forty private rooms. That means four more side passages and an extension to the main corridor. All services and facilities will be installed once the excavation's complete. Mechbots clear the space and prepare it for droids to fit equipment and services we have in storage. If nothing else, we're well equipped with necessities. And, now the manufacturing plants are up and running, there's almost nothing we can't make for ourselves from raw materials on the planet. MMMB1O supplies us with refined metals we can't obtain by ourselves, yet.

The Guardian provided finance for everything we needed to buy from MMMB1O. Now the chaos on Earth means there'll be no further such transactions. Not sure what we'll do about trade. We've no funds. Money's foreign to us; the Guardian planned to take care of that aspect of life for us. In retrospect, maybe that wasn't such a good idea. But money's the entire purpose of people working in the mining concerns. Something we'll have to deal with when the matter raises its ugly head.

Brigitte called in one of the lead mechbots from outside. It took a few minutes for it to be cleared of the dust it brought into the airlock. They're so bulky. The vacuums and blowers really blast the mechbots, since they have no feelings and are as robust as the rock they work on, so it doesn't take long to clean them.

Brigitte stood there, a tiny figure of female beauty standing before a metal giant twice her height and bulky as three men. Her grapholene coverall clings like a second skin. I had to smile. She caught my look.

'Not entirely for your pleasure, Zaphod. Makes it easier to shed dust at the end of my shift.'

'Doesn't stop it being captivating.'

She shook her head at me and grinned before turning to complete her orders to the bots. I watched, marvelling at her organisational and planning skills. She's got everything in hand and didn't take long to finish.

'We'll be plagued by a bit of dust for a while. But it'll be worth it. I checked stores, and we've furniture and equipment for another thirty private quarters, so we'll start production for the rest. I've set a couple of droids on to that. Give me an hour to make sure they're all getting on with their jobs and I might join you in your quarters, Zaphod. Must shower away the muck first.'

I gave her back a stroke and returned to my surgery, spending time preparing emergency packs for the three who'll make the trip to the Chinese base. I arrived at my quarters at the same time as Brigitte, fresh from her shower. She was her usual restrained self to begin with. She worries her husband might be upset, even though she knows he's indulging on the Moon. I explained how important to her health and sanity it is that her needs are satisfied. She relaxed completely as we put theory into practice.

Afterwards, and following our evening meal, I came here to record everything before I forget relevant facts. The inhibitor's still working on Chang. He worked all afternoon with Maddie without further incident. We must keep an eye on him, though. So he's sharing my quarters for tonight. Not a companion I welcome, but needs must.

Record 34: 13:38-27/07/2074 Abdul-Aziz: Terrorist Leader in Space.

The terrorist leader left a report on the log in the spacecraft. It's clear this isn't intended for broadcast and it's probable this is the first time it's been seen since first made. My suspicion is it was made only from vanity.

91

Abdul-Aziz's report:

We maintain what the technicians call radio silence. As we have disabled the communications systems to prevent the slaves from trying to contact the outside world, I think it must be effective. I used one earlier and she admitted they all know they cannot reach anyone outside the ship.

In any case, this message is not for release: I make it only as a personal record for ... well, for posterity.

My false message to Babak will now be common knowledge. I know the corrupt secret service agents from NUSA have equipment that can intercept all messages sent between the different locations occupied by men. They will have found my message and decoded it. They will believe we are heading for the Asteroid Belt. I made the message in coded form, but not so difficult as to make it impossible for them to work out what I meant. And I know they will transmit the message to the base. It means those heathens on Mars will now think we're bypassing them so we can reach their partners in sin on the rocks that spin in far space. That was what I intended. It was a way of stopping them being prepared for our invasion. We are few and it is vital we take advantage of every chance we are given. The big base on Mars will not now be prepared for our arrival. We will surprise them and take over the place more easily. Peace and Glory be to the Almighty!

Later, I must record our progress in this vessel. No one alive now will ever know of us or our work, but the leader has said that we should record everything, even if no one can possibly read our words. I am an obedient servant to the leader and always do as he says. Peace and Glory be to him!

Record 35: 22:41-081.01.01 Annika

Annika is seated at the console bench, alone initially. Her top and skirt reveal mobile patterns of tall trees against blue skies with bright white clouds scudding overhead.

Anni's report:

The situation with Chang, and his news about survivors over at the Chinese base, has really disrupted plans for our defence. It's set us on edge: there's a real tension in the air that hasn't been a feature of our lives before. And we don't like it.

Knowing those moronic bastards, the Cult, are on their way to Mars is very unsettling. No one's in any doubt about their brutality and suicidal ambitions for the whole of humanity. They're not people you can reason with. Irrational to the point of lunacy. But promise some people a future eternity of bliss as an afterlife and they'll inevitably embrace it at the expense of real life in the present.

My parents were devout Catholics. They brought me up in that faith until The Guardian rescued me when I was approaching nine years old. You'll know the rest of that story and about our upbringing on Mangaia. That little patch of mountain surrounded by the Pacific Ocean was a revelation. Taught me the reality about guilt, the truth instead of myths about deities, the rational approach to authority in place of emotional slavery imposed by religion. But, I was raised in that faith and, from time to time, it returns to me, eating into my confidence and peace of mind. Fortunately, I'm rational and intelligent, so generally get over the intrusions. Still, there are times I'm subject to that dreary gift of guilt the Abrahamic faiths love so much.

Enough! Let's move forward. I'm the group's expert on nutrition, hydroponics, and soil technology. I'm also the team's ecologist. The interlinking of fauna and flora in systems that balance themselves naturally fascinates me. It's what I'm trying to create here on Mars. I looked at the necessary food crops as a basis for our existence, then allied their growing needs with the fauna that help keep them growing, breeding and healthy. It's meant bringing insects of various sorts, some fungi, worms, a number of small rodents, birds, and one or two small carnivores. So far, we're in the process of setting up, and most animal life is kept in the cryolab. But I recently needed some insects out for pollination of the fruit and cereals. That meant reviving some smaller birds from their deep sleep in the lab and I'm having to rear the chicks by hand as they're a bit delicate following their long deep freeze as eggs. But we're getting there. It's a lot of care and attention, but it'll be worth the effort. I'm really looking forward to seeing and hearing them in the treetops of the main atrium in the big hall.

I've also been introducing fish eggs into the water purifier, where the adults will feed on our filtered waste products before the water goes through the various plants that take out most of the remaining solids. The fish will be useful protein in time, so I'm keeping a close eye on their development, too. Jai says I spend so much time around the water recycling and purification plant I must be a naiad. He calls me his water nymph, anyway, and when I'm being particularly active, he says I'm a nymphet. Cheeky sod. But I love him, so no matter.

Jai, who's an extraordinarily gifted horticulturist, often works with me in the huge plant halls and atria, where we're raising crops to feed us, and trees for the future. The animals, birds and insects for the final phase of terraforming are also to be freed into these halls over time. It's a constant twenty five degrees in those places, so we rarely bother with clothes, which sort of encourages us to indulge a little more than we perhaps should. But, hey, we're just practicing for the day when I can ditch the implant and start working toward that first baby. Really looking forward to that!

So, that's me. You'll learn what the others think of me as this series of reports accumulates, and I'm happy with that. For now, I need to explain what we're doing to save our future and how Chang's arrival here has caused such an upheaval.

The past two days have been busy. The storm blew itself out, as predicted, at midday today and some of us have been guiding droids to load the rovers with what's required for the trip to the Chinese base. We're hoping Chang's being honest when he says they've plenty of rovers and trailers to carry equipment back, otherwise it'll mean more than one return trip. And a hundred and forty kilometres over this terrain is no fun. We're reckoning on a four-day journey there, a couple of days at the base and another four days for the return. We could do it quicker, but the ground's unknown and could be dangerous.

Chang's buoyant and anxious by turns. He's a strange one. But the inhibitor seems to be acting as expected, except that its period of efficacy is shorter than Zaphod hoped. He's had to have an extra shot to keep him inactive and us safe from attack. But Hoshiko's finished the chastity belt and Zaphod supervised the fitting. It's flexible enough to accommodate his sudden growth when excited, but made from a fabric resistant to cutting. So, at least he's secure. And there's now enough inhibitor for the full return journey. Amber's in charge of that, as none of us trust Chang to administer it himself.

There was an incident this morning after breakfast. Tu was working on the oxygenating plant in the hydroponics centre, trying to increase the volume to allow us to expand the halls, as I want to grow a few more trees. And, of course, he's been busy with the main air conditioning plant to ensure it has the extra capacity to convert sufficient fresh air to fill the new voids the mechbots are making. He was busy in one of the narrow spaces and Chang was passing him the necessary tools when Tu somehow overbalanced and fell off the gangway. He became lodged between two condensers. They're at very low temperatures and he was trapped. Chang eventually pulled him free. By that time, in spite of the external insulation, Tu had extensive ice burns. Luckily, I heard his cries of pain and raised the alarm and we got Tu to the surgery in time for Zaphod to perform his magic. But the replaced skin is still very sensitive and will take a few days to settle.

There's no way he can make the trip to the Chinese base. We have to find a replacement.

There's only Zaphod, Jai or Georgiy. Our medic's needed to take care of his patient, so that leaves Jai and our Ruskie. I know which I'd prefer to risk. And, as it happens, the vote went that way. Georgiy isn't too happy about taking time out from developing the defence system, but he could see it made more sense for him to go. He has much more experience of EVA and, as second nominated driver, his brain activity's already calibrated into a headset for the rover. It's really too late now to start recalibration to suit Jai's brain waves.

They intend to travel in daylight as far as possible: the terrain's difficult enough without having to rely on vehicle headlights. So they're setting off tomorrow morning first thing. The rest of us will continue work here in preparation for our new guests and do what we can toward design and building the weapons we need to defend ourselves. Jai's main skill is in plants and crops, of course, but he's done an extended course, and had practical experience working with space elevators, so he's going to start work to modify the nearest of the two to take the laser we're trying to assemble. It's the cabling to supply power from the fields of grapholex solar panels that may prove the real sticking point. Length of cabling could be an issue. Sarm seems to think she can do something about that. Let's hope she isn't being overconfident.

Brigitte has the extension work in hand and the mechbots have already blasted out the extra space for the enhanced Recroom. They're now working on the new accommodation, so it'll be ready when the Chinese crew arrive. Recroom's nearly ready to be refitted by the droids and we should be able to use it again by this time tomorrow. In the meantime, we only have the Mess where we can gather as a group. Fortunately, the original plans included future use so that room's big enough to house all of us. In fact, the Mess could seat sixty if necessary. But the seating's functional and the tables prevent a really relaxed atmosphere. It's definitely intended to make eating a necessity rather than an extravagance. Still, it'll serve for now.

We all gathered there for the evening meal. It was my turn to cook and I tried out some of the new hybrid crops I've been maturing. The beanpeas seemed to go down well, but the broccoli-spinach wasn't so popular, which is a shame, as it's a good source of nutrition and vitamins. I'll have to do more work on the flavour and texture. Still, it was a talking point that allowed us to reduce some of the tension and anxiety regarding tomorrow's trip.

Afterwards, we remained around the table to chat. Georgiy was indulging in a drop of his home-distilled vodka. He's got the machine, which he made from bits and pieces left over from when we dismantled the spaceship, in his workpod. Uses some of Jai's potato crop to make it. Lethal, if you ask me, but he seems to enjoy the stuff. It's no more than 70 percent alcohol flavoured with the merest essence of the potatoes.

'It's times like this I most miss my single malt.' Zaphod held up his glass of ivory coloured liquid that's one of the substitutes. He swirled the glass and drank, but was clearly unimpressed.

'What do you miss most, Amber?'

She glanced at Zaphod and thought for a few seconds. 'I think it's the thrill of the new season on the catwalks. Always used to love that; seeing what the designers had come up with for the new season.'

'Fashion? Really, Amber?' I was surprised. 'Who was it said fashion was something so ugly it had to be changed often?'

Jai took my hand in his. 'Oscar Wilde, the Irish wit. He said, if I remember rightly, "Fashion is a form of ugliness so intolerable that we have to alter it every six months." And, if you ask me, he was right.'

Amber nodded. 'I know it's superficial and was a contributory cause of problems back on Earth, but I always enjoyed the change in clothes, especially as smart fabrics developed.'

'So, what do you miss most, Maddie?'

'Miss?' She tilted her head to one side, stood and stroked her palms down her bottom to smooth out her skirt. I still don't know if she realises how provocative the men find this gesture. Jai told me they

97

all find it arousing. She sat down again and let her glance circulate, settling on each of us in turn. 'I loved the thrill of speeding along a stretch of well-surfaced road in a car capable of mach one. There's something so exhilarating about taking twists and turns at high speed, knowing there's always that slight risk you might meet someone coming the other way.'

'Really?'

'Oh, I know it's antisocial. And bad for the planet. But we all have our small fantasies and secret sinful desires, don't we?' She turned to me. 'What do you miss, Anni?'

'That's easy. I love to run over hills and fields with the wind in my hair and the sun on my skin, the dew on the grass under my feet. To run over grass and plunge straight into the cool freshness of flowing water. And I miss open air theatre performances, particularly music.'

'Running in your skin over fields? That explains why I caught you skipping through your crops that way.'

I turned to Georgiy and stuck out my tongue. 'It's the nearest I can get to the dream. What about you?'

No hesitation. 'I'm with Maddie. Fast car on an open road. Fab. But also, a spirited stallion to ride bareback over the Steppes, rounding up cattle and camping out under the stars.'

'You're all hopeless romantics. I miss group singing and dancing under a warm evening sun in the open air courtyard of a Mediterranean taverna, with ouzo flowing free and white wine cooling in carafes on chequered table tops. Olives laced with oil and garlic. Seafood caught from the sea that morning. Honey drizzled over pure white yoghurt. And the simple beauty of maidens draped in soft flowing gauze of white and blue dancing with wild abandon to the strains of bouzouki and drums.'

None of us had noticed Tu come in. He stood in the entrance, his skin still showing signs of the recent repairs. He remained standing, unable to sit in comfort yet. He was freshly risen from the antigrav platform where Zaphod had placed him after the treatment.

'And you call us romantics?'

Before anyone could respond to Georgiy's taunt, Chang stood and faced us. 'Decadent, all of you. Do you have no fear of the power and glory of God? Do you not dread your fate in Hell without His mercy? Do you not feel the desire to kneel and worship the one true God and pray for His forgiveness? Is not that a thing you all miss?'

That certainly put a damper on the evening. We all resisted the temptation to put the poor man right, to place the rational arguments before him. It's not the time for that yet. It's something we'll have to work on once the Chinese crew arrive. The last thing we want for you, our children, is the continuation of myths turned to dogma and doctrine aimed at control through fear.

One by one, or together in pairs, we left the Mess for our own quarters. Jai gathered my hand in his and we went back to mine. I've just left him there. I'd have preferred to stay, but I can return when I'm done here. And I thought I should report on the evening before the facts become jumbled by time and new experiences.

We're all anxious about the trip to the Chinese base tomorrow. And concerned about the party coming back with so many who've been brainwashed into fear and obedience. But we can't leave them to die. It's not like they're terrorists; just unfortunate puppets of a despotic state.

Regardless of our fears, we have to hope rational sense and reason will win the day over superstition and false beliefs.

As for the Cult and the threat of their arrival, it seems distant still. It's a constant worry overlaying everything we do and think. I just wish we could be more certain about their plans. But they've been silent since they left the Moon and all we know is that they're likely to be headed our way.

Been in touch with Brigitte. Pure luck she was on coms when I made contact. Great to see her again. Hasn't changed at all: showed me! If anything, she's even more beautiful. Never know how I got so lucky. Not that I'd tell her: women get swell-headed if you let them know how great they are.

Had a great chat for a short while but I got her to bring over one of the senior people so I could pass on the message about the Cult. She brought some hot oriental woman called Hoshiko. Quite a looker! I was expecting a bloke to come, so I asked what her position was.

'Just one of The Chosen. We're all equal here; you can pass the message to me and I'll ensure everyone is informed.'

Odd lot. But Brigitte always said they were a bit funny. Still, if all the women are as sexy as that Jap I'll be there asap, I can tell you.

Explained the secret message I'd found. Told her the Cult's not going to Mars yet. Going to deal with the gangs on the asteroids.

'You're certain about this? It's not some bluff, is it?'

Typical woman: can't think anything's straightforward. No thanks for all my hard work. Read the whole message out to her.

She nodded. 'The inference is obvious. And you think it's genuine; not something planted to fool us?'

Had to be patient. Women don't think logically like us. So I explained how I'd come across the CIA thing and found the message in code. Told her the Cult believe their transmissions are safe; no one's gonna think an automated cargo container would be carrying people. 'They've no reason to think anyone's listening to their messages. No. I'm certain it's genuine. It means you'll have years before they arrive on Mars. That's if that mad lot on the asteroids don't do them all in. You know how tough they are out there.'

She smiled and leant over to whisper something in Brigitte's ear. Brigitte laughed and the Jap woman left. Spent a few more minutes in chat before I had to get on to MMMB1O to let them know the good news. Can't wait to leave here and get to Marion. Brigitte's looking so great and that other woman's a sight for sore eyes. Brigitte says there are far more women than men there, so I could be on to a really good thing!

Record 37: 05:17- 29/07/2074 Abdul-Aziz: Terrorist Leader in Space.

This record is from the terrorist leader's personal reports. Considering he believed there'd be no humans left to read them, I wonder why he bothered. But the mind of such a person is unfathomable, so who knows?

Here is his report:

The journey is long and arduous and time has no meaning for us here in this metal tube, but we do not complain. Ours is a glorious cause and we have women to distract us from the discomforts and restricted living space we occupy. One has just crawled from my presence after I used her. Food is rationed. And water. The droid pilot is converted to our orders and knows to be silent. We detached the rest of the train, destroyed its spare droid pilot, and sent the whole craft back to crash on the surface of the Moon. Unfortunately it missed the base we planned to destroy but collided with an ancient radio antenna site on the side of the Moon facing away from Earth. Only Dutch and British technicians work at that site, but they are heathens and have now been ceased, so another glorious victory to the Almighty. And one less duty for us when we return to finish off the humans on the Moon as our last sacred duty.

One of the women showed signs of being with child so we ejected her into space as a warning to the others. That has left us with only seven pleasure vessels for the twenty nine of us aboard. We have made a rota, according to our individual ranks, so all of us have our proper share of pleasure.

We will all be very glad to get to the mining base on Mars and begin our real task. We will take the ultimate Earthly delight of killing those men who refuse to convert to the true way. It is hard to comprehend their resistance to the truth when it is so obvious to all who seek it. But they are determined to be blind and remain in sin and must therefore be sent to their damnation. If they are so careless with their souls, why should we care? Each man's soul is his own, and it is his primary concern in life. No consideration can be allowed to overtake that of the soul.

We will also, eventually, destroy all their false constructions erected in praise of their Gods; science and reason. They build without faith, so it is righteous of us to destroy with faith all they build in blasphemy. We must be patient in this matter, however, for we have many battles ahead of us before we can declare our task complete and make ready for our own final journey to Paradise.

I rejoice in the forthcoming slaughter of the heathens and the subjugation of their unworthy women, who will serve us until we are ready to ascend to our rightful places.

We estimate we will be in flight for another two months, and rations have been allocated accordingly. If food or water becomes a problem, we will first dispose of the women. Only then will we need to consider leaving behind some of the less worthy men.

Record 38: 11:12-083.01.01 Hoshiko

Hoshiko is bent over the bench, deep in thought.

Hoshiko's report:
I didn't pass on the message from the man on the Moon at once. Brigitte explained that he's her husband, Buzz, a systems analyst who's also something of an astrophysicist apparently. I have to confess I think she could do better. No matter, they seem to be happy with each other.

So, to get back to the reason for this report. I wasn't sure the message was as straightforward as Buzz believes. I wanted time to consider it before passing it on to the rest of the team. I did that this morning, in the mess over breakfast, as we were preparing to say goodbye to those going to the Chinese base.

I waited until everyone was eating and then made the announcement.

That stopped all the talk. One or two cheered. But most of us were suspicious. We had a long and detailed discussion and the outcome was that we're going to act for the most part as though they're off to the Asteroid Belt before they come here. We'll still develop weapons, but should have more time for that.

What made me change my mind? When we discussed it in detail, it was clear I'd given the Cult more credit for intelligence and duplicity than they deserve. They're not the brightest people, after all. Most of what they do is straightforward killing, stealing and rape. They don't usually display any sort of cunning or subtlety.

What really convinced me was the message we received from MMMB1O confirming that they're no longer preparing for invasion. They've passed the warning on to the Asteroid Belt. The miners there are getting ready for the Cult's arrival, which should be in around one and half to two Earth years.

It's obvious the Cult have no idea what they're taking on by invading the Belt. Mining operations are confined to a relatively small sector, but it still covers a huge area of space with vast distances between occupied asteroids. And it's difficult to see how they'll identify which of the thousands are actually in use. They could be decades out there and still not discover all the mining sites.

That's great. Means they might never get back here. And, if they do, it's likely to be many many years away.

It's a real relief to know we'll be safe for the foreseeable future. We're giving ourselves a few days to consider how we feel, but there's a strong possibility we'll start the breeding programme soon. I'm really looking forward to making my first baby with Zaphod. In fact, I'm going to see him right now!

Record 39: 23:12-083.01.01 Amber

Seen from a fixed camera pointing to the small personnel area in the rover, Amber's lying on her front on a reclined driving seat, a light blanket covers her from the waist but one foot's raised, causing the cover to slide down and expose her calf. She's resting on her elbows, fiddling with a small tablet that lies on the seat between her hands.

Amber's report:

It's our first night under the stars of a Mars sky; so clear and bright with all those possibilities out there. The night sky on Earth's been so polluted by city lights and various illuminations made by man that it was all but impossible to see anything of value there.

After leaving my own rover, I stood in the open for a few moments before entering Georgiy's for the night. Chang's alone in his own rover. It's oddly less sophisticated than ours; strange how technologies can diverge when so much secrecy's involved. The Chinese rover has the usual facilities, but his coms are basic as is his contact with the network of geosats launched by the pioneers. I don't know what we'd do without our system: I'm using it to connect my logpad with Marion and produce this report before I try to sleep. Georgiy's scanning some intel he downloaded earlier. We're both still feeling the uplift effect of the news about the Cult. Fantastic!

We covered twenty-eight kilometres today, setting off a little after dawn, around 05:35. We want to get there and back as soon as we can now we're considering starting the breeding programme. Georgiy and I probably won't be first, but we want to be at Marion to share in the joy. I'm hungry for Georgiy, so I'm pleased we're sharing his rover for the nights. It's good to feel so alive.

Three rovers will allow us to ferry nine Chinese back, but Chang assures us they've another four at his base, so we should get everyone back in one journey. If we have a trailer for each rover, we'll also get almost all the necessary equipment back, too. Droids, with a couple of rovers and mechbots, are following us. They'll disassemble the rest of the gear and bring it back after we've set off home.

I don't trust Chang: nothing specific, apart from his attack on Maddie and that instant reaction he has to unclothed women, but there's something else lurking there I can't see and I don't like it. We've got our small handguns just in case, but I hope we won't need them. They were a surprise. Georgiy had one for each of us hidden in an emergency pack in his quarters. I'll investigate that further when we get back. No secrets!

Chang's not wearing his belt, but continuing with the inhibitor, even though there's no chance of him catching me nude on the journey. I administered it, as Zaphod suggested. You have to wonder at the paranoia of the Chinese leadership to inflict such a response on their mission commander. Who else did they think might impregnate their women, for Deimos' sake? Zaphod's doing research to see whether he can turn the poor guy back to normality once he's back at Marion. Can't keep giving him the inhibitor or make him wear the belt for ever!

The journey so far has been more or less uneventful. It's been a while since I drove a rover, but the electroencephalographic headset, that's a hell of a mouthful, let's keep it to EEGH shall we? Anyway, because it only needs concentration, it's a less taxing way of driving over rough terrain than the old manual skills we once used. Mind you, it's important you keep that concentration, which is why we're calling it a day at dusk. Accidents out here can be fatal. It takes a short trial to get used to the way it works again, but my training and the practice I had on the Moon stood me in good stead. Chang uses a less sophisticated system, which, given his pride in the technological achievements of his country, is a little odd. But, considering their peculiar attitudes to personal comfort, I suppose it's not that surprising, really.

It was strange, and oddly moving, to see the base at Marion from a distance. I haven't been out for a while. Recent excavations by mechbots have made changes to our surrounding landscape where they've dumped rock mined from our underground living quarters. It's quite sobering to see how organised and logical the whole operation is. The rubble they extract isn't just dumped in haphazard heaps but laid out in patterns that look a lot like the old dirt roads I remember from my short time in Africa. Eventually, they'll use dozers and the big roller to flatten the rocks and form real roadways. It's good to see that, now they've covered all the routes to the various units above ground at Marion, they've started construction of a road that will eventually lead to our next settlement. That's a very long way off, of course, but you'll no doubt witness it complete and in use, so it's heartening to see the planning and preparation in place on the ground.

The nearest space elevator looks a little odd as you move away from it, its less bulky construction than those on Earth makes it appear so fragile. But it works and is robust enough for the purpose.

I'm really looking forward to creating, carrying and giving birth to my first child. Maybe you're my firstborn, reading this even now. That's a pretty magical idea! I wonder which of us will actually be first to do that.

This rescue mission to the GCC is something we could do without. But we can't just leave them there to …

'What you doing, Amber?'

That's Georgiy.

'I'm reporting the day's activity for the archive.'

'Good. Saves me the trouble. I never said, but I admire the way you handled your rover today. Chang hasn't got your skill. Tomorrow, you lead and he can follow. I'll take up the tail. That way, we might have less near misses!'

'To be fair, he's not getting geosat images in his headset. Has to rely on his own vision and a heads-up screen display. Can't make it easy.'

'I know. Frickin' ancient system. You've got the destination co-ordinates, so there's no need for him to lead. I'd rather have your skills and common sense to keep us out of trouble.'

'Judging by today's progress, we're not going to make it by dusk the day after tomorrow, are we?'

'Doubt it. But let's see how it goes. With you leading, we won't hit the dead ends he took us into today. We'll make better progress. I know we're carrying survival gear and food for any extra days we need, but I want this done as quick as poss so we can get back and get on with our lives. I'll leave you to it, Amber.'

She turns to face the unseen man. A hand reaches in and tugs her drape.

'Phobos 'n' Deimos, Amber! You're so tempting. A man can only stand so much stimulation without acting, you know.'

I'll leave this for now. I think Georgiy has something else on his mind!

Record 40: 23:17-083.01.01 Jannine from MMMB1O

Jannine has changed from audio only to video recording. She's facing the camera on her tablet, her upper part in vision. Her ample breasts are partly concealed by a dark wraparound that could be any length. In the background we see the corner of an unmade bed and, over her shoulder, a moving 3Dee of a male body-builder dominates her wall.

Jannine's report:

Jeez! Thank the frickin lord! Josh come in an hour or so ago an told me that there Cult lot aren't comin here after all! Frickin idiots is goin to the Asteroid Belt. He says they must be frickin stupid. No way

107

they'll ever find all the rocks those hairy apes are workin on out there. They'll be lost forever. Yeah!

I was so happy, I gave Josh a free one. He looked a bit surprised but enjoyed himself. Don't have much technique but he does try, bless him. Alf, one of my regulars is due in a bit. After that good news, he's goin to get more than he expects. Give him a right good seein to.

She stands, revealing the wraparound is short and tied at the waist, as she moves towards the bed. There, she tosses the robe into an unseen area. There's a knock on the door and she moves off screen. We hear a man's voice, expressing delight at seeing her so ready. She greets him enthusiastically and they chatter for a moment. She reappears in picture and raises a hand to her mouth as she moves back toward the tablet. A tall, muscular man can be seen disrobing at the edge of the frame as Jannine leans forward and cuts the recording.

Record 41: 24:19-083.01.01 Amber

The personnel area of the rover, Amber's on the reclined driving seat again. The cover leaves her shoulders bare but her feet concealed. She's using the touch screen of her tablet to make her record this time.

Amber's record:

Wow! Amazing! Never knew I had such an effect on Georgiy. With me and Georgiy it's not just sex; not for me anyway. I love the man. I know he doesn't feel the same, but at least that last session shows he both admires and wants me.

We're close packed in here and, let's face it, he should sleep now. So should I. That's why I'm covered again. Tomorrow's likely to be a heavy day. But I'm sort of relaxed in one wonderful way, but excited in another and don't think I'll manage sleep just yet. I'll continue with this record until slumber creeps up on me.

I don't know what sort of technical advances we'll make by the time you're ready to experience this, my children, so I'll try to give you some idea of what we're doing and how and what the equipment looks like; what it does. You see Reppod and each of us as we report, of course. And the autofacility with Hololinks helps keep you informed about topics as we record. But, here in the limited environment of the rover, those features aren't available. You'll get your sight and sound, not at the highest definition. So, I'll explain and describe when necessary.

It'll be helpful for you to know as much true history as possible, since that's the way we should learn. If humankind had always had true history to learn from, instead of the lies of vested interest, things might've turned out a lot better than they did on Earth.

Actually, I'll use this time to explain a bit about the situation on our home planet. That's an odd term really, since Mars will be your home planet, while Earth remains ours, at least in memory. It's hard to talk about it, you know. We've all got relatives still living back there. Well, truth is, we don't know who's alive and who's already dead in the chaos and destruction we've left behind. I'll try to explain. Start at the beginning, I suppose, so it makes some sort of sense to you.

Earth had systems of cooperation that were meant to ensure everybody was fed and had shelter. They devised a method of exchange called money …

Georgiy appears in the frame, he urges Amber to sit so he can sit beside her, both under the blanket she's using. Amber moves to accommodate him and she switches the tablet from keyboard input to audio/visual.

'I can't sleep, either. Too wound up about this trip.'

'Even after …'

He strokes her thigh beneath the cover. 'Nothing to do with you, Amber. Head's too full of concerns for the community. What you doing?'

'Trying to give our future children some idea of the history of Earth; how money came to be king and …'

'They won't need to worry about that. Leave it for the archive. There are more interesting things.'

'I was going to tell them how leaders became addicted to money …'

'Like druggies?'

'And alcos …'

'Drink's different. Can't compare it to money. Money's about greed and power. Drink's about social things; good company and …'

'In its proper place, Georgiy. But it's a deadly addiction if you can't handle it. That's what happened with money …'

'The more you have, the more you want. Bit like sex, eh?'

'Funny how no one opened clinics to cure that addiction.'

'Sex?'

'Money, idiot!'

'Doesn't matter, Amber. We don't use it.'

'The miners and metalworkers do.'

Georgiy scratched his head. 'Another thing to sort. The Guardian never thought it through properly. Just now I'm more worried about the Chinks we're off to rescue.'

'Me, too. Chang and his gang. Sorry, couldn't resist the rhyme! We'll have to undo years of damaging indoctrination and retrain them in the ways of reason and rational thought.'

'Good luck with that. They're emotionally welded to their faith. It's gonna be hard. People get very steamed up when you question their faith.'

'We've got to do it if we're to make a world fit for our children.' Amber yawns. 'I'm knackered now. You always relax me, Georgiy. Will you sleep now?'

He turns and takes her head in his hands, cradling her face to give her a prolonged kiss. She strokes his back until he pulls away and moves out of frame.

Amber turns back to keyboard input.

It's late and I'm feeling the effects of a day of long concentration on driving the rover with its trailer. The droid's fed us. Temperature out there's now minus 59 Celsius. I'm going to wrap up this account for the moment and get some much needed sleep.

I'll do another report as soon as I can. I have to admit I fear for our safety when we arrive. Chang's attitude to our form of dress was bad enough. Imagine what it'll be like when we have many such individuals to deal with. And we only have his word he's alone in his instant response to naked women. Who knows whether that's true? Maybe they're all programmed with the same genes. Maybe the women are as predatory with men.

Chinese coms have broken down completely, so we've no contact. They don't even know we're on our way. I hope Chang can make them see sense when we arrive. Or there might be bloodshed before this trip's over.

Record 42: 10:25-30/07/2074 Buzz, MB2

Lost all contact with the two EVACs headed for Earth. No idea what happened to them. Had friends take that route from here. Guess I'll never know for sure what went wrong. Worry is they either burned up in the atmosphere or crash landed. Hope I'm wrong and they made it safely. Maybe the reason for no contact is the normal one with Earth now: no coms.

Plans for conversion of the ore carriers are well under way. May even start on the actual work soon, if the engineers and the rest of the community can agree about how we're going to pay for it all. Daft thing is all finances are based on earth, so no one has any money any more. Don't really know what to do without it. The managers will no doubt find a way. They usually do.

Record 43: 20:03-087.01.01 Georgiy

Georgiy, wearing his boxers with plain, unmoving black colouring, is seated with the tablet supported on an unseen surface in front of him. It shows a plain wall behind him and the chair in which he's seated.

Georgiy's report:

Frickin' bastard lied! Every frickin' word a lie! I could kill the … No. No. This won't do. You need to know the facts in some sort of order. What happened. And why.

Trumpsfrackindump! I need to calm down. I'll give it a break. Wait a while.

A second report follows this attempt:

Record 44: 20:18-087.01.01 Georgiy

I'm back in control. I owe you, and the rest of the colony, a calm and accurate report, or this whole frickin business is just so much shit. You need the truth. The colony needs to know the facts. And I need to set it out as it was so I can make sense of it. Sense? Sense! Dealing with that sort of crap? That frickin superstition and hypocrisy! Sorry. Okay. Sorry. I'll control my emotions. Start again in a minute.

Record 45: 20:33-087.01.01 Georgiy

Okay. I'm calm now. Here goes.

We arrived at the GCC yesterday morning, after three nights in the rovers. Had a minor incident on the final evening when Chang stopped his rover right in front of mine and forced me into a crater.

No idea what he was thinking. If the fricker was thinking. Said he'd dropped off at the controls. Moron. Anyway, Amber's quick reaction with the grapple hook got me stopped with no real damage. Her good driving on the tow, help from the droids and my muscle power, none from Chang who said his suit wasn't suitable for heavy work, got my rover back on to level ground. Well, as level as it gets in this area.

He concentrated then. Still not convinced it wasn't deliberate. Not after what happened later.

That last night was tense. I stopped Amber doing records as the journey had been same as the first day, except we covered more ground with her leading. I told her I wanted her to sleep. Truth is, I fancy the hell out of her and we were close confined in there. You can't blame a man!

I also wanted the bandwidth to talk with Marion. All's well back home and the mechbots are doing great with modifications to house our expected guests. Guests! The bugger shouldn't have lied about that! Still, I'm getting ahead again. I'll tell it as it happened.

Yesterday morning, an hour after dawn, we made it to GCC. So different from ours. No space elevator! How the hell did they make it without? Most surface storage is still inflatables. We started with a few of those but the mechbots replaced them with underground storage once we landed. There's a frickin' ginormous cross in the middle of the surface buildings. Also inflatable, it's lit up from within. Weird. Bright green with what looks like blood flowing from the ends of the cross bar and halfway down the upright. Creepy! All the other buildings have the same device on top, only smaller.

Chang stopped his rover a short way from one of the larger inflatables. Amber and I drew up beside him. We'd fixed coms between our rovers so he could talk to us on the journey.

'I'll go in on my own. Explain what we've got planned. Then I'll send for you.'

Tell the truth, I didn't trust him, even then. But we had no choice. Amber and I couldn't just step into the foreign base unannounced.

Who knows what they'd make of that? So we had to let Chang go in first. But I made sure he was wearing our comset and told him to leave it on. He agreed, maybe a bit too easily.

I watched him enter the inflatable, which turned out to be an airlock. He gave a running commentary, explaining as he removed his outer suit and put on the coverall he'd left in the rover when he arrived at Marion. We kept the invisible suit he wore to invade our base: didn't want a repeat of that treachery. I quizzed Amber and realised we hadn't packed proper clothes. Just the lightweight skinnies we use in the rovers; all you need after stripping off the outer suits. They were a bit brief for the Chinese lot. Mine's no more than a thong, and Amber's is a strapless piece that leaves nothing to the imagination. Just one of those details that get forgotten among the complexities of preparation. We weren't bothered. No one's fault really. But I blamed myself for the oversight.

'No more your fault than any of the rest of us, Georgiy. Stop taking responsibility for everything. We're all equals.'

She was right. But I can't help old habits that tell me the oldest man's in charge. Call it an inherited trait, but it's just the way I am.

Chang left the airlock and we watched him his greet the people inside. All female. We assumed the other men were engaged on other duties. There weren't many. They talked in a Chinese dialect, mebbie Hokkien, as that's their most common tongue. The Babelfisch isn't brilliant on translation of Chinese, so we didn't bother. It causes delays and wouldn't have given us much useful language anyway. Seemed to take him a frickin age to explain the situation and I was getting irritated. I called him, interrupting his flow of Chinese. There was a spell of silence, maybe surprise, from the others before he replied.

'I'm explaining who you are and telling them about how you show yourselves so they won't be shocked. Give me a bit longer and I'll invite you in.'

That was fair enough. Better they were prepared than we give them a shock that gets things off on the wrong foot. There was more from Chang.

Sounded like a lot of words to tell them how we'd be dressed when we left the airlock, but who knows how you explain things in Chinese?

Eventually, he gave us the green light and we entered the airlock. Surface suits are hard to peel off by yourself. Amber helped me out of mine, then I did hers.

After we put on our skinnies; mine black, Amber's red, we left the airlock.

Chang, flanked by seven women, pointed a gun at us. Two of the women, one each end of the row, were also armed and pointing weapons at us. We'd seen the movies. Raised our hands over our heads. Waited.

The women seemed fascinated by us and Chang's reaction to Amber was obvious. He'd promised to wear the belt at the base, so we hadn't given him a new dose of inhibitor. I should've realised he couldn't be trusted about the belt. He wasn't wearing it, so I was seriously concerned for her safety. He came at her to satisfy his programming.

'Chang, Lord sire, the Good Book of Upright Morals tells us we must treat strangers with respect. Humble apologies, Lord sire.' One of the women glanced at me and spoke in English through trembling lips; bowed to Chang. Finished, she dropped to her knees and then flung herself full length at his feet.

Chang turned round, grabbed one of the unarmed women and barked a command at the others as he took her off. The women looked at us with uneasy curiosity. Neither of the armed women moved but the other three gathered to talk in a huddle. Amber stepped forward, carefully, to raise the prostrate woman back to her feet. The two with weapons just watched; no sign they were about to loose off a shot. But I was worried about what she had in mind. I moved to help, and deflect attention from her. Amber and I knelt and touched her outstretched hands, putting our palms under hers and coaxing her to rise. She was startled by our touch but she saw Amber and quickly recovered, knelt up and then stood with us.

'You all speak English?'

She nodded. The other women watched; the three who'd gone into a huddle were back in their original places.

Chang had left his headset on and we saw him open the other woman's robe. Then he got too close for us to see any detail. Any case, the movement was rapid and short and we knew what he was doing. Before I could say anything else, he came back. The woman followed, tying her robe. All he'd wanted was penetration and release. What a sad, disrespectful, wasteful imposition.

He marched up to me, wagging his gun in a way that told me he'd never used it in anger. But he stopped short and I couldn't disarm him as I'd hoped. He glared at me, then strode to the woman we'd raised to her feet. Without a word, he struck her hard across her face with the back of his hand. She fell from the force of the blow. I started toward him as Amber moved toward her again.

Chang raised his gun. 'Leave her!' He'd use it if I moved closer.

Amber, though, wasn't having any of it and quickly tended the fallen woman.

Chang shouted a string of commands in Chinese and the other women surrounded us. They forced thin restraint bands round our wrists behind our backs. Marched us to a small cell and shoved us through the narrow doorway. Closed and locked it behind us. We heard them move away. Didn't sound as though they'd left a guard and Chang's headset was still showing the women were with him.

Amber moved very close and whispered. 'Turn off your set. I've disabled mine.'

She'd used internal control to close outgoing coms. I followed suit. We could receive without transmitting. She waited for my signal, then spoke softly. 'I tensed as they tightened. You should be able to work the restraint off my hands, Georgiy.'

She turned her back and I moved round in the dim light of the green leds on the ceiling and felt for her arms. It took time, effort, and pain for Amber, but I released her.

Chang had turned on the woman he'd hit. He slapped her again and shouted at her. The women seemed to accept his actions without protest. Once he'd done with the woman, he led them all down a tunnel. He suddenly remembered the coms connection and stopped. He must've nodded; the image flicked up and down and then went out as he disconnected.

He might come back to check up on us. Amber looked at my binding and worked to loosen it. We spoke softly, listening for footsteps. But there was no sound. We were quiet and said nothing that might indicate our actions.

It took time, but Amber finally managed to release me from the restraint with her teeth. Free, we explored our prison. It was bland, featureless. A cell with four walls, ceiling and floor. The door was the only opening and the square fitting in the ceiling, dotted with small leds, the only light source.

I examined the door. No interior handle and no sign of a locking mechanism. It had slid closed when they shoved us in. I applied my palms to the surface and tested it for movement. There was resistance, but didn't seem to be any lock. Together, we applied as much pressure as we could until the door opened a fraction. Amber was kneeling below me and got her fingers round the edge. I moved my hands once she could hold the door and we were able to slide it open far enough to escape the cell.

We considered making for our rovers and leaving the Chinese to their fate. But we couldn't leave those women at the mercy of that bastard. It was obvious there was more to the situation than we'd been told. I couldn't abandon women who were obviously terrified of their boss. Amber agreed.

No sign of the women or Chang. The whole area was deserted. We heard Chang in our earpieces again but it was impossible to know where he was. Unsettling that he'd reconnected: what did it mean? That sort of confidence, when he had no way of knowing what we were doing, was worrying. Maybe he thought he had to be connected to hear us.

Was there tracking in the cell? No sign of cameras, but they're so small they can be hidden anywhere. We realised we'd have to assume we were visible to anyone watching a security screen. Nothing we could do but keep alert to possible attack and make sure we could see ahead and behind us all the time. We reconnected our sets to each other and Amber turned hers to look behind. That left us able to move more freely, but we were tense, not knowing if we were under observation. All we could do was carry on searching and see what happened.

Chang's headset showed a blank wall with shadows flitting. Could be women, but we couldn't tell. Sounds suggested he was eating. No conversation, just food being gobbled.

Three corridors led off the entrance area, all going down. The left was a ramp, the other two were stairs. We chose the ramp. It was wider and we could walk side by side.

At the end of the slope, a broad flat corridor ran ahead with doors leading off. Everywhere was lit in the flat, dim, green light of emergency illumination. Chang had told the truth about their lack of energy. No alloy cladding on the walls, so bare rust coloured rock surrounded us, here and there patched with black mastic to plug a natural leak. We moved silently along the roughly chiselled rock floor, its temperature barely above zero judging by our bare feet. The first two rooms were empty. Chang suddenly started berating a woman, making her cry. His whole tone was belligerent and bullying.

In the third room, we found one of the armed women on her knees in front of some strange decorated platform bearing another cross and other objects with no meaning. Her feet were bare but she was covered by the same flimsy ankle length gown all the women wear. Hides their skin but shows their shape, looks like a single layer. They'll have the same issues about fabric and laundering that make us wear minimal clothing. Her weapon was close to her knees on her right and Amber, being that side, bent and grabbed it before the woman knew we were there.

She turned and started to rise. Amber pointed the gun at her. And she dropped back to her knees, then fell on to her front with her arms outstretched and her face to the floor.

Amber helped her up, explained we just wanted to talk. She was terrified, her eyes searching for an escape and unable to settle on us. There was nowhere to sit, so we stood in a small circle.

'First, what's your name, please?'

'I am called Ying, Lord sire.'

'And I'm Georgiy, not a lord or a sire, so just use my name, Ying. This is Amber.'

She finally looked at us. Her glance at Amber was curious but her gaze at me held her attention all the time we spoke, her eyes moved to my gens though she tried to hide her interest.

'Chang's obviously told us all a pack of lies about each other, Ying. We need to know the truth from you. We'll tell you the truth about us and why we're here. But we have to be quick. We need information. Do you understand?'

'Yes, Lord sire, Georgiy. I'm sorry. Yes.'

'What did Chang tell you about us?'

She frowned at Amber's question but replied to me. 'He says you are dangerous heathens who will capture us women and use us for your pleasure. We must be wary of your lies.'

'Do you know why Chang came to our base at Marion?'

Again, she frowned at Amber's question and replied to me. 'He went to the heathen base to ask for help as we had an accident on landing. Our water and food is poor. We lost all our men soon after we landed. Only Chang survived the crash unharmed, with the women you have seen.'

'He told us there were more here, three men.'

She shook her head. 'There were eight women and four men in our crew. One woman and three men died in the crash. Chang bravely went into the wreckage to rescue those who were trapped. But none of them lived through the fire and explosion. So he is now the only male left with us seven virgins. God has sent a test for us to pass so we may continue the work of the Lord here.'

'So, Chang lied. Must've been worried about telling us he's the only male. Why, I can only guess. Anyway, we're here to help. We'll take you back to our base. Our mechbots are digging new quarters for you, so you can be comfortable and safe.'

That was too much for her. She shook her head at Amber's explanation. 'No. You are heathens. Your men will rape and torture us and eat our flesh. We know what you do. We have seen, read the reports of those who escaped your evil lands.'

I reached out and took one of her hands in mine. Held her gently. She resisted at first but then grew still. 'Yes. We've heard those rumours. But that's all they are. Rumours and lies, Ying. Tales put out by your masters to keep you frightened of us. If you knew the truth, you'd all want to come and live with us.'

'No. Chang never lies.'

Amber raised her eyebrows. 'If you're not sure about who's telling the truth, let's go back over what you just told us. You said there are seven virgins here. You also said there are only seven women. That means you think all the women are virgin. But you saw Chang take one of your companions when we arrived and use her for sex. You can't deny that happened.'

'You think Chang … that he had … sex with Jiang? She is not ready yet. He took her to teach her the rite, that's all.'

'Right? You mean as opposed to wrong?' Amber was gentle.

'Rite … ceremony, ritual.'

'Ah. What rite is this?'

Ying looked at Amber's feet to reply. 'How to make his erect member go back to normal.'

'I see. Have you been taught this rite, Ying?'

She looked up at me. 'Not yet. Only Jiang. He has taught her many times, but she's a slow learner so he must show her again and again.'

'And Jiang? What does she say about the rite?'

She glared at Amber. 'She has no authority to discuss such matters with us. It is for the man to explain things. We all await our turn to be instructed. Jiang, as the youngest of our group, has been given the privilege of learning this honour first.'

Amber sighed and I shared her frustration at the obvious lies the women had been sold. 'You haven't a clue about the reality here, Ying. Jiang has sex with Chang every time he takes her to 'learn' the rite. There is no rite. All he's doing is fucking her. She's no virgin, of that I'm certain.'

Ying was outraged. 'That can't be true! You lie! Chang is our Pastor and our Lord Sire. He knows the rituals and every single word of the Good Book of Upright Morals. He understands the secret rituals of the Holy Insemination of the Virtuous Pudendum and the sacred ways of the Great and Munificent Jesus Buddha Confucius. He would never violate the trust of the Wondrous Permanence of Spiritual Oneness placed in him before we launched for Mars. He could not do that. He wouldn't!'

Amber took hold of Ying and made her face her. 'You've been lied to. You've been kept from the truth, probably all your life. I can tell you, without fear of contradiction, that Chang's a sexually predatory man. He attacked a woman at Marion with a pointed instrument that might have killed her if our medic hadn't saved her. He attacked her because she refused sex with him. I'm telling you the truth, Ying. And if you don't believe me, I can show you a record of the event on your coms screens if you'll show me where they are.'

But we never got the chance to go further down that road. Chang's coms had been turned off again. He appeared with the woman called Jiang. Her face was stained with tears but she made no sound. He let her go and stepped behind Amber, his gun at her head.

'Drop the weapon.'

She's good. Quick. She tossed it my way and I caught it in time to turn it on Chang. He wouldn't kill Amber: she's another woman for his harem.

Stalemate.

'You've got a choice, Chang. I'm deadly accurate. And I'm aiming at your head. You can either drop your gun, or die. I don't give a shit which.'

'If I drop my gun, you'll shoot me anyway.'

I shook my head. 'I value life. Treasure it. You've shown you don't care about the lives of others. You locked me out of the airlock to die.' I saw his eyes register my truth and gambled on the rest. 'And you let your trapped colleagues burn in your crashed spacecraft rather than try to rescue them.'

His hesitation, failure to deny the truth was enough. Amber's earlier words had their effect on Ying. She was facing Chang and saw the lies in his eyes.

'Chang's penetrated you, hasn't he, Jiang? You're not a virgin, are you?'

She froze for a moment but then nodded, just once. It was enough. Ying moved fast. Her hands connected with both Chang's face and the gun in what seemed like a single movement. The weapon pinged its deadly pulse against the ceiling, taking a lump out of the rock. Jiang and Amber then joined in and disarmed Chang between them. I let them give him a good thrashing before I stopped them. Jiang finished her attack with a kick at his gens that had him screaming and squirming.

I hauled the bastard to his feet. It was too soon for a reasonable talk with him, so I asked the women for proper restraints and we bound and threw him into the cell where we'd been confined. Only we made sure he was firmly bound. Amber took his comset so he couldn't follow our activity. Left the bastard alone for a while.

Jiang collapsed to the floor and wept. Ying tried to comfort her. We were more worried about the other armed Chinese woman. I asked Ying where she'd be.

'I'll show you.' She led me down a corridor. 'You're not going to hurt her, are you?'

'I'm going to do whatever I need to make everyone safe.'

122

She nodded. 'Chang's our leader. Our Pastor. Our guide in all things. We put our complete trust in him as our voice of God in this life. It's hard for us to disobey him, you understand?'

'I'm impressed with your courage, Ying. You did the right thing. I can't prove our ways are right. Not here and now, but I promise you'll see for yourself how we value the lives of all people. No one at Marion Base is treated differently from anyone else. We're all equal. That's how you and your colleagues will be treated.'

'What about Chang?'

'He's shown he's dangerous and selfish. He tried to kill me at our base and now he's threatened my colleague. It's obvious he's been raping Jiang all the time you've been here. We'll try to repair the damage that's been done through brainwashing, but that could be a very long process. Still, we'll try.'

'What's raping?'

I considered explaining but it was too difficult for that moment. 'I'll tell you later.'

'Brainwashing?'

'I'll explain later.'

We reached the area where Ying thought her colleagues would be. It was a large room with little furniture; their church. The other women were praying as we entered and none looked up. It was too easy. The weapon lay by the door. Chang had no doubt told them they were safe while Amber and I were confined. I took the gun and turned to Ying, only to find her also now at prayer. This faith of theirs is an even greater issue than we thought.

I waited until they finished, not wanting to interrupt what seems an important ritual for them. They stood more or less as one and turned to find me in the doorway, armed with two guns. For a moment they seemed shocked, even Ying. Then panic took over and they yelled, screamed and begged for mercy. I let the noise run its course for a few minutes before I shouted for silence. They obeyed at once.

'You're not in danger. I'm here with my colleague to help you. We'll take you all back to our base at Marion and house you there so that you're safe and have enough food and water. How we go on after that depends how you behave. Now, please come with me to where your colleague is with my companion.'

Ying led them from the room past me, their heads bowed and some muttering in Chinese, but all in line and obedient. We made it back to Amber and Jiang without incident and I handed the other gun to Amber. Jiang had calmed after her act of betrayal of her lord and master but seemed more subdued than appalled. I hoped that was a good sign.

'Where do you keep your weapons?' Amber's question was essential.

None of them spoke.

'Look, we don't want to harm you. But there are only two of us and seven of you, eight with Chang. We're in danger. We need to know where your weapons are stored so they can be disabled, not used.'

Ying stepped forward. She turned to her colleagues. 'I have seen that this man is not the savage we have been taught to expect.' It was the only explanation she gave.

Amber nodded at me. 'I'll take the rest to their mess. We should eat together and see if we can't gain some mutual trust, Georgiy.'

I followed Ying down the corridor.

For now, I'll leave this report. But I'll return to it later.

Record 46: 23:07-090.01.01 Amber

Amber is again lying on her front on the reclined driving seat of the rover. She is loosely wrapped in the thin blanket she used previously. Qui, one of the Chinese women, is with her and can be seen to pass occasionally as the record runs. She's dressed in a long, body-fitting, gown patterned with a traditional Chinese calligraphy design and emblazoned with bright yellow flowers.

Amber's report:

A lot's happened since Georgiy's last report and mine. We thought it best that I continue the story of our trip to the GCC. Georgiy's anger and frustration get the better of him. My problem is how to put it down so it makes sense, since I'll have to tell some of it second hand.

I'm recording this during our return journey to Marion. In my rover with one of our new settlers, since the women are wary of sharing space with Georgiy. Jiang, however, much to our surprise, volunteered to go with him. My guess is, as the only non-virgin among them, she feels she at least knows what to expect. They're difficult to read and their customs and traditions are so different from ours that their motives are unclear. Jiang appeared unconcerned about being with Georgiy, though how and why that is I can't say. I know he'll be gentle with her, but how can she know? I do wonder if this is some sort of sacrificial move on her part; perhaps she's trying to shield her colleagues from possible rape, given their beliefs about us. I've tried to allay those fears, of course, but it'll take a lot more than my word to reassure these women. Nevertheless, Jiang did volunteer, so I can only assume she has sound reasons.

Ying and Daiyu are in one of the Chinese rovers. Ying's still doubtful about us and our intentions, but willing to give us a chance to prove ourselves: she's driving, even though she's inexperienced. Daiyu's just obedient and does as she's told.

I've got Qiu. She seems uncertain about Chinese truths the others accept enthusiastically. I'm not sure of her reasons yet, but I guess she's suffered some family crisis that's made her doubt. Zhen and Lin are in another Chinese rover, with Zhen driving. She's obedient from fear alone. Lin's probably open to change. Already signs of doubt from what she says and, if we can get her on her own, she'll probably admit her uncertainties. I hope so; the sooner we can convert these women to rational ways the better.

So, to events at the Chinese base.

Using a mixture of persuasion, bullying, reasoning and visuals from our base, we got the women to believe our offer of sanctuary is genuine and their best chance of survival. They seem persuaded to accept we're not going to deflower them after we let them talk with the other women in Marion. And they watched a patched in shot of the others eating in the mess, which helped them accept we eat normal food and are unlikely to eat them. That helped settle them a bit and, though they're naturally wary, they cooperated well afterwards. They're programmed to obedience, and respect a man in command, so Georgiy assumed leadership and they now do as he asks.

Their droids are something else! Designed by Chang for his use. Accurate copies of Jiang. And I mean in every possible detail. Yes. They have puds and, yes, they take cock and perform with the enthusiasm and passion of a real woman. I know: incredible. Their outer covering is the nearest thing to human skin I've ever come … encountered: I'm not using that other expression, so make up your own jokes. And, yes, the women are pretty certain Chang's made sexual use of the droids. Unlike our androgynous ones, they're not permanently naked: they'd trigger his response every time he saw them! That man might have the best endurance and recovery rate ever, but he's no machine. The droids wear the same close fitting robes as the women, only shorter. Chang said it was so the dress wouldn't impede their movements. Yeah, sure!

There's another thing: Chang. I'll explain about him. Not pretty, but you've got to know.

We organised the rovers and trailers to carry everything we felt was worth having and, on the last day, we took Chang out of the cell. He was little more subdued, especially after I'd given him Zaphod's drug again. We kept him stripped and explained to them why. It outraged the women but also reduced his authority over them. At first, he appeared to accept he'd lost whatever battle he thought he was fighting against us. The women continued to obey Georgiy, organising final

126

collection and storage and getting the droids to do the work on the surface. They've also got machines sent prior to their landing, in preparation, rather like the prep for our own base. There are two dozers, a heavy-duty crane, three surface agricars with multiple tool adaptors: everything from ploughing to seed-drilling and harvesting. Amazing. They wanted to continue a partly successful experiment started thirty years ago growing specially adapted potatoes on the surface. A bit like Jai. Lack of water stopped them expanding that experiment. But Jai will find the machines invaluable.

Their crew of mechbots is also pretty impressive, with some real monsters among the gang. We've sent a party of them ahead with the heavy equipment. I adapted a satnav with the full route for the lead vehicle, the slowest, a dozer. They're much slower than the rest of us but we gave them a head start. Overtook them yesterday. That was pretty weird: driving past a heavy convoy on a planet surface devoid of all other signs of life. They'll probably pass us in the early hours and just continue until they reach their destination. I told Jai they're on their way and he's over the moon.

Back to Chang. Sorry for the diversion, but if I don't put things down as I think of them, you'll have gaping holes in your history, and that won't help your education.

Chang seemed subdued. But it was an act. He carried out a few tasks we set him, without rancour. So we allowed him a bit more freedom than maybe we should. Anyway, it turned out he had a store of weapons the women didn't know about. He convinced one, a pretty little maid called Lei, to take his side. He armed her and the pair came out of nowhere aiming their weapons at Georgiy as we were checking the final list of supplies on the surface.

It was a combination of good luck and their bad planning that let me dodge out of sight as they emerged. We thought we'd dealt with all their weapons; stored them in the trailer I'm towing. They're in a locked cabinet. I had to move quickly.

I wasn't sure if they'd kill Georgiy or take him prisoner. Fortunately, and to our amazement, Jiang jumped in front of him and that made them pause. Enough time for me. I grabbed two guns from the cabinet and dodged behind the building so I could creep up on them without being seen. Chang had no comset, so no way of communicating with us, and he couldn't hear us talking with each other.

I came out of hiding as he moved to have a clear view of Georgiy. To my dismay, Jiang showed open surprise at seeing me. Lei turned round, firing as she moved. Her pulse hit the building behind me and blew a hole in the skin. Air escaped in a loud, squealing rush. I had no choice. I hit her before she could fire again and she fell dead on the spot.

Chang turned at the noise, his gun aimed at me. Nothing I could do. I've always hated guns, ever since my stay in the GUSA where I saw so many people killed by armed citizens. It was him or me. You know the outcome.

We got the droids to bury the pair of them under a pile of loose rocks. We stripped off their suits so recently introduced bacteria will decay their bodies and add more organic compounds to the dust, and gases to the atmosphere. Ideally, they should've been fully recycled, of course, but that was too traumatic for the women. As it was, they were in shock at the whole thing. So was I. Georgiy was white as a sheet through his visor. We all went inside and left the last of the packing to the droids.

Their mess brewed some of their special tea and we sat around drinking that and trying to come to terms with the deaths.

'You had no choice.' Lin was first to speak and I'm glad it was a Chinese who said it.

'Thanks, Lin. You're right. I assume some sort of madness overcame Chang. From the little we've learned, my guess is he felt guilty about allowing the survivors of the crash to burn to death and it upset the balance of his mind. I think he felt threatened by ...'

'He didn't.' All faces turned to Qiu who nodded at each of us in turn. 'I'm sure Chang didn't just allow the men to burn. I believe he made sure it happened. I think his only regret was that some women died with them. He wanted to be the only man left alive with all the women available to him.'

'Like those old Arabian harems?' Georgiy's astonished question brought blank looks from others.

I explained.

'You mean one man had a whole group of women to use for sex?' Zhen looked aghast.

'It was an ancient tradition, prevalent in many countries, including your own, some centuries ago. Most lands where women were traditionally treated as second class citizens, in fact.'

'But that's ...'

'Terrible? Yes. Ironically, we've reinstated it in a form here on Mars. But that's because we need more women to act as mothers than we need men as fathers. If we're to keep the human race going, we have to face realities, and that, I'm afraid, is one of them.'

'Will we be expected to mate with your men and have their babies, Amber?' It was the first time Jiang had asked me a direct question and I welcomed that sign of change.

I nodded. 'Only when you're ready. No one will force you. And if you decide not to take part, that's fine. We, The Chosen, were selected partly because we all have a strong desire to be mothers and we enjoy the fun you can have with men. Your group had more women than men for the same reasons. Chang obviously wanted no competition and eliminated it.'

So, here we are, on our way back to Marion with six new women and a whole gang of identical female droids that also act as sex-dolls. Like we need that sort of competition for the few men we have! We've gathered a lot of essential supplies but we'll need to send back droids and mechbots to collect the less important but useful stuff from GCC. Over time, we'll dismantle the colony and retrieve everything. We need every bit of metal, plastic and all the other materials and equipment we can gather. This trip's proved a bit of a bonus for us in that regard.

129

I hope the men can persuade the Chinese women to engage, so they experience the joys on offer as well as the sacrifices. Once they adapt to the realities at Marion, they should be more malleable. Rape's been absent from our society so long now, and always from the community that formed The Chosen it's difficult to imagine how it was before. We have such a different attitude to sex; even our parents' generation had hang-ups we've never encountered. In a sense, we've been sheltered from something that's a daily reality for many women. Makes it difficult to empathise. Trying to imagine being taken against your will. And, of course, our men would never even think of such a thing. Maybe, once they've had a good fuck, the Chinese women will understand what it's about.

That's another thing: Zaphod will have to fit them with inhibitors: Don't want any accidental pregnancies if any of them suddenly decide to rebel against their faith and traditions: you never know how freedom will affect some people who've been constrained for so long. Rebellion's a strange thing.

Took three days to organise and complete the packing of everything we're bringing back with us. Mostly food, technical equipment, R and D tools and results and, at the women's insistence, one of their larger crosses and the books they use for worship. Georgiy and I wanted to leave them behind to make the move a complete break for them, but they're already traumatised by the changes and their faith's a valuable crutch for them at present, so we gave in. Over time, they'll come to see by our example that their beliefs are nothing but illogical shackles and myths presented as truths.

One last bit of info before I turn in for the night. Not something I want to put in writing, but … I have to report this matter.

It's Georgiy. And, yes, he'll read this next time he makes an entry and I'll have to deal with the flack. But it has to be said.

I admitted earlier I'm in love with Georgiy. I can't help it and sometimes wish it wasn't so. But it is. He doesn't feel the same about me. One reason is he feels I'm too protective, too concerned for his welfare, which he says makes him feel less manly. I don't mean to be like that and, to be honest, I really don't think I'm any more concerned about his safety than I am about any of The Chosen. Anyway, looks like my 'rescue' of him from Chang's attempt to kill him has widened the gap between us. He sees my act as diminishing his manhood, making me some sort of hero when he feels he should be the one doing the rescuing. Stupid. Irrational. Neanderthal. But that's Georgiy. Macho man. Idiotic, but I can't help it. And, I suppose, neither can he. I just hope it doesn't affect our future coupling. I really love fucking with Georgiy more than with any of the other men. There, I've said it. Now he knows. And so does every other Chosen.

Enough. We've a long day ahead of us tomorrow and I need my sleep if I'm to concentrate on driving with that heavy trailer in tow. We'll be back in Marion around midday. I'll be pleased to be back among friends and in my own room. Qiu's now fast asleep. I think she's finding the journey a bit boring, since there's nothing for her to do. I'll have to show her the satnav display and persuade her she can help by being a second pair of eyes looking out for hazards, even though my mental link with the system means I experience every-thing directly as it comes in. Probably best she's occupied for the last day of the journey: she must be anxious about what awaits her and her colleagues.

Record 47: 12:41-092.01.01 Jai

Jai is in Reppod, speaking, rather than using a keypad. He's relaxing with his bare feet on the console bench, his rather hairy chest broad and strong above the boxers that show lush vegetation growing in cultivated fields, the wind gently swaying the leaves as if an ocean of air disturbs the plants.

Jai's report:

I'll do as the others have: introduce myself first. Jai. 32 Earth years. Indian Hindu by birth. Canadian agnostic by upbringing. My parents moved to Canada when it was still an independent nation, and before the disastrous war with Pakistan over the long-disputed territory of Kashmir. I was just five years old. Bearing in mind what happened afterwards, I'm glad they moved! Canada was effectively forced to become part of the Greater United States of America only a few years after we moved there: sort of out of the frying pan into the fire, though without nuclear fallout. Not what we wanted or expected, but probably inevitable under the circumstances. The formation of the GUSA is no more nor less than an example of state bullying. But more of that later, perhaps.

I'm a specialist in plant growth, with a side interest in the science of growing living protein independent of a brain. After an early up-bringing where cattle were sacred, that might seem an odd choice, but famine on the scale I saw would make anyone do whatever they could to feed the many, so don't judge me. I understand the spurious moral issues, but let's stay real on this: non-sentient meat has no sensation or awareness. It can't be described as 'animal', even by the most passionate animal-lover, so let's accept it's just protein that's full of nutrients and flavour, shall we?

Like the others contributing to this journal, I'm one of The Chosen. That means I have qualities and abilities uncommon in humankind, sorry, humanity, sorry abliforms. I'll get used to it eventually. People. That's the one; neutral.

I've developed hybrid plants that can grow in almost all extremes. The problem often isn't growth. It's resultant taste or texture, or both. And some of the plants produce toxins absorbed from the regolith that's the equivalent of soil on Mars. But we're getting there. The latest hybrid sweet potatoes are hardy and prolific. And they taste good. Amazing what you can do with genetic engineering. Now, there's a science that got off to a bad start on Earth. Ignorance and fear had some think eating GM foods would be dangerous; with a few exceptions, that proved unfounded. It was the unknown effects of GM crops left to mingle with naturally growing plants that caused the real problems, as we all know to our cost!

We've none of the inherent problems of potential crop interbreeding, since Mars has no native flora beyond the organisms that exist in aquifers; and they aren't plants in the accepted sense. Not animals, either. A new life form to us that we're still trying to classify. So experimenting with GM hybrids is a lot safer. No danger of the sort of disasters on Earth with GM Oil Seed Rape taking over vast tracts of land and excluding all other plants. Just one of many instances of unforeseen ecological consequence.

Here, sweet potatoes are growing on the surface of a planet with huge temperature variations, no rainfall, and a thin atmosphere that's mostly carbon dioxide with a small amount of water vapour. The amounts of nitrogen and oxygen are growing but it'll be centuries before the air's breathable.

Russia's nuclear bombing of the southern icecap turned out to help in the long run, but at huge cost: delays to colonisation while the fallout settled. And the criminal irresponsibility of those moronic miners in the Asteroid Belt: their bombardment of the surface with dislodged asteroids raised surface temperature and sparked the release of gases from the regolith. But who knows how much more we could've done if we'd been able to settle the planet earlier?

But that's history. In our short time here we've changed the atmosphere more rapidly than expected, especially now we've got the oxygen generators fully functioning. Nitrogen release is increasing since we introduced the mass lichen beds and subsoil cyanobacteria; both results of GM.

I've finally managed to re-engineer the primary legume module to release more nitrogen from the regolith than it needs to feed itself. A more rapid growth in atmospheric nitrogen will help other plants grow. For the time being, we're growing most food underground, where it contributes to our breathable air and benefits from our production of carbon dioxide.

I love wandering the massive food halls, especially with Anni. We wander free, like a couple from the beginning of human existence, when the Earth was still pristine and sustainable. It's like living a creation story from Earth.

Anni and I dance together, marvel at the variety of greens and the colours of flowers, and make love with soft vegetation as our bed. I'm helping her with a project to grow more trees. Had to get the mechbots to delve very deep into the bedrock to allow for the height. Fruit trees are one thing, but these old earth species used to grow tall there; some up to thirty metres! Imagine the heights they might reach on a planet with only a third gravity! Our legumes, the beans and peas, already reach well above head height. Who knows what the possibilities are for trees?

By digging deeper, we also found useful and rare minerals, which help other scientific and engineering projects.

It's important you know why we're so few. Respected scientists talked of a population in the tens of thousands and even millions, by the end of the century. All very persuasive and laudable. But it neglected realities and unpredictable acts of idiocy like nuclear bombs and mining corporation asteroids!

Really, though, what stopped mass colonisation in its tracks, was the exponential increase in global climate change on Earth. Once science became a set of specialisms replacing the wide-ranging discipline it was, a serious disconnect between specialists encouraged specific knowledge but mitigated against general awareness. Climate scientists saw the potential for massive disruption and rapid change caused by irresponsible greed. But they weren't specialists in other sciences that might've understood the consequences.

The melting of the icecaps and glaciers was most misunderstood. It happened far quicker and more violently than anyone predicted.

Well, apart from a few visionaries who their peers discredited as mad, and labelled 'scaremongers'. By the time their predictions of melt rate were obvious, it was too late to stop a self-perpetuating acceleration of ocean level rise. Coasts were inundated and the extra water boosted climate change further. Shifts in ocean and land weights, as ice melted into water, affected plate tectonics that then caused earthquakes and volcanic activity. Politicians and money men were driven by fear of riots to feed and subdue their burgeoning populations. They daren't invest scarce resources in an escape to Mars. Only The Guardian had the vision and means to realise the need for an ark. Thankfully, they'd started preparations long before real tragedy overtook Earth. But that's why we're so few. Our initial plans included two more men and women, but chaos in India and China's withdrawal into deeper isolation stopped their inclusion in the final mission. And all the many planned commercial and state colonisation efforts came to nothing after the catastrophes.

Enough history. But you need to understand the facts before we continue with this record.

So, to current matters. While Amber and Georgiy were rescuing the folk from the Chinese base, the rest of us were busy elsewhere. I was outside this morning, checking the progress of the sweet potato crop and harvested enough for our next two meals for the expanded colony. We thought we were getting seventeen, but Amber says we'll have just six more, all women with no particular skills. Looks like the Chinese expected their men to do all the science with the women acting as playthings and domestic servants: where have I come across such social waste before? Oh, yes, in India, and Afghanistan and Pakistan. Before they merged under the Taliban, which made them even more murderous places for women. The foolishness of tradition makes me see red. Respecting habits and ideas just because they're old is stupid. But the mind-set that accepts faith is one that denies the value of evidence.

Still, new women will add spice to our lives, though I'm happy with

Anni, to tell the truth. The Guardian expected us to form loose bonds with one another, the women giving themselves freely to any man and the men spreading their seed around freely. The women are such beauties that few men would resist them.

It's my duty to impregnate more women when we start breeding, but I prefer Anni. And she prefers me. It's hard for us to include others, but we do it. It's necessary.

Back to this morning, outside. I spotted a small wispy cloud, moving from east to west low down on the northern horizon. Not the first I've seen, but the most substantial. There've been cirrus clouds before, of course, but this was lower and not so wispy. A sign the terraforming elements are having some measurable effect. There are so many unknowns about our attempts to enhance the atmosphere. It's Tu's baby, since he's our specialist, but we're all clued up on the science and fascinated by the possibilities. You're likely to be old before anything substantial comes of our efforts. And I doubt any of us original settlers will see significant changes.

That's another unknown: what effect our living conditions and lower gravity will have on our longevity. Some argue we'll live longer due to the lack of physical stress. Others say we'll die young, because we live underground, away from the sun. We have skylights in as many places as possible. Even through the thickness of the graphoglass, sunlight manages to retain some beneficial rays, so we do get something from the dim light on our skin. All our artificial lighting is calibrated to mimic sunlight as closely as possible, excluding harmful elements that cause skin cancer. Maximum exposure to elements of sunlight that allow production of vitamin D is a reason for our near nudity. And why we exercise naked in the Earthgrav gym. You won't know, but 'gym' originally meant 'naked'.

I'm uncertain whether I should record something else from this morning's session outside. I haven't told the rest of the colony. Not even Anni. I'm not a hundred percent certain I saw it. I think I did, but it was so unlikely, I can't really believe it. Here goes: over to the southwest I thought I saw a column of what looked like smoke. There's nothing there to burn and the geology and atmosphere of Mars mean there's no natural cause. But I saw something, and I can describe it only as like a column of smoke, however impossible that seems. No doubt, it'll remain a mystery and become a joke against me, or a legend told in the future as a fictional tale of unknown threats. Who knows? Anyway, I've recorded it and there's no going back from that.

Okay, looks like Amber and Georgiy are due home in the next hour. We're planning a small party to celebrate their safe return and greet our newcomers. We're a little anxious about the influx of six women, creatures of religion. All we can hope is that they'll be open to rational thought and we'll be able to persuade them of the dangers and basic dishonesty of their faith. Humans are emotional creatures, and so often emotion overcomes logic and reason. We won't let that happen here.

Record 48: 21:57-093.01.01 Hoshiko

Hoshiko, in Reppod, dancing freely to music in the background. Her clothes portray a running depiction of the lyrics of the love song she's playing. As she moves, she gives voice to her thoughts for the record.

Hoshiko's record:

Georgiy and Amber arrived safe and well yesterday after lunch. The music? Oh, that's one of my favourites; Pojo's Joy by Pollie Rollie. (*Hololink of Pollie Rollie in action at a gig*) The Chinese women they brought with them all wear gowns in a variation on graphene fabrics I've been experimenting with. Almost sheer, printed decoration conceals and reveals enough to be provocative. The women don't know this, though. They've all chosen designs in multiple colours that give the concealment they're anxious to maintain. Shyness based on religious beliefs.

137

I stayed with them as Zaphod made his physical examinations and fitted their infertility implants. Lack of sexual experience may make them careless, so we protected them as a matter of urgency.

It was quite funny to have them treat me as an equal whilst they deferred and bowed to Zaphod. I'll have to educate them: don't want our men thinking they're superior! All the women are fit and healthy, with no signs of disease or genetic infirmity, so they'll be suitable vessels for breeding. That's a great improvement for the rest of us, as it means we won't have to get pregnant as often. I look forward to having babies, but don't want to spend the rest of my fertile life as a baby machine. Extra wombs mean we'll be able to be less productive and still increase the population along planned lines.

I wonder how many of you reading this now are mine.

Ying and Jiang seem almost ready to denounce their religion. Jiang's the only one who's been with a man in any way. How she managed not to get pregnant is a mystery, since birth control was left to males. With all of them dead, we'll probably never know what measures they took. No matter; she's safe from pregnancy now until the time's ripe. And her experience with Georgiy on the journey back seems to have made her less suspicious of men in general. It's really curious she's not more deeply psychologically harmed. But the culture she was born into treats women as playthings of men and she seems to accept that subservient role in a way most of us find incredible. Just another example of how tradition and custom can so deeply affect perceptions and outlook, I suppose.

Daiyu's too submissive and could easily be taken advantage of by an unscrupulous man. None of ours are like that. But we'll educate her about her role. Low self-esteem's been bullied into her by an overbearing father and encouraged by church and state dogma. She misses that aspect of life. We're holding a meeting later to discuss the provision of a temporary place where they can worship until they've been re-educated. It's tempting to tell them their beliefs are irrational stories told to keep them in line, but they're so deeply embedded in their psyches that might do serious damage.

Qiu will be interesting to work with. She has more doubts about her upbringing and faith than she realises. As obedient as the others, she has a strong interest in learning the joys of sex and love with a man, but also a strong moral barrier formed by her superstitions and history. It'll be rewarding to introduce her to the pleasures of physical contact but she'll need to be treated carefully if she's to become free without damage to her personality.

Zhen is a real mix of contradictory qualities and beliefs. Much to the surprise of her companions, and especially us, turns out she's a trained astrophysicist who also has abilities in medicine and cooking. An odd mix she's been able to accommodate alongside strong religious beliefs. I've always found it impossible to understand how anyone can hold obviously contradictory beliefs without going mad from the internal debate that must result. We'll have to be careful with her. She'll be the most difficult to break of the habits of dogma and may need help to work towards a rational approach. Perhaps assisting Zaphod with medical issues would be good for her. Though I hesitate to suggest such close working; she's a very beautiful woman!

Lin's probably the most eager and likely to ditch her background. She also harbours a secret only revealed when the group introduced themselves to us. Describes herself as a gardener, but it turns out she's an educated horticulturalist and herbalist. Another surprise! She's also a very good driver: she piloted one of the rovers and Amber watched her progress over the rocky terrain with a sense of awe at her confidence and skill. But she seems unaware her abilities are special and takes them for granted. I'm hoping she'll quickly set an example for the others and publicly renounce her faith. It'll make life so much simpler for all of us once the Chinese women become a real part of our team.

And, talking of the team, the Chinese androids have definitely caused a stir. I suspect it'll be hard to know whether we're talking to

Jiang or one of their droids. She seems unaware of potential complications, but I've already suggested she change her hair style to make her more easily identifiable. She was reluctant at first but I pointed out, as Zaphod was fitting her implant, it was possible one of the men might take her thinking she was a droid, and use her simply out of curiosity. We all know men are easily tempted. Well, tell the truth, so are free women!

Anyway, my suggestion worked and she's asked us to cut her hair tomorrow. Anni's best, as her skill with sculpting seems to have made her a good hairdresser too. After a brief discussion, we decided to keep the covers on their droids. Ours aren't an issue, since they're androgynous.

One thing that intrigues me, as a nanotech, is how they've been adapted to replicate not just the look of a real woman, but also the sensual responses. That's quite some engineering and I'm determined to dismantle one to see if I can adapt the technology for less venal purposes that might serve us.

Most underground changes are complete. We now have too many private quarters, as we were expecting another ten from the GCC. We're going to discuss what to do about that, but it's likely we'll leave them mothballed for future use. Maybe use one, temporarily, for their ritual space.

The expanded Recroom is wonderful, especially now we can also install some leisure equipment from GCC. They brought musical instruments with them, a small portable stage for theatre works, an excellent holographic projector, and some paper hangings that carry calligraphy and ink drawings of ancient Chinese customs to brighten the place up a bit.

The most challenging aspect of the change will definitely be the way we share our men. As things were planned, we had equal numbers among The Chosen and it was easy to satisfy all appetites and desires. The men are all very active, of course, but the addition of female pioneers caused a few issues. Now, we have just four men to share amongst twenty-three women; around six each. The men are generally okay with it, though Jai has a preference for sharing exclusively with Anni. He's willing to move outside their relationship, but I worry for him. Meantime, we've drawn up a rota for each man, sharing their time equally with each of us, and including the Chinese women, even though they're not all sexually active yet. It's a bit clinical, and we've factored in our monthly cycles, which are likely to move towards coincidence. It's an issue with potential for emotional tension, so we're all doing what we can to avoid jealousy creeping in. That would be destructive.

Apart from Jiang, the Chinese women have no experience, so the men are treating them with kid gloves. Their beliefs make sex outside of some ritual contract a sin, and now they know of Chang's deception it's infected them with a serious mistrust of men in general. Jiang accepted her role as sexual plaything but never enjoyed his perfunctory intrusions. She understands he used her as a sheath to provide him with rapid relief, but doesn't appear to recognise what happened to her as rape. She sees what we would define as serious abuse simply as a manifestation of the society that classes women as sex toys at the beck and call of men. It's also possible he took her the first time by accident, thinking she was a droid. That's what he told her, though he never apologised and continued to use her even after he recognised his mistake. It was his idea that the droids be exact copies of her, which suggests he had a serious fixation. And there's even a suspicion Jiang felt somehow special to have been selected in this way. Difficult for us who've been brought up with such different views to even start to comprehend. But if it protects her from serious psychological damage, so much the better. But we do fear for her as she becomes more aware of our attitude to women. Chang's death is no loss. Sorry to be harsh, but, if he'd lived, he would've been a real problem.

In common with our own activity, the Chinese were involved in terraforming Mars. Their plant manufacturing methane and nitrogen is self-sustaining more or less indefinitely, so we've left it in place to make its small contribution to the future of our world. Their crop of modified sweet potatoes can grow as wild plants to add nutrients to the dust there and help more useful gases to enhance the atmosphere. Tu says we've already had an influence. There are measurable increases in the quantities of oxygen, hydrogen and nitrogen in the air.

One final piece of good news before I finish this report: the Chinese developed a way of making a type of paper from certain plant fibres. They brought some with them and I'm eager to see how well it accepts the organic oil and mineral pigments I've been developing. And to see how it responds to the graphite pencils Zaphod and I made so we can draw together. It looks promising.

On that note, I'll leave this. Zaphod should be free for the rest of the night. Our Chinese colleagues' vows of chastity mean the rest of us have more chance to spend time with our limited pool of men for now. And I intend to take full advantage of those opportunities, especially with Zaphod. All too soon, those women are going to learn the delights to be had with men.

Record 49: 15:19-128.01.01 Jannine from MMMB1O

The astute among you will notice a skip in dates here. Following Hoshiko's last record, there were others from The Chosen, but these were mostly comments relating to the Chinese women and their progress at Marion. Nothing of any real interest regarding this history and nothing that won't be covered by the following reports.

I continue this account with the next record from Jannine at the metal working base on Mars. It appears exactly as I found it.

Jannine appears relatively close-up in the frame. Her shoulders are bare and she looks a little odd with her head wrapped in a gaudy scarf that conceals her hair and shows only her face. Her face betrays uncertainty, perhaps even fear.

Jannine's report:

They come with no warning, the Cult. Security should've told us. Mind you, they jus care bout savin their own shit lives. That's what you get when guards are interested in nothin but money. No loyalty. Not professional.

But that's beside the point. It's the terrorists I'm tellin you about. But I have to be careful 'cos they don't like us keepin records nor nothin.

They hijacked an empty ore train. Right after they'd done MB3 with that bomb. Took out all the men. Kidnapped some women.

They took hardly no time changin a carrier with life support took from part of the base what wasn't destroyed. Cut corners and got the train back on route to Mars. Set off here.

MB2 said they was goin to the Asteroid Belt; frickin idiots! If we'd known they was comin here we could of got ready, like.

The ore train what they took was an empty on its way back to fill up again. Brought it back here with their captive women.

Incomin ones land on their way to the Asteroid Belt to pick up new techies and supplies for the miners. Our guards was waitin for an empty what was due. Security thought the incomer were that one. The droid pilot give standard answers when they hailed it. I got all this from a Cult shit when he was fuckin' me. He was laughin about how thick our security guards are. No checks, even though we'd heard what the Cult did on the Moon. Security's full of morons who only know to follow orders. But no one give no orders about this one 'cos no one knew!

You'd think that couldn't happen, but MetCorp don't give a toss about us. We're just their ticket to a quick buck. We work. We get paid. Nothin else, they don't care about. They cut corners. All profit with them. Jeez, you wouldn't believe the accidents we've had. All covered up as 'natural' disasters by Security. No one complains: next in line for the riskiest job if you do. And they pay us enough to make it worth our while. That's everythin here: every problem's got a price, and every worker.

Anyway, upshot is Security let them land. Droids do it every trip and they've been workin more than five Earthyears now. Not me. Only been here seven months, about. I lose track. Most everythin's automated. Still a real sight to see those massive containers make soft landins, not hardly even kickin up dust. One worker said it's the engines they use. He explained, like but it were all Chinese to me.

It's the mechs what they sent in to sort out I feel sorry for. Never stood a chance. The terrorists just gunned them down. Old-fashioned ballistic weapons. I mean, on a spacecraft! Even I know you don't shoot a frackin' gun on a spaceship! But they just don't care, see? They marched the captured women in front of them through Security. Used them like shields in case anyone fired on them. But Security weren't ready. Intel said the ship was empty, so they never thought to ask questions.

The Cult shits shot everyone they come across. Panic everywhere. No one in charge. No one even armed for frack's sake. Murder. In two hours the Cult had the whole base. Can't call them soldiers: no honour. Not like professional troops. Can't call them freedom fighters: don't care for freedom, jus killin everyone what disagrees with them. That's everyone, so they shoot first and don't care who's still alive.

Once they'd got the base, they parted the men left alive and us women. Took us to the mess. Made us strip. Left us naked. Any woman argued they shot her. Left her on the floor as an example to the rest. They took the men to Recroom. Made them strip as well. Someone said about coms and Government troops comin soon. They laughed. Said there was no coms now. One destroyed it all on arrival.

Jeez, they're organised like that. Knew what they was doin, what they needed. I was with the other women. But we heard what they did to the men. Sorted them into them willin to help and them not. Matter of money for most. Let's face it; that's what we're here for. Who'd come here for anythin else? Me, I'm workin for that new

Lamborghini; always loved fast cars. Well, I was. That's before I heard what a frackin' waste of time and effort that is with Earth not good for nothin. Now I'm stuck here frackin shits, for free!

Men what was unwillin they shoved into the airlock. Opened it and made willin workers in suits shovel the bodies outside. Left them in a heap. Another warnin to the rest. A few with guts tried to fight back. The shits just took them out. Don't care at all about life. Want everyone dead anyway. Just stayin' alive long enough to finish the job of endin' the human race. One told me that's their aim. I let him do me and never asked no questions. They beat you soon as look at you, so I just spread me legs and take the buggers in, give them what they want and say nothin. They think that's what women are for, so I suit them.

The men what agreed to help, they marked them all with a burn on their foreheads. Nasty. Used a sort of modified label-laser. An Arabic word it is. No one knew what it said. I got one of the shits to tell me while he was fuckin me. It just says 'kafir'. That's their word for heathen. Worryin really, 'cos they're always shoutin 'death to the kafir!' They shout a lot. Mostly it's rubbish. They shout at us all the time. 'Undress!' or 'Cover your shame, whore!' They took our clothes. Burned them. Left these black sheet things you wrap round you like a towel, most of us don't bother. Cept we have to cover our hair with a scarf. Mad. They want us stripped, anyway. No style. I mean, I like a fuck as much as the next woman, but this lot – it's just a quick in, shoot off, and out again – don't try to pleasure us.

Never understood women complainin about it. I mean, natural isn't it? I'm a good Catholic girl; do me confession regular, like. Been doin it since I were thirteen and had my first fuck. With the Father that was. Me penance for the sins I'd confessed. That first one was a taste. I liked it, even if he were a bit rough and ready. No one had never took no notice of me before. He said I were beautiful. Undressed me. Touched me gentle like and made me wet enough to take his cock. It were a bit quick but I felt somethin I'd never had and

145

I wanted more. After that, I went to confession every time I'd fucked one of the lads. The Father always made me fuck him as me penance. No punishment really, except for when I said I enjoyed it and he spanked my bare bum. I said I didn't like it after that. But I did. The Pastor on Mars was different. He didn't want to fuck me as penance. Had to do Hail Mary thingies an all that stuff. I asked him why not but he said it weren't right to fuck me. I said I liked it and he said I were bad, like. The shits killed him soon as they saw that dog collar. Shame really. He were a nice bloke.

Never get why some women can't just let it happen. It's what we're for, isn't it? If they could just see they only need lie back and let him go at it. Soon as he's shot his load, he'll be away. Same for them Cult shits. Just do it and let the buggers go.

Talkin of that, here's one after some. Better hide this and fuck him.

Record 50: 18:56-12/09/2074 Buzz, MB2

Whoever sorted passwords and security protocol for the N.U.N. servers didn't do a very good job. Your average hacker wouldn't get through, but anyone works in the industry, knows servers and multilayer protocols, like me, can easily find a route.

Wouldn't believe what that database holds! Incredible. Looks like every member government used those servers to back-up data, including stuff from their defence organisations. There's over fifteen exabytes here. No wonder it took a while to complete the back-up! So far, I've done a search to extract links to defence programs from the most advanced weapons nations. The NUSA, China and Neurope are easiest. The Chinese stuff's in their bloody pictograms, and I'm not even going to try to translate that. But the other stuff's in standard English. Encrypted, of course, but I can decrypt. I've got the program up and running. Looks like it'll take a couple of days to get plain text with its graphics. Then I'll have a real good look at the stuff. Fascinating.

Always been a bit of a nerd about weapons.

Already had a look at the stuff on there re telescopes and astronomy; passed the info to my colleagues here. This stuff I'm into now is just for personal interest and won't be any use to anyone else now Earth and its power brokers are finished. But I get a real buzz out of learning about it.

Record 51: 16:43-129.01.01 Georgiy

Georgiy is pacing the Reppod area in front of the consoles. His fists are clenched. His boxers are an angry solid red. As the report begins, he's talking, almost to himself, as if unaware he's recording.

Georgiy's report:

As much as any man, I love women. Maybe more. But, by frick, they can be difficult. And now we've got 23 to cope with. There's gonna be trouble. Already has been.

And now we learn the message from MB3 was crap. The message from the Cult they told us was genuine was a smokescreen. The shits have taken MMMB1O and will no doubt be on their way here as soon as they organise themselves. No coms with MMMB1O; we got the message via MB3 again. This time Buzz was apologetic about his previous mistake; said he'd come across the original message by accident and had to decode it. That's why he thought it was genuine. Looks like the shits aren't as frickin' idiotic as we thought!

Update on our situation.

Now we know for certain the Cult are on Mars, we've got to get our fingers out and build a weapons grade laser.

Snags: none of us is a weapons expert. We're having to find out whatever we can from various files on our servers. Not a lot of good so far. But there's a manual for industrial lasers and that's been useful in getting us started.

But we've hit another snag. The machine itself is under construction, with Tu and Sarm managing some of the fundamental engineering. But Brigitte took it into her head to physically test the cable length for the power supply from our fusion plant. Actually took the stuff up in the space elevator to make sure we hadn't mismeasured it, which wouldn't be surprising, given the length we need. Turns out she was right. Even with the extensions, it's a good five thousand metres short! She was able to feed out the cable as she went up and managed to stop upward progress before she lost the free end. That takes some work and guts. I've yet to thank her properly. Mind, since it's Brigitte, that'll be a pleasure.

Problem now is how to get the necessary grade of cable in the quantity we need. We can adapt some from the stuff we retrieved from GCC, but it's not enough. It's not like we're after standard cabling. This has to be capable of taking high current from the fusion plant, married to output from our array of solar sheets. Sarm's got mechbots and droids making a wind turbine from scrap we have on site. It'll be a vast structure with massive lightweight sails. All I can say is 'thanks' to the techs who solved the problem of mass production of graphene sheeting. Brilliant! While wind power might help, we can't rely on it for what we need. It's got to be absolutely constant and powerful enough to drive a weapons grade laser. That means only the fusion plant married to the solar panels will do it. The wind turbine will act as a back-up for our domestic needs while the laser's in use.

So, that's our most urgent task and we're all trying to think up ways we can adapt, butcher or even make the necessary cabling. Our manufacturing plant was set up for smaller and lighter needs, since the pioneers had already brought most of the essential heavy stuff. The idea was we'd slowly build more manufacturing capacity as the base grew and became established. But we don't have time to work like that. Not for this project. So, we're giving the matter a lot of thought and things are getting pretty tense.

Having that frickin threat over us is taking its toll. Yes, we're all professionals. Yes, we're all trained astronauts, with all that means in terms of discipline and self-control. But we're human beings, too. And our frickin survival's at stake here. This shitty Cult: shame the UN didn't destroy the whole frickin lot of them when it had the chance a couple of decades ago. But it was the usual story of too little too late, and the inevitable vetoes from China, Saudi Arabia and, much to my shame, frickin Russia!

Anyhow, point is, we still have the Cult to deal with. And, bloody idiotic and illogical they may be, but those frickers can never be accused of missing a chance to take advantage of trouble.

Which takes me back to the problem with the women.

Qiu invited Zaphod to discuss surgical technique with her. Turns out she's another surprise: wasn't chosen by the Chinese just for babies. She's a qualified surgeon and has other skills as well. Anyway, long story short: she and Zaphod hit it off. Now she can't get enough, and the other women are mad because she's breaking this rota they've got set up. I thought Hoshiko would be most miffed, since she fancies she's in love with Zaphod, whatever that means. But she's been as good as she could about it. It's the other women giving the Chinese girl bother for hoggin' the doc.

Don't know whether I should step in or leave them to sort it out. Want a laugh? Was a time on Earth, in certain societies, when women were thought to have no interest in sex, but that's never been true. Eager as any man, given the freedom to choose. Why wouldn't they be? Fucking's nature's reward for procreation. Women play a greater role in that than we do, let's face it. It's easy for us. We can fuck and leave. Women have to carry the produce; babies. And they have that built-in biological need for a provider to ensure the family's fed and sheltered. Modern women try to overcome that biological imperative, but it's there inside them and it's bound to surface from time to time.

The upshot is that Qiu and Amber had a bit of a fight over Zaphod. I mean, fists, feet, hair pulling and a tumble on the floor before he separated them. Amber was due some time with the doc and Qiu walked in just as they were about to couple. Seems Qiu took off her wraparound, elbowed Amber out the way and tried to drag Zaphod on to the bench with her. Normally, Amber would've dealt with it sensibly. But, to be honest, I'd just rejected her. I mean, that incident on the trip back with Chang. It's hard for me to deal with. Men rescue women, not the other frickin' way round.

Yeah. Okay. I know. Old fashioned. Macho, stone-age man; I get all that. But it's still in here. Can't deny how I'm made. Amber saving my life makes me less of a man with her. It'll take something special to change that back to how it should be, that's all I'm saying.

Anyway, we're now in a quandary about what to do with Qiu. Tu and Zaphod think we should let the women deal with it.

'It's their domain, Georgiy. They know best how they feel and what they need to do. It'll make things worse if we interfere. Leave them to it, eh?'

Zaphod's right. I know he is. But I still feel partly responsible. I tell you, sometimes I can see why those religious types keep their women under the thumb. Makes life a lot simpler. Well, simpler for men. I know, I know! Irrational outdated thinking. But the fact of the matter is I hate discord, and I especially hate it when the women aren't happy. Can't help it. It's the way I am.

'Leave it, Georgiy. Get involved and you'll only make it worse. They'll sort themselves out far better left alone to deal with it.'

Tu had a point. I agreed with him. But I couldn't just let this rankle. Had to do something.

Yes. It was a mistake. I admit it. Probably made matters worse.

Anyway, I gathered all the women in Recroom. Didn't tell the other men: left them out of it. I made Qiu and Amber face each other and explain their actions to the rest and each other. That way, I thought, we'd clear the air and could get on with the important stuff.

Wrong!

Seems Qiu's the jealous type. Wants Zaphod for herself. Now she's experienced sex with a man she wants more and she wants it with

Zaphod. He wasn't there, so I spoke on his behalf. Explained there are only four of us and we have to share ourselves among the women, including those who haven't opened up yet. 'You will.' I said, 'Once you've ditched your old-fashioned ideas and got rid of the guilt your god dumped on you.'

Another mistake. Never understood why people are so attached to their faith. I mean, they're demonstrably wrong and mad ideas. How can anyone believe something when there's no evidence for it? Any case, all these religions are frickin' full of contradictions. Faith's just about choosing which bits of so-called sacred texts you decide to believe and then ignoring the rest. A recipe for madness. Bloody stupid. And I told them so.

Amber frickin' saved me again. Bundled me out of the room before the Chinese women scratched my eyes out. I tell you, that was some fierce protest. They'd have torn me limb from limb if Amber hadn't got me out. And, like the frickin' idiot I am, did I thank her? Of course I didn't. I just stormed off and left them to it.

I'm a disaster.

Maddie enters Reppod. She's displaying exotic dancers on her top and skirt, but they're caricatures, not sensual beings.

A fool. They'd be better off without me.

'No, Georgiy, we wouldn't.'

Maddie's here. I sense a lecture coming on.

'You know, Georgiy, for a man with an IQ exceeding 200, a well hung cosmonaut, and Marion's own antediluvian macho-man, you can sometimes be surprisingly stupid. Tradition warring with your intellect, is it? Just because Putin and his great-grandson used to ride bare-back and act like gangsters, doesn't mean the Ruskie in you has to run the same track. Look around, see the women here for what we are. Individuals with a common gender. People first and women second. And, yes, we all know religion's a fool's game invented by the powerful in order to keep the flock obedient to the shepherd. Hell! Christ himself used the term 'flock' to describe his followers and called himself the shepherd. If they can't see the logical message in that, are they likely to see the real truth?

'But a fool you ain't! And, no, we wouldn't be better off without you. In fact, we'd be far worse off. So cut the pessimistic self-pitying crap and be in my quarters in an hour for a damn good fuck! Got it?'

Maddie leaves.

Away she goes, swinging those hips and all but flaunting the most tempting tits that ever adorned a woman. And I'm supposed to stay here and concentrate on this report when I know she'll be waiting and wanting me in an hour's time?

Okay.

Penance for my idiocy. I'll write some more and put her out of my mind, if the image of her doesn't put me out of my mind first!

Enough of sex.

The problem. The cable's too short. We don't have the means to manufacture enough extra in the time we have left. Solutions?

There are always solutions. We're all frickin' geniuses. We have the combined brain power of an army of university professors allied to the common sense of the scientist, the courage of the cosmonaut, the tenacity of the pioneer settler and the physical endurance of the athlete. If we can't solve a problem it's insoluble.

Sorry, have to take a break. Brigitte's just appeared at the door and we're not supposed to let anyone other than The Chosen near these reports. Be back once I've dealt with her.

Georgiy exits from the frame. There is a brief period without activity and he then returns. His boxers have taken on a series of mechanical devices marching over an industrial background. This time, he sits on one of the chairs and addresses his words direct to camera.

17:16 – 129.01.01

Back.

Frickin Deimos! It's coincidences like that that make less intelligent, sorry, less rational people, believe in fate and all those other superstitions. What was it I was I thinking about, writing about, when Brigitte interrupted me? Lack of cabling for the laser. And what did she come to see me about? Lack of cabling for the laser.

She's been doing some research, having concluded we've no chance of making the stuff ourselves in the time available. For reasons only clear to the female mind, she looked up detailed files about the aborted Indian mission. Yep. Not only the Chinese, but the Indians were intent on staking a claim here. Both nations were at war at the time, not with each other, and their leaders wanted to deflect their citizens' attention away from conflicts that couldn't be justified. Result? They both did the space job on a shoestring without proper planning. Frickin criminally irresponsible, sending people into space without proper preparation. But we all know what frickin idiots most political leaders are, don't we? Oh, sorry, you don't: except from the history you've read.

Anyway, seems there's some dispute about whether the Indian mission was actually aborted or whether, in fact, it simply failed. Cut a long story short – she gave me all the details she's found legally, and by hacking into files stored on government agency sites stored as backups on the Moon. Her husband gave her access. I didn't ask how. But there's clearly more to that lovely lady than meets the eye. And, let's face it, she's an eyeful already. Oh, sorry, you can't see her. (*Hololink to Brigitte*)

See what I mean?

Anyway, upshot is that the Indian Mars mission, the one the world thought ended up shooting into deep space, may actually have reached Mars. May even have landed! How the frack they kept that secret is beyond me. But they've been a bit obsessive about security because of the war with Pakistan. Seems to be a strong possibility the spacecraft made it here. And the landing site's less than two hundred kilometres away.

She hacked into a survsat, shifted its orbit to cover that part of the planet in more detail. There's definitely something there. Looks like a smallish base. Signs of damage and no indications of life from the intel she's already seen. I had to chastise her for interfering with the satellite but I'll thank her for her great work. Could turn out to be the answer to our problem. Who knows? Missions have to be equipped with cabling for solar power and fusion power plants at a distance from living accommodation.

I told her to try coms. See if she can get a response now we know there might be someone out there. Hell of a long shot, but if they've actually set up their own base, they might have the cable we need. I can't believe the only thing stopping us from defending ourselves is a length of suitable cable! Fuck me! Now we've got those supplies from the Chinese base, we should have enough gear to construct the lasers to weapons grade. Only the power's defeating us. And we can fix that only by using the right cable.

I'll call a meeting later to talk over the whole situation with everybody. We've only got a narrow window to finish our preparations, and we need time to make sure we've got the laser in place on the space elevator in time to blast the shits. Simple maths says we need to raise the laser a hundred kilometres above the surface to give us a range of around twenty-five kilometres to the horizon. We'd prefer more, but we'd need even more cable. And, no matter how good the cable is, we'll lose some power due to length. Compromise. So, we're looking at achieving as much as we can get. At present, we've got enough to take us up to about sixty kilometres, which gives us a horizon at around twenty kilometres. Does that extra five kilometres make much difference? Absolutely. There's a natural break in the mountain range around twenty five kilometres away. Means any convoy would be forced into single file, which makes it easier to pick off the vehicles one at a time. At the twenty kilometre horizon, they'd be able to spread out across the whole field, so there'd be multiple targets. Too great a risk. It's certainly worth the effort of a trip if we can manage it.

So, we need to complete the lasers and ensure their power sources can be connected. We're not weapons engineers. Obviously, we'll continue building the lasers and, if the worst comes to the worst, fire them both from ground level, but that'll add the uncertainty of atmospheric distortion and weakening. And the terrorists with their suicide bombs might just get too close for comfort.

Right. That's me done. I've got a hot invite from Maddie, and no man's going to pass up that delight whilst there's breath in his body and blood in his veins. Well, I'm not, anyway!

Record 52: 03:56-14/09/2074 Buzz, MB2

Working late for the lads doing obs on a new terrestrial type planet they've discovered. Lucky I was; had Brigitte on.

I'd sent a message about the Cult arriving at MMMB1O, as they need to know: they're probably next on the list.

Well, Brigitte says they're convinced they'll be under attack soon, so they're trying to develop weapons in readiness. Talk about coincidence! Never let on I've been looking into it. She wanted to know if we've got any weapons experts here. We're all astrophysics and astronomy scientists. And them from the mining works are techies and grease monkeys, with their crop of sex workers. No one knows about weapons.

But I said I'd find out what I can and get it to her. Made out like it would be difficult and involve all sorts of secret code-breaking; stuff like that. Well, with a woman like Brigitte a man's got to keep her impressed. But I won't waste any time. Soon as the stuff's finished translating, I'll send it. Not letting anything harm my woman.

Brigitte will be proud of me. She'll be well impressed!

Record 53: 19:03-126.01.01 Abdul-Aziz: Terrorist Leader in Space.

The Martian base is ours. We have destroyed their entire means of communicating with the outside. Unfortunately, no communication with our High Command has been possible for some weeks now. In fact, I am convinced none of them continue to live on Earth and they have fulfilled their part of our sacred mission to end all life on that debased and corrupt planet. In any case, I have authority to act as I see fit and I know our duty and what we must do to fulfil it.

Today, I personally executed forty-seven kafir heathen men. Seven I put to the sword, detaching their foul heads from their defiled bodies. Ten I shot with weapons given us in the name of the Almighty from the conflict on Earth. Twenty-nine I placed outside on the planet's surface under the harsh test of the Martian atmosphere. None could summon up the faith to continue their existence. And the last one I personally flogged to death at the punishment post, for he was the most vocal in his denial of our truths. I lashed his heathen flesh two-hundred and fifty seven times before he expired. We gloried in his agony and the heathen men and women were shown a lesson in what it is to disobey and disrespect we who are superior beings.

Between us, we have removed a total of two-hundred and ninety eight men. Seventeen women proved too recalcitrant to be of use. They will beg for deliverance long before we put them outside, where all will expire from lack of faith.

We have now a respectful cache of seventy-seven females to serve and provide delight and pleasure. Some were sullen but a beating explains to them why they must comply.

Record 54: 20:47-134.01.01 Madonna

Maddie is sitting on the edge of the console bench with the displays behind her, her crossed legs are swinging slightly off the floor. Bare feet. Her skirt and top show explorative schematics of droids, both surface and internal.

Maddie's report:

So, to bring you up to speed.

We had the meeting and did further research, using Brigitte's access to secret government files. Useful info! And we've discovered a lot more about the Indian mission. It's hard to understand why a country would want to hide a success like a Mars shot, especially when most others were criticising them for their failure! But we think, well, Jai does, they were scared Pakafghanistan might try to destroy their efforts. As it is, it's from there that the Cult hijacked the mission India put in place in an effort to show they were trying to 'rescue' the failed mission. No one knows why they went to such elaborate lengths to hide it. But the government there had grown more and more paranoid toward the end, so who knows what might have been going on in their minds?

Anyway, I digress. The upshot is we've tried on as many wavelengths as we can to contact them, but got nothing. So we're taking a trip. Now we know there's something to look for, we've used survsats for a more thorough search. We've found what looks like a small colony 187 kilometres to the southwest, in an area where early geologists expected to find another large aquifer.

Brigitte volunteered and, since we can't spare the men, she's taken Qiu with her, and a bunch of droids and mechbots for labour. Qiu thinks she was chosen by lots, but Georgiy rigged it. A useful way of getting her from under Zaphod (pun intended) and lowering the tension her jealousy's been causing.

I've modified headsets for their rovers and they've taken a trailer each and two upgraded droids to control the rest and the mechbots. They've taken three Chinese droids as 'gifts' to ease the hoped transaction. We don't know how many people are there or in what condition. It's odd to think they're here without contact with the rest of the Marsper colony and without anyone knowing. Their colony's fifty odd kilometres to the southeast of the recognised route between us and MMMB1O. It's a surprise we never spotted them, as we've been watching that route. But we've been looking specifically for movement along the surface, so the stationary base could easily be missed, seen merely as an unusual feature rather than the danger movement would've signalled.

There's signs of damage in the higher resolution pics we gathered. Looks like an explosion, which may explain Jai's recent sighting of what he thought was a column of smoke in that direction. No signs of life or movement on the surface. But pics of Marion from the survsats only rarely show signs of outside activity, so that's nothing to go on.

The pair set off four days ago and their nightly reports have them more or less on target for arrival at the base today. Fingers crossed – for the love of iron oxide, there's an anachronism for you! Anyway, let's hope they find life and that the base has enough of the cable we so desperately need. And that they're willing to part with it, of course.

Here, we've persuaded Ying and Lin to explore their natural desires and they've given up their virginity. Both have ditched their long gowns for our loose tops and wraparounds. Ying's is the shortest I've seen and she smiles every time she sees one of the men. It's like she's making up for lost opportunities, which I suppose she must be. Lin's working with Jai, which isn't the best thing for Anni, although she's not the jealous type. Yet another surprise: turns out Lin's qualified in biology and is actually a help around the plant voids.

The Chinese women continue to surprise us with hidden talents. They acted like they were just pretty breeding machines, but all, apart from Jiang, who's a great cook, have some sort of scientific or engineering skill!

Lin's also an expert with poultry and has enhanced our chicken production facility by employing some specific GM knowledge from

China. Given a few more days, we should be able to produce enough eggs to actually eat some instead of allowing them all to produce new chicks. It's still odd seeing wingless fowl wandering around on four legs. They look obscenely naked without feathers. Makes me wonder: why do I have such an odd reaction to avian nudity when I'm all in favour of it with people? Some inherited memory from religious forebears, no doubt. Still, their meat's full of flavour and tender as you could wish. In fact, I'm cooking chicken tonight, with help from Jiang.

Zhen's a real puzzle. She says she wants nothing more than to raise a family. But she's not willing to have sex. Because of the lack of male partners, there's been more girl on girl than most of us want, and she's happy enough to engage with us for that sort of pleasure. But she's adamant she won't let a man penetrate her until she's married. That's never going to happen. Marriage was never an option for The Chosen, and the only available men are Chosen, so she's either going to have to go without forever or change her views.

Signs of chinks in the armour of some of the Chinese women (sorry, pun completely unintended!) are more evident in some than others. Jiang renounced her faith almost at once. She's a lot less stressed now she no longer has to serve that cretin, Chang.

Her attitude to her rape and abuse has shielded her from inevitable psychological damage that could otherwise have destroyed her. It's a cultural idea I can't get my head round, but she really doesn't seem to feel abused. More cheated out of her freedom to decide which man she takes to her bed. Now she's got a choice, she's having sex with all the men as often as she can, which is pretty often. She's as active as the rest of us anyway. Zaphod says there's a possibility it's denial re-inforcement. But even he thinks it might simply be that her culture and indoctrination make her look at the whole thing in a different way. It's so alien to us. But we're all keeping a watch on her, in case she becomes disturbed. Maybe she is just rejecting those shackles she was brought up with, rebelling like a teenager. Let's hope so.

I saw her dancing in the corridor the other day, completely uninhibited and joyful in her movement to some music from way back. It was Polonium Rides Again singing You Conquered My Move; great song! I had to join in with her and we laughed and danced together until, eventually, Zaphod arrived on his way somewhere and joined in. He's a mover. It was great to just dance; a real change from the tensions of our drive to sort out this weapon of defence. Of course, it ended in the inevitable when Jiang dragged him off to her new quarters. I say, dragged, but he went willingly enough. I confess, I was just a bit envious, but, hell, poor woman deserves some real happiness now she's free.

Our two volunteers should reach the Indian base very soon. It's all unknown territory, but our satnav and the survsat give a good idea what to expect. They're keeping in constant contact and so far all is going well. No accidents or disasters. They did see an unusual outcrop at one point and Qiu took samples. Initial analysis on-board looks like it's bauxite with a good proportion of titanium oxide, so a worthwhile find for the future, even if the rest of the trip turns out to be wasted.

Sorry, called away to look at a droid that's been badly damaged in an accident with one of the big mechbots. They can be buggers to work with; their sensors are less subtle than the droids' and they move so fast sometimes. Anyway, I'll continue this report when I'm free again.

Record 55: 21:15-18/09/2074 Buzz, MB2

Fuck me! Stuff they've been developing … I tell you, those are some pretty sick minds. Ignoring most of the more … imaginative … stuff and concentrating on laser technology, as that's what they need. Any case, the rest of the stuff I've found is so advanced, and designed for mass destruction, it's no use to them. I've got the search engine extracting everything on lasers. Big search, so it'll take a while. Get it off to them as soon as it's done.

Record 56: 23:17-134.01.01 Jannine from MMMB1O

We've got to keep away from our men. They've threatened to castrate anyone what so much as looks at us. Issued orders to the men to sort a mission for that new base over the other side. Them high-fallutin clever clogs are supposed to be settin' up some sort of ... Utopia, yeah, that's it. As if! They're goin to go out there and blow the poor buggers to Hell and damnation. Still, they do say none of that lot believe in God or Heaven, so who knows where their souls will end up?

All the same, we don't want the shits to hurt our fellow Martians, so we sort of messed up their plans a bit. It were dangerous. But we delayed their start by a few days. And Privates, who's got the biggest cock I've ever seen – too big even for my frontie – somehow managed to put one of the coms dishes back in place. Can't move it, mind, so we can only send and receive twice a day, when we're in line with one what feeds our signals to the Asteroid Belt. Managed to let them know what's happenin. Course, the frackin shits found what we'd done. Someone said one of the converts grassed. They cut off Privates' head in front of us all so we'd know what would happen if anyone else tried anythin on. Didn't stop some of the boys sortin the grass, though.

Record 57: 01:39-19/09/2074 Abdul-Aziz: Terrorist Leader in Space.

It came to my notice that some converted men who pretended to the faith have been obstructing plans for our mission to the far base, where the ones they call 'superbeings' live in palaces of plenty and excess. We questioned enough traitors to find a core of fifteen who have been acting against us.

We publicly flogged, and burned them with hot metal, and they screamed like women, so we unmanned them and then stoned them to death, in the way we deal with false women, since these are clearly not men in the eyes of the Almighty. The rest now know the consequences of such disobedience and are fully committed. They have declared themselves servants to the true way, bowing and praying to the Almighty as is proper and right. There were two women who also were persuaded by the traitors to act against our cause. Both were dealt with in an appropriate manner until they expired. Such is the fate of those who are false.

Record 58: 21:23-19/09/2074 Buzz, MB2

Brigitte's not there. They say she volunteered for some mad trip to find that Indian mission everyone knows frackin' crashed on arrival. Why? And why'd they let her go for no frackin' reason? I'd already sent them the data but if I'd known before, I wouldn't have! Stupid bastards; risking my wife's life! Well, they'll get no more from me. She'd better be safe, that's all I can frackin' say.

Can't believe it. Two women alone on the surface when those Cult shits are loose there. What are they thinking? If I was there, this would never of happened. I'd never let her go on such a dangerous trip. No man would let a woman do that.

But I'm not. Can't be, yet. Soon, maybe. Then I'll give the stupid bastards a piece of my mind!

We're well on with modifications of the ore carrier to take passengers to Mars. Onward trips to Earth have stopped, so we've got a couple that were in the system, waiting. No structure to deal with trade here or on Mars now, so we commandeered them.

Tugs that tow the trains are a bit more sophisticated; take about ten technicians for transport to and from for things like leave and re-organisation. But even they're really built for profit, so life support's pretty basic.

We need to transport up to five60 individuals, so we're converting this first carrier to hold one80. Once it's fitted out, we'll test it with volunteers and then start on the next two. With the capacity in the tugs, we should just have enough to take everyone. We're making some life support stuff on site, using 3D printers for parts we used to get from Earth.

I wish the buggers would get the job done so I can get to Mars. Brigitte! My Brigitte, is she safe? Shit, I can't sleep now, not knowing. But the comsat's out of range at the moment. I'll have to wait to get another message to Mars. Get on with some work to keep me occupied.

Record 59: 11:56-137.01.01 Tu

Tu sits at the consoles. He rests his chin on his hands, elbows on the bench. Music plays in the background – I recognise it as Drowning on the Mountains, by Jehovah's Child; a pretty cool track for something recorded so long ago!

Tu's report:

Catching a brief moment before lunch. I've left Lin working on modifications to the beef production unit. She's got a real feel for that work and I prefer to work with plants, so we make a pretty good team. I'm letting her deal with the protein side of things; helps her feel like one of the community.

Anyway, my reason for this report is activity at the Indian base. Yes, it is the Indian base, so rumours and our research proved correct. Brigitte and Qiu reached the place yesterday and found it like a disaster site. There's been a huge explosion and they started searching for signs of life. But they're weren't too hopeful, given the devastation.

Brigitte sent a full report, and it makes sense to include it here, since no one but The Chosen can access this recording facility. I've forwarded a copy to Buzz, as I gather he was a bit annoyed Brigitte had gone.

163

Brigitte's report:

We arrived mid morning. There's stuff scattered over a wide area. Looks like the result of an explosion. Loads of damage above ground. We started searching for the airlock but couldn't find it at first. Qiu started at the eastern end and I took the west, both of us with droids and mechbots as a team going over the ground and shifting rubbish where it looked like it might obscure something. Qiu first found signs of possible life. The airlock was almost completely buried in metal fragments and lumps of rock all mixed with dust. It took a while for the mechbots to clear it away, but we found the entrance. The control was damaged but I worked on it with a droid till we got it working.

I went in first with the same droid. Tested the atmosphere. It was a bit smelly, but fine. I called Qiu and we waited until the cleaners had dealt with the dust.

It was pretty dark down there. Looked like only emergency power was working; a strange blue light that makes it hard to see detail. We decided to stick together, as we were going into the unknown and no one responded to our coms. First room we found looked like a horror film. Blood everywhere. But no bodies. It stank of gore and Qiu was sick. It took me all my time not to throw up. We tried the next rooms and found five personal quarters empty. Personal effects all there, like the people expected to come back to them.

We called out, hoping anyone alive would hear us. Without our skintights from the surface, we felt a bit vulnerable. Not knowing who we might find and what they might feel about meeting us wearing our rover skintights, especially after what Jai said about some Indian customs. It was unnerving, to tell the truth, and we were jumpy.

Qiu reached for my hand and I was happy to have the contact. It seemed to get darker the further we got inside. Glad we had droids with us. They used their illuminators to give us more light when it grew too dark to define anything. We passed the kitchen area and found uneaten food on the counter. Looked okay; not rotten or anything. Next we found their Recroom. Empty. Didn't look as though it had been used recently, but a big screen was flickering on and off, making the place really eerie. The flickering shadows felt full of unseen threats. We got out of there quickly and examined the rest of the living area. Nothing and no one.

It was cool down there, standard underground temperature, so not too cold to bear. We decided to look at their production areas, in case anyone was left alive. But we weren't hopeful. First area we entered was stinking: their protein plant looked to have no power and the meat had died from lack of heat and food. Smelt terrible and we left there as soon as we'd called out to make sure there was no one living. Next was their mech area. Nothing living there, but we found a huge stock of cabling of various types in the store. We're going back to examine that later. Looks promising.

The horticultural area was last. Felt a bit warmer and there was a slight hum of ventilators and pumps. It's a huge place, with a great variety of plant life, some of it several metres tall.

It was there we found them. Two men, both in a bad way. One had burns and the other looked ill. The one with burns was unconscious but the other one stirred when we came into sight. The look on his face was utter confusion. He tried to get up from the ground but he was too weak. I sent a droid back to our rovers to get med supplies and food so we could see what we could do for them. My med knowledge is only basic but Qiu's good, of course.

She did a diagnosis on the ill one, that's Rakesh (*Hololink to Rakesh*). Seems he's just suffering from starvation and shock. He rallied quite quickly. Akash (*Hololink to Akash*), the other one, Qiu helped by treating his burns with the emergency micropore in the medpac. He's still unconscious, but she fitted a drip-feed and his vital signs are improving.

Rakesh found his voice once Qiu had given him the stimulus and some food.

'Thought I'd died and gone to heaven and you two were angels.'

165

It was such a cliché we both laughed. That seemed to make him a little more confident. We introduced ourselves and explained why we're here, where we're from.

'There's only me and Kash. The rest died of some sickness we must've brought with us, or when the fusion plant blew up. We think that might've been sabotage. Maybe one of our team was a Cult member. He was killed when he went out to the fusion plant and it exploded. We think he did it with one of their suicide bombs.'

We ate together and he explained they'd collected all the bodies they could. Well, in reality, since Kash was badly burned, Rakesh had done it all himself but he's too modest to admit it. We got the droids to organise the mechbots to bury the others on the surface. They were stored in the protein store; one reason for the smell.

Once Rakesh understood our problem and what we need, he directed us to the store we'd seen earlier and the mechbots gathered three great reels of suitable cable and some connectors. We guess from what Rakesh told us there's about six thousand metres there. Should be enough. It's loaded on to the trailers, along with some other stuff we've salvaged. There really isn't much we can bring back with us, but I think Jai might be interested in some of the plants.

We're not equipped to carry such stuff, so we're leaving the auto systems, such as they are, to keep the plants as healthy as possible. I disconnected power from the manufacturing facility, and repaired and reconnected the supply from the solar sheets. That had been blasted out by the fusion plant explosion, which is why they had almost no power when we arrived.

We're giving Kash another day to recover a bit more, as he's still very ill. Then we'll set off back home with the stuff, and our two new men. Rakesh was a bit weak to begin with but food and Qiu's excellent care has restored him somewhat. In fact, he showed an interest in Qiu she was happy to indulge. We've moved out of the horticultural space into private quarters, now there's power. It should make Kash a little more comfortable and it provides us with privacy when we need it.

Qiu asked him about the mystery illness and their files are attached for Zaphod to examine. He might be able to identify the cause and make sure we don't carry any lethal infection back to Marion. Not much point getting the cable there if we kill everyone with some bug. In fact, I suppose we should really stay here till we know it's safe. There's enough food. And now the solar's working again, the place is comfortable enough. It's Kash we're concerned about. Qiu says he needs skin grafts and she can't do that here, as their medic centre was damaged by the explosion.

I think that's all I need to report for now. Ask Zaphod to get back to us as soon as he can with his results. We'd like to be back at Marion as soon as we can.

That was the end of Brigitte's report.
Tu continues his:

Zaphod's working on the data they sent over. Doesn't look good. First indications are that whatever killed the Indian team wasn't a natural pathogen. He suspects it's another manifestation of the Cult's determination to put an end to all human life. Phobos knows why they think their particular deity would welcome the destruction of something he's supposed to have created. It's bollocks.

Brigitte asked Rakesh about their mission. He told us what he knew. India's Mars project was already in place on the Moon with the spacecraft in orbit, so it wasn't affected by the war, except there were problems with the chain of command. They finally launched a month after us and their flight took longer because of the increasing distance between Earth and Mars. Their landing was okay, and they set up successfully. Then the illness came and they had no way of fighting it, as they couldn't identify the cause. The explosion in the fusion plant was the final straw. They kept quiet on coms because they were worried about an attack by the Cult. Ironic, considering that's what brought disaster anyway. Rakesh is convinced they had a Cult member among

167

the crew and the bastard deliberately let them land on Mars before releasing some sort of virus to cause the illness. Looks like it could still be here to infect us.

We've asked Brigitte to put the cable in the open, uncovered so the atmosphere and solar radiation can work on any bugs that might be contaminating it.

We're not much further on with preparations for the defeat of the coming attack. But construction of the laser's going better now Brigitte's husband has accessed secret weapons research info for us. Georgiy, Maddie and Amber are examining those files so they can get a better idea of exactly what we need to do to make the lasers powerful and reliable. It's a lot more complicated than we realised.

Something called 'blooming', caused by vaporisation of surface material on the target, can seriously deflect the power of an aimed laser beam. There are ways of dealing with it, but they're complex and we don't know whether we can make the equipment to counter it. But we're working on the problem. Looks like Buzz could be a real asset for us. Must make sure we keep him sweet.

The construction team's continuing on what we've designed so far, but they're having to make sure there's space for any modifications to deal with this blooming. One way round it might be to use pulses instead of a steady beam. All way beyond me, I'm afraid.

Ah, lunch is ready. I can smell the unmistakable aroma of Jiang's excellent cooking. Making my mouth water. I'll be back after we've eaten.

Record 60: 22:58-21/09/2074 Abdul-Aziz: Terrorist Leader in Space.

We have now completed preparations for the mission to the far base, which we discover is called Marion. Named for a female who first stepped on the planet, I understand, though why they let that happen is unclear. It indicates the moral degradation of those in

168

charge that they glorify a woman in such a way. It is rumoured that women there are treated as equals with men. This is unacceptable and very bad; against everything in the sacred texts. If it proves to be so, we are duty bound to ensure all those women know their true place and serve as required before we end their existence. It is clear no such woman could ever attain the state of perfection necessary to enter Paradise. We must, however, make them understand their wickedness in their failure to learn their rightful place in the world.

We three who now oversee the Cusp have discussed the problem of leaving the base here unguarded. Several converts who showed promise we have allowed to demonstrate their devotion to the faith. Six proved their worth by dealing with disobedient fellow men in ways as harsh as any could expect. They have shown they know the proper place of the women and have been allowed to use them as required. These six men will be protectors of the base in our absence. No member of the Cusp wishes to miss the opportunity to do our proper duty by destroying the special base for which we are bound at dawn tomorrow.

We have equipped ourselves with an industrial laser, modified by some converts so it will melt metal structures at a distance. And we permitted some technicians to convert three reserve mining machines into guns. Their original purpose was to inject explosive charges from a distance. They now fire those charges over longer distances. Our ballistic weapons are ideal for close work and we have our traditional explosive vests, to be worn by six converts when we make the final attack. If we were greater in numbers, we would, of course, accept the honour to be martyred by wearing and exploding these vests ourselves. But we are too few to indulge in such sacrifice. Perhaps, at the end of our trials for the Almighty we may permit ourselves this greatest of all honours.

There are now twenty-seven members of the Cusp still existing. We have lost two of our original number. One disappeared without trace and we have no knowledge of his whereabouts or his fate. It is a sad loss as he was a particularly strict user of the women and always left them wailing after he had taken his pleasure. But we have had no sign of his being anywhere here and believe he has performed some unknown sacred task and been rewarded with instant transport to Paradise. The other lost member I would rather not describe here, but feel I must. He was discovered lying with another man! One of the converts. They were naked and joined as a man may join with a woman but with his part in the man's basal orifice. It is the greatest sin and we dealt with them in private so that no others may be stained with their vileness. It is enough to record they both ended this life in agony and dread and will never know the joy of Paradise.

So, each of the pressurised rovers will contain nine of us and two converts with their bombs. We have dedicated droids programmed with directional guides to drive the vehicles. And we have seven large earth-moving vehicles, three of them great heavy dozers to crush and flatten obstructions. These each have a dedicated droid driver and a large mechbot to act as mechanical aid should we need such help.

We have supplies of food and water to last the expected duration of the journey and our return, since we expect to destroy the enemy base and therefore will be unable to top up our needs in those commodities. Our food is basic but wholesome; a small price to pay for the glory of fulfilling our duty.

I tremble with joy at the prospect of setting out in the morning to complete this stage of our sacred mission.

Record 61: 23:11-139.01.01 Zaphod

Zaphod is walking up and down to and from the door to Reppod. He holds his hands at the back of his head, clearly in some form of turmoil. His boxers show an abstract pattern in violent colours, swirling and clashing.

Zaphod's report:

How do you tell someone who's volunteered for a rescue mission that they may die or never be allowed to come home? That's my task with regard to Qiu and Brigitte. And I have to make the same decision about the two men they've rescued, if Kash recovers.

I think I've identified the cause of the infection at the Indian base. Without actual samples, I can't be absolutely certain, but the docs Brigitte sent over give most of the info I need to come to a pretty clear conclusion. Not a virus, but a man-made bacterium based on e-coli, modified to make it rapid in spread and incredibly virulent in those unable to fight it. I'm guessing it was stolen from some government biological warfare lab by a member of the Cult. From the DNA and body fluids I have on record for both our women, one appears susceptible and the other may be capable of being a carrier. Until I can discover an antibiotic, I daren't let any potential carrier back into our base. In fact, until I've found a way of eradicating it from living tissue, I daren't allow any of them back here. The risks are too great.

For the time being, I've organised a temporary shelter above ground, in one of the original inflatables we used when we landed. It's complete with airlock, dedicated water and air supply and a store of food to last the four of them for a full Mars quarter. Mechbots are currently constructing a geodetic anti-radiation dome to make the occupants safe from that danger as well during an extended stay, if that turns out to be necessary. We've placed it effectively 'behind' our other external buildings so they won't be in the line of fire when the Cult start their attack. It'll take about seven days to complete and I've made sure it's big enough for all four of them, though my instincts tell me one of the women won't live long enough to make that journey.

Once they arrive, I'll organise a droid to take samples from the men, to see what allowed them to fight infection. I can then apply that resistance to the rest of us and build it into our DNA to protect us and our future children. The pathogen may be short lived or eternal. I've no notion at present, though I'm conducting tests through a model I've set up on the computer. Whoever manufactured such a bug was clearly insane; but that's par for the course (sorry, old golfing term) (*Hololink to golfing info*) with those involved in the military on Earth. If it was released there, I fear it'll wipe out the majority of any survivors who make it through the climate change shocks. They'll be in poor shape anyway, following the violent storms, lethal winds, warfare and civil riots. Chances for anyone still alive on Earth have to be assumed to be dire indeed.

I haven't publicly identified which of the two women is at risk of death. In fact, I haven't warned any of them of the reality, only that we need to put them in quarantine for a while, until we can identify and defeat the organism they're now carrying. It's dishonest, but I believe it to be the kindest way under the circumstances. There's nothing I can do to prevent the death. And it's cruel in the extreme to warn them of their impending demise when they're likely to last no more than a couple of days anyway. A case where ignorance is definitely bliss.

I've told them about the danger of the pathogen for the rest of us, so they know why they're coming home to quarantine. There's a danger that the bacterium may be immune to external conditions here and survive the journey. That means we'll have to disinfect the cable, and everything else they've brought back that we need to use for our defence. I'm working on that right now. Has to be something strong enough to kill the bacterium, capable of application outside, but not likely to cause harm to those who apply it. Normally, radiation would act as a disinfectant on the surface, but I daren't rely on that with this strain. We'll have to use a droid, probably the one I use for sample collection since I can't risk that one coming into contact with the rest of us. It'll have to stay in quarantine until I've found a solution. I'm no specialist in epidemiology, so I'm working partly in the dark. The data bases on our servers are useful, but they're no substitute for an experienced and intelligent specialist in a situation like this. And time isn't on our side.

We've learned that Kash is a world-class expert on weapons grade laser technology! Typical of our current trend in problems that we find exactly the help we need only to discover we can't make use of it. We daren't risk bringing him into our midst. I'll have to treat his burns remotely, through the same droid I've organised for the samples. It's now also programmed to deal with the delicate surgery. As soon as we have him here, I'll use samples of his skin to grow enough cells to replace the burned sections. The sooner we can heal his physical wounds, the sooner we'll have access to his expertise.

I told Brigitte to set off. But progress is slow. They're having to move gently to avoid further damage to Kash and the large reels of cable are slowing their progress. Estimates are they'll take seven days to return. At least that gives us time to complete their quarters and equip them with everything we can to make them comfortable. Brigitte continues to provide us with details of their journey and the state of her three companions. I hope we don't lose that contact. Qiu's less used to our coms and may not be an ideal link with the party if Brigitte becomes infected with the virus.

Hoshiko arrives. Her clothes reflect her calm state of mind with their serene scene of a lake in a green landscape. Herons and cranes lazily glide across the blue sky.

'You think it's fair to keep them ignorant of their true danger, Zaphod?'

'Sensible and kind. There's nothing anyone can do to physically help them. I'd rather they didn't spend their last days in fear of a painful death.'

'What about honesty?'

'Sometimes we have to tell lies of omission to protect the innocent. I'm not happy about it, Hoshiko, but where's the value in telling them the truth? I'd just be assuaging my conscience regarding our vows of comprehensive honesty. Sometimes, the physician has to be more than just a scientist, as you know.'

'Agreed. I came to you for some personal time. Are you free to share, Zaphod?'

'My rota has Zhen down for the end of tonight, so definitely!'

I've reported all I can for now. I'll return afterwards, if other info comes to light.

Record 62: 10:19-24/09/2074 Buzz, MB2

Some clown called Zaphod's been on – Zaphod! What is he, some fracking fictional character from ancient sci-fi? Claims to be the doctor at Marion. Said he'd come on to reassure me about Brigitte. Says she's fine at the moment. What the frack does that mean: at the moment? I tell you, I'm steaming. They send her out there into danger and then come on and tell me she's fine, 'at the moment'! Claims she volunteered. Yeah. Like hell she did. She was forced. I know these academic types. So-called geniuses with no heart. They blackmailed her into going for them so they didn't have to get their dainty little feet dirty.

This Zaphod character says he's in constant touch with the party. Party? I thought she'd gone with another woman. Says there's four of them on their way back to Marion now. So, I suppose that might be seen as good news in a way. Maybe.

I'll wait to see what the fracker has to say next time he calls. Better be good if they want any more intel from me, that's all!

Record 63: 20:14-141.01.01 Zaphod

Zaphod is hunched over the console, a slim sheaf of printouts in his hands. He's staring at these as the record begins and it is some few minutes before he starts to speak, scratching his head and then looking up at the recording station he's using. His eyes betray his exhaustion but his voice is steady and calm.

174

Zaphod's report:

Sorry for the break. But you'll understand the motivation. A bit longer than initially intended, but I've been working on solutions to important issues.

We must remember to try to give you a picture of everyday life as well as report the troubles we're currently living with. You need to know as much about our reality as possible if you're to form an accurate impression. So, I'll try to include some domestics, as part of your education.

It's evening (well, the time tells you that). We've eaten: a delicious meal of sweet potato, fresh root vegetables and simple roast chicken, followed by fresh fruit salad. The only ingredient missing was wine. But we'll eventually grow and harvest grapes and make wine, I'm sure. We're supposed to stay free of drugs, even the ubiquitous alcohol, because of the dreadful damage they did on Earth. But alcohol's been with mankind from the dawn of civilisation and, as a social lubricant, it has true advantages over other narcotics. Now we have the means to prevent alcoholism, we can afford to risk the occasional episode of overindulgence, so I'm not following that particular prohibition. Cocaine and the opiates, those so-called leisure drugs that ruined so many lives, we can do without, especially since we've developed more effective, non-addictive, painkillers. But the odd glass of wine, scotch, rum or vodka won't go amiss with responsible use.

The enhanced mess is working well, though it seems a little underoccupied with just the current cohort. Still, it'll fill in time, mostly with the arrival of you now reading this, I hope! Everybody else is in Recroom, indulging in much needed entertainment. They're watching a 3Dee; pure escapism to help us relax. I'll join them as soon as I've brought you up to date.

News from the Indian expedition.

As expected, Qiu is ill with the infection. There's nothing I can offer, other than the palliative care they have with them. It seems her death's inevitable. This fracking pathogen introduced by the Cult is intended to be lethal. I can only hope whoever developed it to wipe out humanity fell to its vile destruction and suffered a long and painful death! Sorry. Most unlike the doctor's response, but I can't abide the sort of evil self-indulgence that consists of shedding all humanity in the selfish hope of saving a non-existent immortal soul. It's anathema to me, and, I expect, every decent human being, including you Marspers.

Brigitte's coping with the others, and the recovered Rakesh is at least able to help her with Kash, who's apparently recovered partial consciousness. They're keeping him calm with the medication I suggested. I only hope it lasts the journey, otherwise the poor man's bound to suffer.

Because of the speed they can manage whilst keeping shaking and rattling to a minimum, they've only covered seventeen kilometres today. At that rate, they'll take at least the estimated week to be here. Week: there's an anachronism, for you! (*Hololink to Earth calendar*) Their food and water should last, if they're sensible. Brigitte's a woman with a good head on her shoulders. I still haven't told them the full details of what's involved on their return here. No point giving them anything else to worry about. Anxiety can be a serious drain on energy and morale on the road, and they need all the courage and strength they have just to make the return trip.

To be honest, I'm using this session to take a break from a problem I'm finding very difficult to solve. I need to discover a cure, or at least a treatment, for the bug those evil creatures have infected the Indian base with. And it's proving very difficult. The tragedy is increased by the fact that the best person to help me in this is Qiu, the very person I'm trying to save and the one person I can't have stand by my side to help solve the problem! If she manages to survive, and that's not likely, I'll make damn sure her value is properly understood.

Enough. I think that movie calls with its opportunity to relax me. And then, some passion with one of the wonderful women who surround us, followed by sleep, so my brain can work unimpeded by consciousness in search of a solution. And so I can forget, for a while, the threat of attack by the Cult.

Record 64: 21:10-141.01.01 Jannine from MMMB1O

Took lots of time to get it all sorted for their mission. One of the frackin shits wanted to take some of us with them to be fucked on the road. The one in charge – we call him Fusty 'cos his beard's proper smelly – he said no, so they went without us. But they left some of their converted boys in charge. They say they're comin back to fuck us all before they kill everybody here!

Must be mad to tell us that. I mean, we not got nothin to lose now, have we? So, we sorted ourselves and got the guards away from each other. Amazing what a bloke'll do if a few naked women promise him a treat. Tied the bastards up (oops, sorry about the bad word!) and then got some of the men what hadn't gone bad to shove them outside. This was a bit after the Cult had set off.

After that, we worked out who we could trust and who'd really gone over to the side of the Cult shits. There was about thirty traitors. The other men put them outside. Don't take long to die out there. Nasty, though. I didn't like to look.

So we're back to normal duties. I've got one of me favourites waitin for a good seein to so I'd best stop now.

Record 65: 23:16-25/09/2074 Jeremiah: Soldier of the Almighty.

This short record was amongst a whole batch of what appear to be purely personal notes culled from the many hours of recordings made secretly on the journey of the Cult from MMMB1O to Marion. Most of these are irrelevant, many illiterate or simply incomprehensible, but I've included this one, and a couple of others later in the account, to illustrate the mind-set of foot soldiers of the organisation.

Jeremiah's report

Days are long. Journey is boring. No women are aboard to pleasure us. It's forbidden to pleasure yourself. Tension among the troop confined to such a small space for so many hours with nothing to do. Some men fought each other. No one's been killed but there are some injuries. The troop leader ordered a public flogging to give an example to the rest of us in my rover. I was picked to wield the strap. I marked his skin with seven stripes but he never made a sound. Brave man. The others behaved after that. This sacred mission must not be diverted from our aim. It's too important. Vital.

Record 66: 22:17-147.01.01 Annika

Annika's on her back on the soft sofa in Reppod provided for that purpose. She has an arm behind her head and one knee raised as she looks toward the camera. Her clothes reveal a panorama of the main food hall with Jai appearing from time to time as a natural explorer through the lush growth.

Annika's record:

I'm taking a break at the end of a long day, before I see if Jai's free to share some personal time. In common with most of the rest of the team, I've been working on the lasers. I'm only useful as a go-for in this, as I'm not a mechanical engineer, only a genetic one!

Zaphod's deep in work on the potential solution to the infection problem. I know he's missing Qiu's input on that.

Those bastards!

It's hard for anyone with a civilised attitude to comprehend why they'd do anything so foul to others of their species. But the Cult have proved themselves over decades to be less than human and more criminally lunatic than any other group of extremists. Let's be honest,

178

all religious extremists are sociopaths, but the Cult's definitely the worst of a very bad bunch. I find it hard to hate, but I willingly make an exception when it comes to that lot.

Anyway, to the matter in hand. A belated record to keep you up to date with happenings here.

First, the current situation regarding Zaphod's truly heroic attempts to create some mechanism to defeat the infection. He's isolated the actual pathogen and plotted its DNA. That's given him a clue about how to defeat it. As usual with GM, however, it's not simple. He needs to develop an intervention that'll allow the bacteria to continue to thrive in the host but be inactive. Even better would be to get it to seek out its more virile companions and render them inert or destroy them. Like I say, a complex problem. But he appears to be on the right road, if current tests on lab rats are anything to go by. They're not real rats. We'd no intention of bringing a pest like that to Mars! They're collections, kept alive in a life-support solution, that represent every type of cell in the human body. An excellent research tool, developed by one of the university teams back in England about forty years ago. Oxford, I think. Anyway, they allow comprehensive human experimentation without causing harm to any living creature. And they're really helping Zaphod.

I was in the exercise room earlier, doing my statutory two hours at Earth gravity. Got to keep bone density and muscle mass at peak. Zaphod came in for a break from the task, and to do his own session. He watched me for a while: looked exhausted. I was a bit wicked, made an exhibition to tease him. It worked. We're not supposed to interrupt physical training sessions in the Earthgrav, as it takes a deal of power to maintain it for those periods. But making love in Earth gravity is so different from the Mars version. All of us indulge from time to time. Surely the extra energy expended must count as part of our physical workout?

I was certainly more relaxed after, and Zaphod seemed less stressed. He's a generous lover. Something to do with his concern for others. Hopefully, my intervention helped take his mind off difficult issues for a while.

On that; Brigitte's fine and is utterly unaffected by the infection. Now they've arrived and taken up residence in the inflatable, Zaphod's managed to get a droid to take body samples from them all. That's how he identified and isolated the pathogen. He's using the samples in his tests for the treatment. Much to our amazement and delight, Qiu survived her infection and is now recovering, though slowly. Rakesh is fine, and eager to get out of quarantine so he can make a contribution. Kash is still poorly, but the skin grafts Zaphod managed with stem cells have already taken well. Seems he'll recover fully with few signs of the original burns. But he's still weak. Brigitte and Rakesh are taking turns to nurse him and Qiu.

I feel so sorry for them stuck on the surface with only the basics for survival. But it's the best we can do. We're desperate for Kash to recover enough to apply his expertise to the laser. Time's moving on. We have fewer and fewer days before the terrorists attack. In fact, we're a bit concerned they're continuing to move at the same rapid speed as when they set out. We'd hoped the rough ground might impede their progress a bit more. They've now changed direction slightly to make for the Indian base, which is nearer to their original course than GCC. The fact that they know about it, and can locate it, means they have better navigation aids than we thought. Hopefully, they'll waste enough time at both deserted bases to give us a chance to finish our defences. With luck, their pathogen is still active at the Indian base and will kill the bastards. We're unsure if they carried the bug with them and infected the mining base before they left. If so, the whole lot there could well be dead by now. It's horrible not knowing. We're continuing our defence preparations so we'll be prepared as fully as possible when they arrive.

The extra cabling has been thoroughly blasted with lethal radiation and tests show it's as clean as we need. We're now connecting it. It's a delicate and complex task because, as you'd expect, the Indian connectors are a different type and totally incompatible with ours. That's a hangover from Earth. Manufacturers that should've made basic commonality a priority for convenience of users decided they'd make greater profits if they made all their fittings unique. Fuckin' mad, of course. But that's the result of a society built on profit above social need.

I remember my dad used to go mad every time he needed to replace a part for the plumbing or electrics at home. Always involved a real search for the right make and model to fit what we already had installed. It would really wind him up if that model was no longer made. He'd have to replace the whole of that part of the system. More cost, more wasted resources. Such lunatic waste and all to allow those with wealth and power to retain them. Greed and addiction are terrible, but they were actively encouraged by certain groups on Earth even though their excesses threatened to make the planet uninhabitable. Which is exactly what's happened.

The scramble for escape grew frantic toward the end. Some commercial space operators had plans in place for their crews and most favoured customers. A number decided on the other Moon bases. They were few, but they'll eventually have to move as those colonies become unsustainable. Most opted for one of the three moons of Jupiter. Why? Clever marketing convinced them they'd get more for their 'bucks' out there. In reality, it'll take them years to arrive and they'll find those moons totally unprepared for colonisation. But there's no way back for them. There's a wonderful irony that the system the wealthy put in place is the one that lied to get them to shell out for what turns out to be maybe the biggest scam ever. Good riddance to the lot of them!

Their general consensus was Earth would quickly recover once the population had been decimated by the various catastrophes. But we always knew there's no chance of that happening for centuries. Long ago, we realised the home planet would be hostile to human life for two or three millennia. Maybe even longer, now ice in Antarctica's melted to the rock in enough places to cause further local temperature rises. Along with methane from melting permafrost, it's helping create a runaway effect in climate change. Some even say Earth could go the way of Venus!

Our greatest blessing is that The Guardian, though formed by extremely rich and influential people, represented the rare altruistic side of wealth and power. Men and women who understood the reality of their privilege and decided to do something positive for the human race before it was too late. Their investment and expertise saved us, The Chosen, as a way of ensuring the species continues and may even flourish.

It's why we have our own rules. Why we have no leaders. Why we have no money. Why we don't tolerate dogma. And why we rely on open-minded scientific guidance to direct the way we do things. With the emphasis on 'open-minded'. We're all too well aware how certain scientific disciplines and individuals can become so entrenched they become as inflexible and hidebound as those who stick to a faith.

We exist in an uncertain universe with its own laws, indifferent to life, and we've got to live according to that reality. Otherwise we'll simply repeat the errors and drastic faults of our ancestors on Earth.

So, those of you reading this in my future always be aware of your roots, your history, and the appalling outcome of the greed, selfishness, indifference and partisan attitudes of your forbears. Read your history. Learn it by heart. Let it be always at the root of your decision making process. Only by learning from the past can we avoid its failures and move forward to a better life for all.

Sorry, that became a bit of a diatribe. Had to be said, though. We're all passionate about creating and maintaining a world where all have equal opportunities of social contribution, interaction, enjoyment and fulfilment.

Back to the unpleasant present. As things stand, we've only a few days left to build, deploy and eventually use weapons of destruction. The threat we're fighting wants to put an end to the most daring and creative experiment humankind has ever devised. We're a cooperative, intelligent, creative and loyal group. Against us is a fanatical group determined to destroy all life.

Jai enters Reppod. He stands between Anni and the camera she's using until other cameras automatically engage to include them both from more than one point of view. His boxers portray an exact match for Anni's clothes, continuing the moving panorama. For a moment, he appears transfixed by her. But he sits in the space beside her and she rises to allow him to move until he rests against the end support with her head in his lap. He looks at the displays and receives the info she's recorded.

'They're not the only threat, though, Anni.'
She nods. 'I know. I was coming to that.'
His hands play with her hair, shoulders, and upper body as they talk. She stretches up and caresses his flanks.
'Suppose some of them do come here?'
She briefly stops moving her hands. 'Do you think they will?'
'We're the obvious destination for anyone looking for a more permanent home.'
'The ones on their way to Jupiter can't come back, though, can they, Jai?'
'No chance. One way trip to extinction. Be okay for maybe three, four years after they arrive, but then they'll run out of resources. There's not enough out there to keep a colony going. That marketing must've been really something. Talk about being hoist on your own petard. What in the name of Deimos is a petard, Anni? (*Hololink to weapons of England in the Middle Ages*) Oh. Well, now we know.'
'It's the lot on the Moon and the other miners with their floozies here on Mars I'm more worried about. And the gangs on the asteroids. There's some pretty rough types amongst them.'
'It'll come down to survival, I suppose. What we've got here makes

us sustainable. There's nowhere else available. We'll have to adopt and adapt. Makes our dream of Utopia rather redundant. But I don't think we'll have any choice in the end.'

Anni rises and stands. She takes his hands in hers and pulls him upright.

'I don't want to think about that now. It's bad enough we have to kill those others just to survive. I need a diversion, or I'll never sleep, Jai.'

'Me, too!'

They leave Reppod hand in hand.

Record 67: 20:12-148.01.01 Jannine from MMMB1O

Jannine is at a small table, her bare back to the camera. We see small bottles and items of make-up on the surface in front of her. We watch her reflection in the mirror applying this rather obviously to her face as she talks.

Jannine's report:

We got proper organised and we're makin extra weapons. Turns out the manager had some anyway. But they killed him straight off so we never knew till one of the lads bust open the office. Found a locker full of guns. Not enough for all of us, but plenty to kill those frackin shits when they get back. They're learnin us to shoot so we can all help.

I'm in demand. Must be me big tits. And me juicy frontie. Doin it free. Till we sort out what's happenin now Earth's gone quiet. I mean, is anyone down there still alive? Anyway, off out for a meal with Stewey. I'll give him a good fuck after. Never had him before 'cos he never had no money. Now it's free, he's catchin up. Good at it he is an all. Nice to have proper grub again after that crap the Cult shits made us eat.

184

Record 68: 23:10-2/10/2074

Another brief insight into the workings of the minds of soldiers of the Cult. This one appears to have been the leader of one of the groups in a rover. He styles himself a Soldier of the Almighty.

Jawid's report:

Progress is too slow. The larger earth movers achieve only a certain speed, so we have to stick to that. They're all originally from my old homeland in the NUSA, actually from my father's company, though I daren't let the others know. Typical of his crap and degenerate crafts-manship that they're so slow. The journey's taking longer than we hoped, and our food and water supplies could run out before we return to MMMB1O. But that's not important. We'll do what we must. It's the will of the Almighty, as set out in the Holy Texts, and must be completed.

I directed the droid pilot to whip a disobedient man who'd caused a fight. It wouldn't do it. Refused, point blank. I demanded it obey my orders. It said something about the 'Prime Directive', whatever that might be, and I grew angry. I nearly finished the moronic thing but the men reminded me it drives for us. We need it.

So I beat the disobedient man myself. In my anger I lashed him a bit too much. Now there's only twenty-six of us. We buried the body under a thin cover of dust and piled rock this Godforsaken planet calls soil. Why would anyone want to live here? It's a Hell.

A second report was made almost at the same time as that above, this one from the nominal leader of the terrorists.

Abdul-Aziz's report:

Images from the satellite we can access show something man-made

185

off our route. It may have food and water. If there are people there, they must be destroyed anyway. We did not know of this place when we set out. Now we are approaching it. We are ready to destroy and kill all we find. Unless there are women we can first to use for our relief.

Record 69: 21:09-151.01.01 Hoshiko

Hoshiko is seated right on the edge of the comfortable sofa, her bare feet apart and her elbows resting on her knees, her hands holding up her head. Her clothes display flames that appear essentially artificial; a simulation of fire rather than the real thing.

Hoshiko's report:

My turn again, as Zaphod, who should be doing this, is resting after his intense period of research and development, so he can concentrate on properly evaluating the results.

We've reached a point in the construction of the lasers where we really need practical input from Kash. He's recovered enough to move around and can talk again, now Zaphod's repaired the damage the blast did to his mouth. I'm really impressed how our medic controlled the droid to do that remote micro surgery. The operations were difficult and exacting, but Zaphod never lost concentration. He guided the droid's every tiny move using UHD cameras relayed to the screen in his surgery. That droid's now quarantined with the four. It's a Chinese one. At least it can act as a servant for them.

So, Kash is advising, but he can't physically interact with us till Zaphod's tests are complete. If the antibiotic proves effective, we'll release the four of them. It'll be a small risk, but the Cult's getting closer, so time's very short. It's either a tiny chance of further infection, or the strong probability of annihilation.

Zaphod says it'll take a lot more time and experimentation to change our DNA so we can't pass on the infection, even in a dormant form, to our unborn children. That's an issue we'll worry about once we've rid ourselves of the immediate threat.

Rakesh, Qiu and Brigitte are growing more restless with their prolonged confinement, and I don't blame them. We desperately need Kash hands-on to make the modifications. Meantime, Maddie and Sarm are working with Georgiy to make the tools they need to build the components Kash has identified.

Zaphod's medical training is mostly in treatment and surgery to deal with injuries and space-related issues. He's not a research scientist for such complex matters. But, typical of him, he's doing everything he can to solve the problems. He's organised all sorts of safety controls. The mechbots excavated a small lab for him, and the droids made it impervious to all intrusion and escape of biohazards. Zaphod had to work from plans devised on Earth to deal with biological weapons, using info obtained via Brigitte's husband, Buzz. He's proved a real asset and is setting up a link so we can bypass security settings installed by Earth authorities. It's a complex process because of the coding, but he thinks he can manage it. It'll be useful to have full access to all the secret files stored on those servers. We have capacity to transfer yottabytes of data to our memory banks. Excess storage was built in, and our manufacturing plant can make more hardware for the future. Transfer speed's a slight nuisance, but we can deal with very large amounts if we're willing to take the time.

Once Buzz gets us access, it might be best to have him here so we can use his expertise. I know Brigitte would love that. But, as things stand, the Moon bases don't have the means to build a spacecraft from scratch. Everything's assembled there from kits designed and built on Earth. With things the way they are, there'll be no more modules available. Buzz says engineers there are modifying an ore carrier.

Interaction between our two communities will cause tension and difficulties, as the Moon bases weren't set up with the same aims as our exclusive community. What I mean is they have people on the

Moon who profess various faiths. We'd have to vet everyone who wants to transfer to Marion. Fortunately for Brigitte, Buzz is a rational guy. She says he has no superstitions or other hang-ups.

So much will need to be agreed between us. We've different views and attitudes on so many things. There are their commercial interests. Then there's the problem of STIs. We have to consider that if we're to build a proper shared community. Their personnel are from lots of different social groups and states, some of which aren't noted for their concern about such things.

I shared some private time with Zaphod before I started this report. You nearly witnessed that, as he came in here with me.

'Take off your clothes, Hoshiko, and show them what you really look like, how stunningly beautiful you are.'

I did. 'And you.'

He did, too.

Then I remembered. 'Our own children could be watching us, Zaphod. I don't think it's appropriate for them to see us making love, do you?'

'Maybe not.'

We went to his quarters. I left him sleeping. I do love that man.

It's hard to explain, but I don't think we feel sexual jealousy about sharing partners. Sex is an appetite. We share food, so why wouldn't we share sex?

But I have deep and positive feelings for Zaphod I don't experience with other men. I enjoy them all. Variety's good. But there's a real difference between sex with Jai, Tu or Georgiy and making love with Zaphod. With the others it's all sensation, fun, and physical satisfaction. But with Zaphod it's more intense, like sharing our very selves. We connect in a way that doesn't happen with others. I asked him and he feels the same. He actually finds Brigitte the sexiest and really enjoys what he calls their shagging sessions. I have to admit, even though she isn't one of The Chosen, she's got the most amazing body. But he says with me he finds a deeper level of intimacy and connection, something he's willing to call love. It's a profound emotional bond that is more than mere sensation. Wonderful. I hope all of you experience it when you're old enough.

We've declared, for breeding, we want to share with each other first. We all decided from the start; once we're ready to breed, the woman will stay with one man until she's pregnant. Changing partners can obstruct fertility. Different sperm cells fight with each other and stop any of those little wrigglers actually getting to the egg. So we've each chosen the man we want to be the father of our first child. Zaphod for me. Anni wants Jai, Maddie doesn't mind but fancies Georgiy. Amber also wants Georgiy. I hope there's no conflict. Maddie knows it's important for Amber, so maybe she'll have Tu instead. They'd breed one of those mixed race children who often turn out outstandingly beautiful. But it's up to her. In this decision, the men have no say.

Only one couple at a time will try to breed initially, until each has produced a healthy infant. After that, it'll be up to us how often we get pregnant. The non-Chosen women will still have fun with the men. But they won't be allowed to get pregnant until all of us Chosen have completed our first pregnancy. Then they'll choose the man they want to father their child. Now, we have two extra cocks, Rakesh and Kash, to add into the mix. They're both unknowns to most of us at present, though Qiu's had both and Brigitte's spent time with Rakesh. We'll have to see if they make any difference to our choices.

So, that brings you up to date. We all hope Zaphod's work will result in the release of the four trapped on the surface. Then we can finalise the construction of the lasers. They're our only effective option for defence, so have to be as accurate and efficient as possible. We'll have one real chance to destroy the attack before they reach us. We must make it pay, or all these words and images will be just so much wasted data storage.

Record 70: 11:18-152.01.01 Jannine from MMMB1O

Jannine is in bed with the covers up around her neck. She's looking into the camera on her tablet. A discarded item of clothing, red and lacy, can be seen draped over the headboard behind her.

Couple of the lads fixed the coms dishes proper. They even move like they did. So we've told everyone what needs to know. Even sent a message to that lot on t'other side. I saw the vid of them replyin. Right good-lookin bloke. Hot woman behind him. They're like gods, they are. Gonna breed a new sort of human to carry on the race on Mars, they say. I tell you, that bloke can fuck me full of seed anytime he likes.

Ah. Here's Stewey for some more.

The camera moves off Jannine and shows an unsteady angled shot of a short man entering through the open door to the room. He pulls his tee shirt off as he enters and tosses it to cover the tablet and blank the image.

Record 71: 17:35-08/10/2074 Jeremiah: Soldier of the Almighty.

Another pair of reports gleaned from the slightly chaotic record I've been able to access from the terrorists. I've included these two as they demonstrate the fragile nature of life as a member of the group, and their priorities.

Images are lies! Something was but not now. All gone. Rubbish on surface. Underground chambers empty of much. No life support. And dark. We find water. Fill bowsers. Small food stock we take all. No life here. One man say signs on doors Chinese. I beat him for lies. Chinese inferior and cannot to space. He insist he right. I beat again. His body underground. Twenty-five loyal go forward on sacred mission. No women there for our needs. One broke droid very like woman, with all parts. Not able stand. But can lie. We use for pleasure and take.

19:18-08/10/2074 Abdul-Aziz

The men started fighting over who should next use the new female droid. I made a list and told the men to wait their turn. I reminded them of their reward in Paradise where there will be plenty of virgins for all. We must be patient. It will all be worth it. I keep the droid woman in my rover. We are now seven not nine, so we share in pleasure more now.

Record 72: 18:03-155.01.01 Jai

Jai lounges with his bare feet on the console support. His boxers display wild animals prowling through jungle.

Jai's Report:

In a few days we'll know whether we're going to survive or not. Well, we might know. The Cult may take longer to arrive. But they're definitely on the move. After taking over the miners' complex, they could have access to satellites that allow satnav. We don't think they can access our own HD survsats, which means they could have some difficulty actually locating us. We're hoping so, anyway, as it gives us a bit more preparation time.

Rakesh and Kash are both very open and honest about the state of weapons technology in India. Neutron bombs were used during the war with the Pakis over Kashmir. Sorry, that's my ethnic background seeping through. But I've every reason to hate those bastards. The entire country was overrun by extremists decades ago and various factions were encouraged by the extreme government there. India did

191

the world a favour, even if too late in the day, by wiping out the whole merged state of Pakafghanistan. Unfortunately, it didn't rid the world of the different cults, and there's every chance those here on Mars have brought such technology with them. We don't know.

Looks like whoever goes up in the space elevator to operate the laser will have to stay for a while, depending on when the attackers arrive, as they'll need to get rid of them all at a distance. I feel sorry for the pair who go up. It was never intended to be used like that. It'll be cramped and uncomfortable. Food, water and breathable air will all be issues. We're working to ensure the best conditions we can. Haven't decided who's going. But I doubt it'll be me. We need people who know the technology.

On a happier note, as you'll realise, Zaphod's vaccine works. Kash, Rakesh, Qiu and Brigitte have all returned to the fold. Kash went straight to the workshop where we're building the lasers. He's used his expertise to make the modifications. That guy knows his stuff; a dedicated and determined engineer and scientist. The work's now done, or as finished as we can make it. Power units are all connected and ready to be plugged in to the lasers. Tomorrow, we're taking them a few hundred metres from our above ground constructions. We'll connect them up and run tests from ground level. Then we'll take one aloft for further testing, if we have time before our attackers arrive.

As we can't do tests in darkness, we're having a bit of a party tonight to welcome the others back into the fold. That'll be some celebration after their long confinement. And I'll get to talk in person with these two new guys from India. I'm just a little nervous, to be honest. We share a background I escaped as a child, and I worry they may still be wedded to either Hindu or Buddha, or worst of all, Islam! There may be resentment from them about my agnosticism. I'll have to deal with that, as will the rest of the team, in much the same way as we've been working on the Chinese women. A task that's slowly succeeding.

Qiu's been helping Zaphod with the research while in quarantine by sharing her knowledge. With her input, he's worked out what modifications are needed to do the GM on us and protect our future offspring against the Cult's pathogen. That's a bit closer to my area of expertise, so I've contributed some knowledge and help on the Genetic Editing. He's ready to start the actual process and, as always seems to be the way with medical pioneers, he's going to work on himself first, to make sure there are no complications. We don't like it, but he's not going to change his mind. The rest of us will be fixed over the next few days, once he's certain there are no unwelcome side-effects. Computer models and the labrats suggest it should be safe and effective, but there's nothing like real work to convince a scientist a hypothesis is sound enough to be labelled a theory. Then we'll all be safe for the future and you, reading this, will never have to worry about being accidentally infected with the bacterium, should it turn out to survive for so long. All indications are it'll naturally die out over time, once there's no one to either carry it or be infected. But only a lengthy period will tell if that's actually the case.

I'm still working on the surface-growing potatoes, experimenting with traditional hybrids and some GM. I've been testing the DNA of tardigrades, identifying and extracting those elements that allow them to survive so well in extreme conditions. I've finally isolated the necessary components and engineered them into the potato hybrid we prefer for flavour and texture. It's early days yet, but lab specimens are doing well. I've only told Anni; can't keep secrets from her. I'll let the rest know once I'm sure I've succeeded. Bugger! Just realised, they'll all know as soon as they come here to do their next reports. Oh, well.

So, sorry guys. No doubt others are trying to keep things to themselves until they're more certain of outcomes. Such is the nature of scientific experiment, after all.

Anni arrives at this point and sits beside him. Her clothes match his pictorial display. They embrace and kiss.

'So, you're in here, my soulmate and love. Wondered where you'd got to.'

Both turn to face the sofa behind them.

'You're surely not suggesting we use the couch, Jai? I mean, someone might come in and catch us. It's not the same as when we're in the plant halls.'

'I wasn't suggesting ...'

'Can we actually exit the recording, Anni?'

'I don't know.'

We leave the recording at this point as it carries no further relevant info.

Record 73: 20:40-155.01.01 Jannine from MMMB1O

Jannine is lying on top of her bed with a pale pink pillow under her head, her almost black locks spread out around her rather unremarkable face as she holds her tablet above her with the camera pointing down. Her upper torso, visible to the tops of her breasts, suggests she's undressed. The bedclothes beneath her are dishevelled and not particularly clean.

Jannine's report:

We was waitin' on the attack on the posh base. Turns out the Cult shits changed course to a base we never knew was there. Nowt there but a few mounds on the surface.

'Hey! Boris.'

A large man arrives and plonks down beside her, his arm pushed under her neck as she allows the tablet camera to pull further back and show them side by side.

'Finish what you're doin, lass. I can wait.'

'Sure?'

He nods.

She continues.

No one knows what happened. But the lot at, what they call that posh place? Oh, yeah, Marion. God knows why. Anyway, the lot at Marion know about the base. They got some settlers with them now. Mebbie they're not as snobby as we thought. Charlie said he's told Marion the Cult shits are on their way. But they knew anyway.

'Hey, Boris, I can't concentrate on this if you're doin ...'

Record 74: 24:07-155.01.01 Jai

Jai is sprawled on the sofa on his belly, propping his head on his hands. His boxers lie beneath his feet, one of which is raised slightly, waving as he speaks.

Jai's report:

I began this report at 18:03. Anni's beautiful distraction, which I explained to her will now be on record, was a wonderful break from other realities. She wasn't worried about us being recorded. Said it's a great way to educate you in how a man and woman can be when they're in love. And, if I'm brutally honest, the attack's now so imminent we want to take full advantage of every chance to be together, in case we fail.

It's now nearing 24:09, which would really freak out those on Earth. Our day's longer, of course. Anni and I ate after our beautiful session. No one interrupted us, although we were so into each other we may not have noticed!

The others expressed their pleasure at my work on the potatoes and I'm hoping to have a really useful crop of the new variety in the near future. Nutritious, full of flavour, good texture and able to grow outside with some under-regolith irrigation. The other advantage of such cropping is the small, but growing, effect on the atmosphere.

Ultimately, we hope to develop an atmosphere that'll allow us outside without breathing equipment. We want to make it similar to Earth's, but without the damaging proportions of carbon dioxide and methane we're currently using to make a runaway greenhouse effect. We lack fossil fuels, so there won't be the pollutants that caused death and disease on Earth.

Anyway, you want news. The four from the quarantine bubble joined us for a great meal. Rakesh and Kash are as rational as we could hope. Both are from religious backgrounds. Rakesh was raised a Hindu and Kash a Muslim. They'd already seen the stupidity of such superstitions long before they were recruited for the Indian mission. Science is their fascination. Their specialisms are very useful.

Qiu's pleased to be back amongst us and has claimed Zaphod for the night. He's very good with her; the medic's philosophy of doing whatever's best for his patients, I suppose. But her time with the two Indian men has shown her she can have a good time without the good doctor. Brigitte's happy to be with us again. We all thanked her for her sterling efforts on the surface. The success of that mission was largely down to her determination, courage and initiative. She's taking a rest now she's no longer one of only two outlets for the Indian guys. Zaphod's passed them sexually fit for coupling and they've been made offers by other women. They believe they've entered some sort of paradise. Which, in a sense, they have. Our women are very beautiful, including those pioneers who stayed after they'd finished setting us up.

I broached the possibility of colonisation by some from the Moon. Brigitte's the only one who looks on that with great favour. She hopes her husband can be in the first lot to arrive. It's still a distant possibility, but I've no doubt it'll become a reality in time. And then we'll have to deal with the disruption that influx will cause in our small community.

It's a very challenging environment on the Moon. None of the inherent advantages we have. They don't have the natural resources for atmosphere, and many chemical components are missing, so growing food is difficult. They rely on solar mirrors for heat in their cold times and for much of their power. Regular imports from Earth helped them out with certain food basics and more difficult component manufacture. That's ended now, of course.

They're currently putting together the manufacturing capacity to modify ore carriers to transport them here. It'll be some time before they're ready. They'll need our agreement to live here or at MMMB1O, at least to begin with. That's something we'll debate once we've overcome the present danger.

The thought of an invasion of less than perfect specimens into our midst fills us all with dread, to be honest. We're a small group with our own set of rules and a growing number of customs that could easily be damaged by less sensitive and less intelligent people. I don't want to give you the idea these Moon people are brutes, or un-civilised, but we're undeniably a superior form of being. Along with them, will come some from the mines on the asteroids. Some of them are convicted criminals who were given the work as an alternative to prison, so they present a real threat to our way of life. Such is the situation now facing us. Our own form of Eden is under more threat than we could ever have imagined. Yet, I suppose we were always likely to be subject to such disruption. I mean, as soon as the idea of our Mars colony was voiced, those on the Moon and the Asteroid Belt must've considered it an attractive alternative.

Time alone will tell.

I'm finishing for the night. I left Anni in my quarters. I was due to be with one of the pioneer women according to the rota, but I put her off. I want Anni, especially now the Cult convoy is moving so close.

Record 75: 22:19-09/10/2074 Jawid: Soldier of the Almighty

This report from the terrorists shows how their thought processes and impulsive actions sometimes work against their best interests.

Jawid's report:

The leader in our first rover's been corrupted by his sense of power. He's commandeered the only source of pleasure open to us. He's no right to such action and I told him so. My men, loyal and true to the Sacred Cause, backed me up. He threatened to beat me. But I deprived him of his leadership. He's not fit. It didn't take him long to stop his struggle in the thin atmosphere of this unholy planet.

There are now twenty-four of us and I've divided us into equal parties. Six in the lead rover and nine in each of the other two. Each rover will have the woman droid for one day at a time. The six sacrificial men who'll take their explosive vests into the base at Marion aren't true believers so don't count for any privileges. I've devised a rota for the woman droid and the men are now content.

Satellite images showed another base. Not the one they call Marion. I sent the slow dozers off on their own, along the direct route, so they wouldn't slow us down while we checked out the other base. Without them, we can move at very good speed. So much so, that I think we may abandon the heavier equipment completely.

I hoped we might find food and water. Maybe more woman droids. But there was nothing on the ground apart from ruined equipment. Many small burial mounds surround the entrance to underground chambers and a sign showing a death's head was placed there. I read the words, warning of a deadly infection. We had a discussion but, in the end, my wisdom won the day and we left the place without exploring further. Some men thought it might be a trick to fool us into thinking the base was unoccupied. They thought it was the Marion Base. But I've seen the survey satellite pictures and that's a much more extensive base with activity on the surface.

We did find some scraps of potato under a shell of protective material one of the sacrificial men identified as Grapholene. The vegetables are old and dry but we've brought them aboard for if we need extra food later. When we get to Marion, we must preserve some of their buildings until we check their food supplies. That way, our mission needn't end on Mars and we can continue our Sacred Cause to the Asteroid Belt. There are many different places to visit and destroy there and we're a small party with limited means. It'll be good for us to move out and start a new battle once we've finished our work here. Our Almighty will be greatly pleased with our efforts and will reward us fully when we reach Paradise.

I dream of my seventy-two willing virgins all vying for my attention and providing endless pleasure and delight as they serve my every need. Imagine it! Paradise must be the most wonderful place possible.

Record 76: 14:56-11/10/2074 Buzz, MB2

Brigitte says the Cult's moving close now. Wish I could be there with her. Had words with that Zaphod bloke. Seems smarter than I thought. Brigitte says he saved the lives of them they found at a base we thought had never got going.

Her people have modified their weapons with the info I sent. She's really impressed with that. Says they're as prepared as they can be. And this guy from the Indian mission means they've got more hands-on expertise.

Who'd have thought the Indian mission could of made it after all? Everybody was positive they never even made it to the planet. That distraction technique worked on everyone. Hacked the N.U.N. reports and couldn't find anyone apart from the Indians who knew the mission had landed. Even their government's own security files didn't show the outcome.

Very nervous about Brigitte there in Marion. Says she's got the best people to be with in a fight. I know she'll do everything to get through this. Can't wait to be with her again. Shouldn't be long now before the ore carrier's ready. Hope I'm in the first group to go.

Record 77: 23:47-159.01.01 Amber

Amber is leaning cross-legged against the edge of the bench. Her clothes show a parade of male and female catwalk models wearing a range of highly improbable clothes. Music plays as a background to the images and she taps the surface with her fingers in time to the beat. Actually, it's a surprisingly good track, given that it's positively ancient. For the aficionados amongst you, this is Buzz Aldrin's Love Child with Rust on my Heart. I've downloaded it for personal use!

Amber's report:

We've been busy since the last report. Very busy.

Tomorrow, two of our group enter the space elevator with one of the lasers. As is the way with these things, it had to be named. So, it's Captain Marvel, after a comic strip superheroine from way back when. The other's named The Wasp, another female superheroine. I wonder why we name weapons of destruction in the female gender. Surely women are progenitors, carriers of new life, the less aggressive human sex and therefore less likely to kill? But it seems to have been so since the beginning of the paternalistic era and we clearly haven't lost that subliminal influence. Unconsciously sticking to all the crap in the Christians' Bible, the Muslims' Qur'an, and most other frickin texts that tells us women aren't just inferior to men but the root of all evil! We's obviously wicked!

It's taken time, energy, imagination and a lot of skill to put together weapons with enough power to disable the threatened attack. We're all pretty exhausted.

Once Kash could contribute, it made a real difference. Before that, we were working with guesswork and the info we got from the files Buzz accessed. But a man with knowledge and hands-on experience of lasers as weapons, gave us a real chance of building what we need. It's meant manufacturing some components and adapting others from

200

existing equipment, which has temporarily put that stuff out of commission. Let's face it, if we don't defeat this threat everything else is irrelevant anyway.

We finished construction a couple of days ago. We've been on the surface, first testing Captain Marvel for power and accuracy. She's … it's pretty impressive and we've altered the landscape, albeit only slightly and at a distance. But the power's incredible. I've dealt with the raw power of rocket fuel in its many forms, but this light-gun's amazing. To watch it vaporise solid rock in less than a second and blast a deep pit in the side of a mountain is quite something. In fact, once it's done the work we need, we're thinking of using it to open up more caverns underground. It leaves less debris than explosives and certainly makes less noise and dust! Neater finish, too. Might be a problem with residual heat but we can always use a bit of extra warmth. The Wasp proved even more effective. As that one's designed for use on the surface, it's more powerful. It'll be used at close range, since our horizon here is only around 4 kilometres. At that distance, it'll vaporise most metals in less than a second. No chance for anyone occupying a vehicle hit by The Wasp.

Afterwards, we manoeuvred Captain Marvel, which I suspect we'll shorten to 'Marvel' quite quickly, into the space elevator. It takes up a deal of space in there and I'm glad I'm not one of the pair selected to travel with it. That's going to be a pretty intimate few days.

We decided the best combination was a man and a woman. They'll need something to entertain them during the slow ascent and waiting time. Sex is pretty damned good for that. They have to be a pair who enjoy each other's company. We had to avoid using The Chosen for this job. For a start, we're too precious to risk on a mission that might end in death. And, secondly, a duty like this will enhance the status of those who perform it and give them more respect around the place.

Kash volunteered, and who'd refuse that offer? He's such an obvious choice that his selection screamed at us. But which of the women to send? He volunteered to spend time with all the willing women.

Zhen's the only who's excluding herself from that area of activity now. Still clinging to her faith. It's a useful psychological and emotional prop for her, but I'm sure she'll eventually come round. In the end, Kash and Katniss were chosen. Well, they selected themselves. They enjoy each other's company, have great sex, and are attuned in various technical matters that'll be useful when it comes to discharging the laser. I think Katniss may find the confinement a bit difficult, but that's probably true for all of us.

Hoshiko's engineered a new protective skintight for Kash, as his Indian spacesuit was too bulky for the space elevator. We could've used the more distant one, which has greater space, but it's too far from the power sources. The one we're using is really designed primarily for personnel and small item transport. But there's just enough room in the capsule and the facilities are adequate for two crew. Once the attackers come into range from their high viewpoint, they'll have enough time to don their skintights, open the hatches and programme the system to hit their vehicles before any of them come close enough to do us any damage.

We all hope they don't get hurt in the process. They'll be pretty exposed up there, and we've no real idea what weapons the terrorists have. We know they've got explosives, since the mining complex has a huge store for use on the asteroids.

The Asteroid Belt's far too distant to come to the rescue. By reputation, the gang there's a pretty cohesive conglomerate, driven mostly by the promise of profit, but carrying the pioneering spirit that helped open up wild lands back on Earth centuries ago. It must be a real issue for them to know MMMB10 has been invaded and they can't do a thing to help. But they've sent a ship. It'll take a good two years to reach us, though.

The Chinese base attracted the Cult. They then diverted again and went rapidly to the Indian Base. Our vehicle tracks are plain in the regolith there for them to follow! The fact that they found those bases suggests they have access to HD survsats anyway.

Kash speculates the Cult may have brought nuclear weapons with them from Earth. We don't know. We've had no communication from the terrorists. Long ago they learned not to warn of their proposed activity.

Rakesh and Kash both experienced terrestrial nuclear war, and say it's terrifying. But no one really knows about the effects of such explosions here. Our atmosphere's so different, we're definitely dealing with an unknown.

Zhen reluctantly admitted skills in astrophysics and nuclear fission. She won't elaborate. But, with help from Georgiy, she's come up with some calculations. The fallout from the sort of bombs the Cult might have here could spread to a spherical diameter of between three thousand and two hundred and twenty thousand kilometres, depending on the actual power of the bombs.

Fortunately, Mars isn't an easy place for aircraft. We use drones and small entolopters for close survey work, but they have short flight times and limited ranges, and none is able to carry a big load. The only way of delivering such weapons on Mars would be through missiles or rockets fuelled with bipropellant, and we've good reason to believe no such delivery mechanism exists at the mining base.

So far, the images we've had of the convoy shows them travelling in pressurised rovers with trailers and an escort of ground movers piloted by mechbots. These trucks, used for bulldozing the terrain and dumping rubble in craters, are massive, heavy and slow. Latest intel shows they've abandoned the heavy gear completely and are moving forward at the highest possible speed. Doesn't look as though they're stopping overnight. From current progress, we estimate they'll be in range of our high laser in three days.

Katniss and Kash ascend with Marvel first thing tomorrow. It'll take them a day and a half to reach the necessary elevation. There are multiple cameras on-board, so we can be sure both of them remain well, and act as additional eyes and ears for the approach of the attack. We can do a couple of hours obs each and really concentrate so we don't miss anything. That'll give Kash and Katniss chance to relax so they're fully prepared when the time comes to trigger the weapon.

If the Cult continue at their present rate, Katniss and Kash will have a day of waiting once they reach target height. It's going to be a difficult time for all of us. But harder for them, as they'll be responsible for the lives of the rest of us. That's some burden. They're up to it. But all The Chosen feel we should be doing the deed, even though we accept the risk's too great. Our team spirit's really come to the surface in this crisis.

We had a sort of party this evening. Good food. Entertainment in the form of music and dance from myself, Sarm, Kash and Katniss. She's taking the synth version of her guitar up with her; to help occupy her time. Kash is taking his as well! They'll perform duets. Actually, Katniss has a lovely singing voice and Kash isn't too bad. They might come back with new songs. I let the music and mood get to me and stripped to dance in freedom. Not something I'd normally do with an audience, but it felt right; a homage to our joy of freedom. It sparked a mood of frivolity and most of the others joined in.

I made that sound like we had an orgy. No way! We just danced, nothing more. And laughed. The sort of laughter that comes naturally from a release of pent up tension. It was a good way of gaining relaxation so we could all sleep tonight.

In fact, I'm now the only one still up, apart from Daiyu, who's on coms duty. We keep up that habit, even though we only hear from the Moon, and they communicate at specific times dictated by their position relative to Earth and the comsats. Very occasionally, we get a message from the Asteroid Belt.

I hoped to persuade Georgiy to my bed after the dance, but Katniss had a yen for him and I couldn't rob her of what might be her last chance of that. Kash persuaded Brigitte to relax her rules. They had pretty regular sex whilst cooped up in the quarantine pod, and they've taken a fancy to each other.

I don't know when anyone will get to continue this account,

although we're determined to have some record of what could be our last days. Generally speaking, we're dealing well with the threat. It's coming to an end now. Soon, we'll face real danger. We'll deal with it as best we can. At present, we're not thinking beyond that. We're all just hoping for a positive outcome.

For once, many of us have realised, on a personal level, the attraction of praying to a deity. Those with a mind-set dictated by faith, must find prayer a real comfort. Pointless in practice, but it helps them deal with anxiety. We, with our rational attitudes and use of reason and scientific evidence, have no comfort blanket and deal with each crisis in a logical way that makes no concessions to our emotional needs. But I'd rather live with the uncertainty of rational thought than the false hopes promised by dogma based on superstition and arcane ritual.

Still, you'll never be troubled by such considerations if all goes as we hope. There'll be problems to come when new people arrive from the Moon and the Asteroid Belt, but we'll deal with those as they develop. For now, let's get over this ultimate danger.

Record 78: 21:10-14/10/2074 Jawid: Soldier of the Almighty

Marion's now only days away. Tomorrow, we prepare for battle, as there are signs the people there know we're on our way. Satellite images show movement on the surface and some unidentified device taken to their space elevator. We can now see the top part of that Devil's lift, but no capsule as it's too distant yet. There's a natural rocky barrier across our route but a gap will let us through. Looks like a road's being built from Marion in the direction of the base we left behind. It makes sense for them to construct such a road. But we don't understand the reason for a second barrier, close to the base, stretching either side of the road. Bit of a mystery.

One of the sacrificial converts suggested they might've built it to restrict our forward movement. But that's stupid. I beat him a few times for his foolishness.

'You'll get us all killed before you finish your task, with your insane pride and certainty!' he yelled.

I don't allow such insolence. It sets a bad example. I put him outside and he gave up life so easily I know I was right. One less mouth to feed, though we don't give the sacrificial men the same rations we eat. They'll all die at the end of the mission anyway and it'd be a waste of precious food and good water.

Tomorrow, we get ready to fight. So tonight I've taken the woman droid so I'll be calm and ready to lead the men in our Glorious Holy Mission of Righteous Death.

Record 79: 22:12-14/10/2074 Buzz, MB2

First carrier's complete and under test. Had a look inside. Astounding what you can do when you're fighting to survive. Nothing special, but it's equipped with all we need for a safe flight. Accommodation's a bit public; six to a unit and no private washing facilities. At least they've made the heads (toilets for them who don't know) relatively private. All organic matter will be stored to offload on landing so it can be recycled on the surface or in the growing halls. We know the value of recycling.

Starting on conversion of the other two carriers in three days; testing on the first should be done by then. We're gonna use another three to take our useful equipment. And enough inflatables and life support for us when we arrive. Bit of a logistical nightmare. A lot of what we need is being used. Looks like we'll have to upload it in stages, with the last lot here living in very basic conditions until they can go to the carriers. Hope I'm not one of them.

Brigitte sent a brief message. Says she's well and they're ready for the Cult. Wish I could stand with her and join that fight. She'd be so proud when I rescued her from those shits.

Record 80: 09:14-161.01.01 Jannine from MMMB1O

Jannine, sitting on the bed with her knees raised and apart, a light negligee wrapped loosely about her, is resting her elbows on her knees as she talks into the camera on her tablet. A raunchy number, banned on Earth, is playing in the background. For those who care about such things, it's Obscure Galaxy gigging with Between Her Thighs, a track I wouldn't be seen dead with.

Jannine's report:

Last I heard the Cult frackers was gettin close to Marion. Daft frickin' name for a base. No one knows what'll happen. Least we warned them. Mebbie they'll help us if they beat the frackin' shits. We could do with a bit of tech help. Everythin's auto and we lost most of the good techies 'cos the Cult killed them. All we've got left is the labour force and us. Well, whores is always wanted by men wherever they are, aren't we? We're like the reward for their work. They paid us well and we got to keep our money. Better'n that place I worked my ass off on Earth. No pimps nor drug barons here. Every cent my frontie earned went right into me credit account.

Almost had enough for that Lamborghini. But looks like Earth's a goner. Don't want to go back there now. Climate's fracked and there's wars all over the shop. People fightin over water and food and everythin else. Loads of floods and tornadoes and things like that. Everyone says they're probably all dead anyway.

I'll stay here. Take me chances with the miners. Mebbie hook up with one of them god-like men at Marion. They're all real fit. Seen them. Only four. Four cocks with all them hot fronties on offer. And all them women looks happy. Them guys must be fuck machines.

Talkin' of that, here comes Mackahinny. He keeps it up for hours. Always makes me cum least three times. Yeah. I'll do him okay.

Record 81: 18:37-161.01.01 Madonna

Madonna, pacing the area in front of the consoles, wears her clothes with a very fast moving road race shot through the front of a land vehicle on Earth. The terrain is rugged and the vehicle twists and turns alarmingly. Fortunately, she has the accompanying soundtrack turned down low so we hear her words clearly.

Maddie's report:

So, my turn to file a report.

Kash and Katniss are up in the space elevator. They've got coms, of course, and they're making reports, which we'll add here to keep you informed. Really, we've given them that to do as a way of keeping them occupied, so they don't have time to mope whilst they wait for the final moments of action. In reality, we've connected their coms to this system, so everything will be recorded anyway. It'll only be basic audiovis; none of the sophisticated input of PaSe, but it'll give a live feed. It's two days now before the Cult's expected arrival at the horizon from their viewpoint. A delay caused by the Cult's peculiar ritual of a day of prayer before they attack. There'd been rumours of this, but we never expected them to do it here, especially on the surface. But that's the measure of their faith, I suppose. You have to admire their dedication, even if it's misplaced and based on vile beliefs.

Marvel's in position. They ran another test on it earlier (I refuse to refer to the bloody thing as 'she'). Aimed it at Phobos. That lump of rock's twenty-two kilometres wide and around six thousand kilometres from the surface. It's predicted to collide with Mars in around a hundred million years, so anything we can do to reduce its size must be a bonus! The idea was for them to identify a small spot with the long-range sight, train the laser on it and fire to check how accurate they are. Our furthest horizon on the ground is less than five kilometres and they'll be covering a distance nearer twenty-five from the

208

elevator. Our lives depend on this thing working, so it's vital they're accurate.

Results are spot on. They blasted a small hole in the little old moon, exactly where they meant to. So all's looking well for the day of the attack. It's a bugger just sitting waiting, though.

Sarm had a brill idea a few days ago. We sent out our mechbots with heavy moving equipment and they dug trenches, piled up the rubble on the far side of the ditches. Made a barrier about five kilometres wide on the direct line of the Cult's route. They'd already started constructing a rough road that'll eventually end at MMMB1O, and the barrier crosses that so it should look pretty genuine to the Cult. We've left just enough of a gap in the defence ditches to allow one vehicle through at a time. That way, we've more chance of picking off each one in turn, rather than trying to fire on a line of the buggers.

We've identified at least seventeen vehicles, three of them pressurised rovers that'll carry about eight to ten occupants each. The big dozers and grabs, guided by mechbots, are now way behind. We guess they'll have droids with them. Of course, the Prime Directive protects us from any destructive action from robots. There was an idea, way back in the early part of the twenty-first century, that the PD could be overturned by clever coding. But it's now so well encrypted and so intrinsically embedded in the circuits that it's no longer possible to undo it. We know; we tried. All that happens if you attempt to change it is the poor old bot, whatever type, has a system meltdown and ceases to function.

We can still only guess at their attack plan. Could be as many as thirty suicide bombers in those rovers. There's a group of larger vehicles with them, one of which appears to be carrying a biggish device we can't identify. But they have what look like seven heavy guns. We're guessing they've modified directional explosive drills normally used for mining. They pack one hell of a punch. So they're the prime targets, since they could be fired even from over the horizon, not too accurately, but might do some real damage. Rakesh thinks they'll be accurate enough once they reach line of sight to inflict real damage to surface units at our base. The heavy stuff's still progressing but it'll be days before it catches up. No sign of missiles or rockets in the gear they're carting.

Here, we're all in limbo. It's hard to concentrate on certain things when you're facing a death sentence, especially when so much is unknown. We might never have known about this danger if not for those brave souls who alerted us from the Moon. We'd have carried on, blithely ignorant of our impending doom. Those last moments then would've been fraught with terror and pain. We all say a daily thanks to those brave people.

We live with uncertainty as a way of life, because we're strongly agnostic. None of the superstitious crap about some bearded deity in the sky overseeing individual lives and, apparently, destroying them when they fail to come up to his peculiar standards. What a way to live your life. Zhen clings to her faith. But the other Chinese women have seen how we live, the way we are with each other. They've even admitted we're a generally good and generous bunch and they're all seriously questioning or rejecting the dogma they were forced to live by.

So, no real projects being undertaken at present. But we decided to start our rota to determine who's going to have a baby with whom and who's going to be first. Jai and Anni are a no-brainer, of course. They're a married couple in all but name: free-living, as we all are, but definitely a love match and ideal to form a baby. Zaphod's happy with Hoshiko and she's delighted. That left Tu and Georgiy for me and Amber. I fancied Georgiy as the father of my first child. But Amber has her hopes set on our Ruskie and her dreams of a family bond with him are much deeper than mine. My feelings are confined to the pleasure of sex with him.

So I'm spending time with Tu, developing interesting variations on the common theme and finding we've twists and turns in common. Quite adventurous. Rather exciting, in fact. So we're going to be a couple and leave Georgiy free for Amber. She hoped for more enthusiasm from him, but he's a Neanderthal: still thinks it's the man's job to dominate and the woman's to act as subservient vassal. Amber, for all she loves the brute with every cell of her being, isn't about to be his sex slave, or any other sort of slave. So I guess they're going to have to work on that relationship. I've a theory that Georgiy's secretly as much in love with Amber as she is with him. He just doesn't want to admit it, even to himself. Especially to himself!

So, we just had to decide who's going first. Zaphod ruled himself out; he needs to be fully available for the first birth and that would be difficult if it was Hoshiko. Jai and Anni volunteered and we're all happy for them to go ahead. Zaphod's removed her infertility chip because it'll take a good two months for her to return to her natural cycle. God, imagine unregulated periods again. Rather her than me. Mind you, I'll have my turn soon enough. We decided it was okay for them to start the process now, since there's no chance of a pregnancy before we've dealt with the Cult. This way, we might have something new to celebrate when we've settled our future existence. Knowing those two, they'll be in the Eden of their plant caverns copulating like the proverbial and indulging in pleasure at every opportunity.

Tu enters the frame and Maddie moves provocatively.

'Not jealous of them, are you Maddie?'
It's odd, I see him every day clad in those pants that hide very little. There's no disguising the gens waiting for action, especially when he's ready. I love that he's built like a prime athlete, toned and trim with muscle where it belongs, tall as a man should be, skin a lovely shade of bronze and torso devoid of hair, unlike Georgiy. Took me a while to really appreciate Tu's smooth skin, but I prefer it now. Certainly a lot better for the tongue. And he does taste rather delicious.
'Not jealous, Tu. But always ready for some loving.'

211

He's keying now: his chosen method of input. But I can see his words on screen.

'Maddie's skin glows with health and she's the same beautiful shade of honey all over. Under that brief top, magnificent breasts proudly declare their desire for freedom and the short skirt emphasises her firm buttocks. I know every centimetre of her body, know how she responds to my touch, my kiss, my eventual plunge into that inviting cavity she's so ready to share.'

'Stop it, Tu. Unless you're going to do something instead of just talk about it.'

'The couch awaits. It's a matter of seconds to remove my covering. See? Simple as that. And now, yours. But I'd rather watch you reveal your delights.'

I've stopped the report here, for obvious reason. But I wanted to provide evidence of the way their sexual and affectionate activities became substitutes for the obsessive materialism that had earlier been a major cause of the chaos and destruction on Earth. Without money and work related ambition to distract them, The Chosen naturally took to sensual activity to disguise their anxieties and survival worries. Call them abliform if you will, the reality is that people are animals at base.

Record 82: 20:37-15/10/2074 Buzz, MB2

Yeah! This is my last report from the Moon. Been picked for the first carrier and I'm due on the next transport. Was going to take us all at the same time, but decided it made sense to do two or even three trips. Got the tugs, so power units are no problem. Engineers and mechs will go last, once they've done the other conversions. Leaving my quarters for someone else to use till they leave. Had the servers packed up and placed in one of the storage units. Two telescopes are coming, too. Organised the IT for that as well.

They made the changes because we're running out of essentials faster than expected. The fewer people left on the Moon, the better. We're heading for MMMB1O, as they've got spare capacity. Be looking to go to Marion as soon as I can after we land. Should take about 162 sols, with the current location of Mars in relation to the Moon.

Had a last short chat with Brigitte. They're about to engage the Cult, maybe tomorrow! Once we're in the carrier, I won't have chance to contact her till we land. I'll have to beg a coms spell: can't wait all that time to find out if she's okay.

The Moon will be deserted once all three transports leave. Everything for the future of the human race, all the important history, will be housed on Mars, so we're taking what we can. It'll be a longer trip because we're trailing seven carriers. Difficult, too, as we're fairly crowded. Opportunities for stargazing are almost nil. Everything's pretty basic. At least they've organised living quarters for men and women, so there'll be chances for entertainment on the flight.

Right. That's it. Been called. See you on the other side!

Record 83: 23:46-161.01.01 Madonna

Madonna and Tu are together on the sofa, relaxing. They move and replace their clothes, both showing firework displays with a sound-track of classical music. There's tongue-in-cheek humour there. I think I recognise the music as Variations on a Theme by Thomas Tallis, which is one of my dad's favourite pieces. It's very pleasant but I can take or leave it. He says it reminds him of his place of birth.

Maddie and Tu's report:

We're all allowing ourselves to sink into pleasure whenever we can. 'And that was some pleasure, Tu.'

We're conscious each time might be our last. So we treat each other with special consideration. It makes the whole experience rather wonderful.

'Will our frankness and honesty turn them on, our children, Tu?'

'Will it arouse their sexual desires and make them seek a partner? I hope so, once they're old enough to appreciate the emotional and physical pleasures of such delights. They'll experiment. Try various moves and play with one another as they learn what's involved in giving and receiving this ultimate pleasure.'

We hope you'll each find the wonder and satisfaction that a complete and well-executed act of sex gives. And, maybe, if you're lucky, you'll find the real pleasure to be had from loving your partner. We hope so, anyway.

Tu bends and kisses her and leaves Reppod.

He's off to do his stint on coms. I'm free, but I'll need to sleep soon. So, to complete the report I started earlier. Katniss reported back with their activities. Here's what she says:

'Most of you don't know much about the technology, so I'll make this simple. Sorry if I come across as patronising. Not my intention.

'We fired up the gun this morning. Initially all appeared well. But it was soon obvious the heat exchanger was producing more residual heat than expected. The confined space means there's no natural dissipation, so some build-up's to be expected. Our real concern was the potential for distortion caused by excess heat. We tried modifying the refrigerant circuits but only achieved minimal reduction in excess heat. Then Kash had a brilliant idea. We suited up, depressurised the capsule, and opened the hatch we'll use for firing. Space can deal with any amount of excess heat and the equipment quickly settled to its proper working temperature.

'We'll have to operate the gun in the vacuum of space anyway. Now it looks like we'll also have to prime it in a space environment. So, one lesson learned. By the time we'd sorted that out, it was getting late, so we packed up and restored our atmosphere. Stripping off our biosuits had the expected effect, so this report's a little later than intended. But you'll have seen all that on your screens. We're about to eat now. By the way, Kash wants Zhen to know he really appreciates her extra ingredients, which make our otherwise plain food much more palatable. I second those thanks, Zhen. Great idea!

'I'll report again tomorrow. I hope!'

So, vital lessons learned and a real chance of success tomorrow. Tomorrow. What will it bring?

I'll leave this for now and sleep. Fill you in on progress next time. Who knows when that'll be, or what I'll have to tell you, or whether I'll even have the chance to do this ever again?

Record 84: 05:33-162.01.01 Georgiy

Although this is named as Georgiy's, it's more accurately a compilation of his report in Reppod and records taken from various on-site cameras. Where necessary, I've added narrative to make the action clear.

Record:

Okay, let's cut the crap, shall we? This is it.

Georgiy here, just so's you know.

Katniss was on lookout this morning when she first saw the Cult appear on the horizon, moving forward slowly. They're in the open close to the natural gap. Hoshiko was on duty here and watched via the space elevator cameras at the same time. She logged it as 05:24:02. The double sighting's verification enough. Amber's taken over coms now, so Hoshiko can rest for when the bastards get in range of our ground-based defences, if they do!

We checked yesterday with the Moon base and, through them, the Asteroid Belt. They lost their comsats for the Belt because of Cult activity, but they've partly restored coms now. Between them, they've reassured us all movement and activity from the direction of MMMB1O must be the Cult. They either killed or enslaved all legit occupiers there. And the people they left behind have now restored some normality. They've told us they're not leaving the base until they know for certain the Cult's been destroyed. So that gets shot of any doubts about the shits approaching us.

I've tied screens here into streams from the space elevator, so I can see what Katniss and Kash are doing. Nothing at present. I've audio as well, to relay activity as it happens.

Ah, there's Katniss. Looks weary. And Kash. Doesn't look much better. None of us slept well. How could we? They're suiting up now. The skintight biosuits are great protection and pretty manoeuvrable once fitted. Buggers to get on in a hurry.

'Amber here Georgiy. Kash and Katniss are preparing for action. I'll keep you informed as things develop.'

Sorry about that. It's how the link works.

'Yeah. I know. I'm watching, Amber. Only relay anything I can't access, eh?'

Don't want to be interrupted. But it's good to know she's on top of the job.

Katniss is helping Kash first. He's almost completely in, apart from the helmet. Now he's helping Katniss into hers.

Both ready. Takes a few minutes for body heat to make the springs operate so the multiple layers of fabric cling. Not doing an EVA, so they're using hose connections for bodily function protocols. Low gravity means the containers don't weigh much, but they have to make sure they don't tangle the hoses with each other or equipment. Moving's a bit awkward, but you've got to be prepared when you're suited up. No one wants a skintight full of piss or, worse, shit.

Helmets on. They'll tackle the hatch soon as depressurisation's complete. Now 06:17, so they've done pretty well to get ready. Be about thirty-five minutes before they can open the hatch. They're now visible to anyone in the Cult convoy who looks through binos. Nothing we can do while we wait. Kash is checking the laser and Katniss prepping the sights to make sure they can lock-on before firing.

Shit! Kash tripped over his hose. Disconnected? Katniss is looking. It's fine. No sign of a breach. We agreed we wouldn't interfere, but it's tempting as hell to tell him to be more careful. All our lives depend on them getting this right! But it won't help if I dip in with caustic comments. Bite my tongue.

Amber on coms: 'We're now all interconnected with each other and the space elevator. We need quiet unless anyone spots something unusual, so Kash and Katniss can concentrate.'

'Yeah. Thanks, Amber.'

Stating the frickin obvious.

Twiddle thumbs. Whistle tunelessly with impatience. Watch the screens for errors or actions that need correcting. Keep shtum, Georgiy. I'm doing this as much to keep myself occupied as to let you lot know for posterity.

Finally! They're opening two hatches. That takes about four minutes. The tech's pretty good.

Cameras show constant forward movement from the Cult, still approaching abreast. We reckon they're far enough away for the elevated laser to do real damage before they all pass through the gap.

07:00 precisely. They've switched on the laser, warming up the gun. They'll test fire once, well away from the Cult's position, to check integrity, before they try it on the target. Want to make sure the bastards get no warning.

Test firing okay. Seconds pass slowly. Each one a heartbeat. No alarm or action from the Cult.

This could be our last day. But we have to believe we'll do this. We'll succeed. Imagine the party afterwards!

I should tell Amber I love her. I should. I do. It'll be public. Might be the last chance before … and, for all my pretending not to, I have to face facts. I feel more for that woman than for anyone I've known. Should tell her. Kept her at arm's length, even when we're having sex. Best ever! I'm … admit it, terrified of commitment. Always was. Not manly to be in love. Not manly to let feelings dictate actions. It's not what men do. But I can't be dishonest. I love the damn woman. I do. Fuck!

Tell her.

I will.

Tell her. Now!

'Amber?'

The slight background buzz falls to silence.

'Georgiy?' Her voice.

'Look. Soon it might be too … too late. I need you to know. I need to tell you.'

'Spit it out Georgiy. We might all be dead in a few hours.' Jai butting in. Alright for him. He's always been close to Anni. They're like bloody coneys: fucking every hour they can.

'Georgiy?' Amber again.

'Amber. You have to know. I love you.' There. Said it.

Silence.

Shit, she's upset. Doesn't she feel the same? Made a fool of myself. She doesn't feel that way about me after all. Shit! I should … what does a man do when a woman rejects him like that? Publicly. I mean …

Amber enters Reppod.

'Georgiy!'

Bugger me! She's here.

She throws her arms around his neck. They kiss. Kiss again. Embrace as Georgiy stands to hold her.

'Frackin' marvellous!'

'About time, you daft brute.' She kisses him again.

They separate. 'Shouldn't you be on coms?'

She punches his arm. Hard. 'Hoshiko's taken over again, moron!'

She kisses him again. He sits and she sits on the bench, facing him.

Any other time we'd be at it right now. But that'll have to wait. She's staying. Waiting here with me until we have to man the ground defences. Together if we fail. Together if we succeed.

'We'll succeed, Georgiy. I know it.'

07:03 They've sent the first blast.

A hit! One of the outer trucks comes to a halt. For an instant, the vehicle glows red, then white. A small explosion and it's nothing but wrecked metal.

The convoy's still coming.

'Cease your fire! This is an escape mission from the Mining Base.' The voice sounds Indian.

Shit! What now?

Everyone talking at once. Chaos. The convoy's still moving forward. Is it the truth? A lie? The base told us they are all there. This has to be the Cult!

'Jai, Kash, Rakesh; talk to him. Identify him.'

Talking now in a language I don't know. Hindu? Gujarati? Who knows? A rapid exchange. Still plenty of time to blast the bastards if they're not legit. I'm sure they're not. But we need to know for sure.

'Jai, what do you think?'

The others continue to talk in their exclusive language, shutting us out.

Jai comes over. 'I think he's lying. I think he's a Cult extremist trying to convince us he's legit. I think that's what he is. I don't trust him.'

'Kash. Katniss. Blast the bastard into oblivion.'

'But suppose he's telling …?' Kash is full of doubt.

'Can't risk it. Them or us. Simple as that. Blast the shits to hell and back.'

'But he says he's carrying women and …' Kash is still unwilling.

'Katniss. Up to you, gal. Do it. We don't have time for debate. Has to be now. Or you two are in serious danger. That's a laser on top of their truck to the left of the rover. Take it out!'

One camera zooms in to one of the larger vehicles moving beside the rover on the left of the three already through the gap. A weapon's mounted there. Movement. A couple of people in suits working on the machine.

'We're legit! We've escaped the Mining Base. Truly we have.'

'Supposing he's …?' Kash is agonising over it.

The laser atop the rover moves, turning to lock on target.

I call over coms to the convoy, now they've opened up. 'If you're legit, renounce your faith and all its tenets. Call your Almighty a shit and a fraud! Do it. Now!'

Silence. Slight background chatter from those on the ground.

'Now. Or you're history!'

A cry of some sort. Meaningless. Then a second cry, 'Glory and Peace to the Almighty!'

'That's it. Do it! Now!'

Katniss fingers buttons. Another blast. A hit on the truck carrying their laser. It keeps moving. A bright flare. Small explosion. Their machine's nothing but scattered shrapnel. The ejected crew stagger on the ground in flames …

The elevator camera images flicker. Die. Blank screens.

No contact with the elevator.

'Katniss. Come in Katniss.'

Nothing.

'Kash. Kash, come in. Copy?'

Silence.

I try various frequencies in hope one's still operating.

Nothing.

In coms, Hoshiko says nothing there either.

We have to find out if Kash and Katniss are okay.

No intel from their cameras. We're blind to the outcome. All we know is the Cult's laser's dead and they've lost a truck. How fast will they move? What's their strategy when they reach our horizon? How long before they're in sight at ground level?

We must suit up. Get out there. We need to defend our base. Defend our lives.

Record 85: 07:11-16/10/2074 Jeremiah: Soldier of the Almighty.

They devils! Have high weapon melt trucks and bodies. Men die in Martian air. Demons, all! I call retreat till more prepared. Attack complete shock. Infidel ask why God not warn. Is test of faith. Determined to duty. I beat fool question belief. He not speak blasphemy no more. Not allow heresy. He plead soft words. Beg mercy. Say not mean. But I hear words. He insult Almighty and expect not punish? He fool. Dead fool.

One less bomb destroy base. No matter. Member Cusp take place. As first convert fail before. Still six walk bombs destruction heathen pigs. They luxury and insult Almighty their words and actions.

We less fight. But we prevail. We right and God protect. We move forward. Faith do Holy duty we given.

08:17-17/10/2074 Jawid: Soldier of the Almighty

The laser was unexpected. Far more powerful than the one we'd modified for transport here. Ours is destroyed. But not before we got a shot at their tower and hit their weapon. So, we are even now. They have no laser and neither have we.

The men were troubled by the suddenness of the attack. We have regrouped and taken time out. I led the men in another prayer session to build their faith and confidence. Knowing we are in the right makes

221

the difference. I reminded the men that God is on our side. The kafir have no God to defend them. We will obviously prevail.

Tomorrow, we will attack at dawn and they will not be ready! We will prime our guns to take them out on the ground. How dare they attack us this way? We are disciples of the Almighty. We are the Cusp! Do they not know who they deal with? Are they so deluded they believe they can triumph over us? Fools! Demons! The Devil must be with them. But we have the Almighty. We are stronger and we will win this battle.

Tomorrow, we will kill them. Kill them all. And take their special women and show them they are not special at all. Just servants of men along with the rest of their polluted and degenerate gender. We will make the bitches howl as we fuck them. They will beg for mercy and plead with us to let them serve us for the rest of their miserable lives. And we will. We will take the foul bitches on the rest of the glorious journey. Use them every day to show them their place. And they will worship us as their masters, just as they should. I told the men there are plenty of vessels for pleasure at the base. They can take their fill when we are victorious. They all renewed their vows and are now fired up to succeed. Tomorrow! We will win and we will fuck the lot of them!

Record 86: 07:42-162.01.01 Zaphod

Zaphod is in Reppod. Other reports from individuals and automatic recording devices set up both in and outside Marion have been merged with this to make sense of what must have been a somewhat chaotic situation at the time.

Zaphod's report:

I've taken over from Georgiy. He, Brigitte, Rakesh and Maddie are suiting up to visit the space elevator. We've sent a couple of droids to survey the Cult, as we're now blind to their movements. They move

222

quickly, but it'll be at least an hour before we receive any intel from them. Moving at the speed they managed for their journey, the Cult convoy could be on our horizon very soon. Jai, Tu, Anni and Sarm are suiting up to prepare Wasp. Hoshiko and I are on coms here and in Comspod. Jiang's organised food for us all. We've broken out hand weapons for everyone in readiness.

Jiang appears at the door with food. Zaphod invites her inside and she enters rather gingerly, as if it's a mystical space.

'Thanks, Jiang. Hoshiko been ...?'

'I've fed her. You were last, Zaphod. Eat. We all need strength. Zhen and Daiyu have gone to pray for success.' Her shrug says all it can about her feelings on that score.

We're not fighters, warriors. All scientists and peaceful technicians. But our lives are under threat and we'll do our best to defeat this scourge. Maddie contacted our forward mechbots to get them to create small pits and hills out of the regolith to impede their progress as much as possible. It won't make a great difference, but every minute counts if we're to be prepared. The bots will return to base if it looks like they may be attacked. Droids are installing pole-mounted cameras to give us another two kilometres of warning of the approach. Should really have planned that earlier, but we were so focussed on the laser in the elevator, we rather let that blur our vision. Like I said, we're not soldiers here!

Still nothing from the elevator. No coms. Our real concern is for Kash and Katniss.

As well as coms, Hoshiko and I are keeping obs on our horizon, so we're prepared for full action as soon as necessary.

We've got links up and running for everyone, so we can view and hear the parties on the surface. That'll give full audiovis here.

They've just about finished suiting up, Maddie last, with Rakesh helping her fasten up.

Right, they're in the airlock. It'll be a while before they're all out there, so I'll just rest, eat, keep an eye on the horizon scans, and wait till there's something to report.

#

Maddie and Rakesh have taken a rover to the space elevator. Brigitte and Georgiy are touring the main site in a last check for vulnerabilities. I'll stay with them for the moment, as it'll take the other two some minutes to get to the elevator.

#

Maddie and Rakesh are now within visual of the space elevator. The capsule's static, judging by the view from Maddie's headcam. The distance scale's measuring it at twenty four point 3 kilometres. Too high to be reached by any abliform.

Rakesh has his vis on highmag. Scanning the capsule. Angle's pretty oblique, looks like the walls are intact. Can't tell about the side facing the attack, not from this viewpoint. No discernible damage to the underside. There's a hint of smoke from the far side. He's got one of the droids ascending one of the tensors, with a strong tether attached. They can move pretty fast, but it'll be a while before it reaches the capsule. The Cult could be here in moments. No intel yet from the droids we sent out.

#

Tu and the others have Wasp ready and aimed at the spot on the horizon we expect the Cult to appear. No sign of them at the moment. Brigitte and Georgiy are at the elevator, in another rover. The four of them can do nothing till the droid's reached the capsule. Be another few hours. Nothing we can do but wait.

#

No sign of the approaching attack yet. The worry is those guns they're trailing. Fortunately, they can't use them accurately till they're within sight of the base. Even then, the miners from MMMB1O tell us they're only really accurate at about one k and none too reliable even that close. They're not intended for offensive use but as remote tools to excavate slopes on asteroids. But that won't stop those shits from firing them randomly. They won't care what they hit, who they kill.

#

Intel's in from the droids on survey duty. They report the Cult convoy is stationary and the men appear to be outside. They're praying! Bugger me, that faith of theirs must be strong. No sign of further forward movement. The droids will stay on station as long as they can. Their power sources allow around thirty-two hours, so they'll be okay for now. We'll send reliefs as necessary.

And the pole cameras are in place, so we've got sight for another 2 kilometres. The Cult convoy's stopped just inside the gap in the range of hills, spread out again but not moving. Our droids are monitoring from hiding. Their skin camouflage makes them almost impossible to detect.

15:27

The climbing droid's reached the capsule and is trying to gain access. Its headcam gives us its actual view. Oh! No need for the airlock. The quadrants are still open. Not good news for the occupants. It's climbing in.

Oh frack! Kash is a goner. Suit's burned. Skin exposed and blackened. Still and dead. Those bastards!

It's found Katniss. She's under some fallen gear. Lifting that out the way.

'Careful! She's probably injured.'

Suit's intact, as far as we can see. Droid's closing the hatches. Starting pressurising protocol. Gone back to Katniss. Examining her. She's on her face. Back of the suit looks okay.

'Take care turning her. She may have broken bones.'

Slowly moving her on to her back, having cleared the area.

'Take it easy.'

Droid's checking integrity of the suit. Looks okay. But she's been in there too long. Life support's still connected but vital signs very low. Have to wait for full pressurisation before she can be released from the suit and properly examined.

That droid's using the time to repair some electronic damage. The Cult's laser got in a shot at the same time the pulse from Katniss finished it off. Looks like it caught Kash direct and dislodged some equipment from the ceiling. That's what trapped Katniss. It sliced through the edge of a quadrant but the self-healing system's made the seal secure. Starting the descent. Looks to be working normally.

All we can do now is wait to see what she's like once she's out of the suit.

#

Capsule's fully pressurised. The droid's unclipped her helmet. She's breathing. There's a pulse.

'Strip the suit off. Slowly. Carefully. I need to see all of her.'

Katniss is deeply unconscious. No reaction to movement, but her vital signs are improving a bit now she's free. Must be tough, to survive that and spend all those hours in the suit. If she recovers fully, it'll be some sort of ... I was going to say 'miracle', but such things are fiction. Still, we can hope.

I'm programming the droid to make the medical examination and any interventions necessary. It's one of ours, so it's already pro-grammed with the basic info. Just needs a top up to do the complete job.

They're on their way down. It'll be a day or so before they're at ground level. Who knows what the situation will be by then?

Record 87: 10:19-163.01.01

This report, cobbled together from records provided by various sources on site, describes the attack on Marion. I've added narrative to provide a better experience of what actually happened and merged most of the info into a single report, with two notable exceptions, which will be obvious.

The attackers are visible on the horizon, as daylight colours the dark sky. All base personnel are outside, armed with portable pulse guns. Their rovers are out of line of sight and the colonists mostly cluster round the laser they called Wasp. They're a good distance in front of the buildings. A couple of heavy mechbots continue to dig pits and pile rubble beside them, making a direct vehicular approach hazardous. Two droids, one Chinese, arrive swiftly in front of the attackers to join the colonists.

The convoy rumbles forward. A mining gun stops and fires. The charge falls short, but makes a crater to further impede progress.

Rakesh takes the seat at the laser and aims the projector at the truck towing the gun that fired. The cab glows white hot and explodes, scat-tering hot shrapnel over other trucks and a rover.

Another pulse. The gun behind the truck glows red hot. White. Explosive charges stored next to it blow-up in noisy blasts that create a pall of smoke, dust and rocks.

A second gun fires a charge. It explodes quite close to the laser. Lumps of rock and clouds of smoke shower the defenders. A large lump of rock hits one.

'Pull back!' Ying's cry is instantly followed and they drag the laser farther from the convoy. Two pioneer women carry Zhen out of danger, loping across the broken ground, and leave her beside the airlock before returning to the laser group.

Another explosive shot lands some distance from them, making a wide crater.

Rakesh aims the laser and fires again. It blasts one of the rovers. Men inside try to escape. Those not burnt are killed when they explode. Must've been wearing suicide bombs. Nearby vehicles are spattered with debris, flesh and bone.

'Got an idea. Back soon as I can.' Maddie crosses the rough terrain and vanishes through the airlock.

Those inside the two remaining rovers appear to have grasped their danger. The heavier trucks move into place as shields. Rakesh has the laser prepared and fires. It hits a guarding truck moving to protect the rover he was after. The vehicle explodes and briefly flares into flame. Explosive charges near the towed gun burst in a series of bright flashes.

The remaining rovers separate and move toward their target as two attack groups, their accompanying heavy vehicles in front as shields. Rakesh targets another truck but the shot goes wild and only damages a front wheel. The truck's disabled and the others swerve to avoid it. One of the second attacking group's guns fires a charge at the space elevator. It explodes short of its target.

'We have to defend the laser. It's all we've got.' Tu's warning comes as another explosive charge bursts a short way from the group.

Brigitte crouches behind the machine and uses her wristpad to transmit code to their mechbots. They turn as a group and form a wall of defence. Rakesh aims between the mechbots and hits another truck. It bursts into flames, its explosive charges blowing up in a rapid series immediately afterwards.

Abruptly, the two attacking rovers come to a halt. The attackers' trucks suddenly stop moving. The whole convoy is now static, no more than a kilometre distant.

Jawid: Soldier of the Almighty

We regroup. Move forward more cautiously now we know their evil ways. The high laser fires no more. We beat it! It's dead and we live on to fight.

Our trucks move as our shield and their other laser, sited on the ground, can't deal with all our vehicles at once. We must win now. We move forward, closing the distance until we see the men on the ground with their puny weapons in their hands. But they have women with them. Surely not? Their women fight? Unholy, blasphemous heresy. We move for …

We can't move. The droid's stopped driving. I berate it. Tell it to move forward. All our other vehicles are stationary. Nothing moves forward or backward and we're exposed. In the open. I don't understand. What's become of our robots? Why don't they respond to my commands?

Out of the rover before it's destroyed.

Rakesh uses the hiatus to target a truck directly in front of a rover. It blooms into red and white fire. The gun's charges explode together behind it and the rover's exposed. As he aims at the rover, it empties of men. They scatter quickly before the vehicle takes a hit and showers the ground with debris and smoking metal.

An explosive shell lands next to the laser. Rocks and dust rain down on the defenders. Rakesh stumbles as debris hits his helmet. Two others go down.

Sarm takes over the laser controls. Qiu and a pioneer woman organise a team to carry the injured out of danger. The attackers' vehicles stay still. Sarm aims at the truck shielding the remaining rover. Her shot goes wide, but hits the gun behind the neighbouring truck. It disintegrates and its charges explode, blasting dust, rock and shrapnel over the area around it. One of the walking attackers falls. No one goes to his aid.

Sarm adjusts her sights to the back of the rover. Another explosive charge zooms overhead and lands behind the laser. The shockwave and debris unseat Sarm before she can fire. Stunned, she rises unsteadily and retakes her seat. Aims again. Fires. The back of the rover flares into brilliant colours as the metal vaporises. Only two of the men inside escape before flames and heat engulf the rest.

Maddie returns from the base. 'I sent a program shift to their droids and mechbots. They're disabled now. It's just the men we have to deal with.'

That's a game changer. The colonists look out at the attackers. Eight men are scattered over a wide arc. Another two remain on one of the last guns. Sarm aims at that. They fire first and the blast unseats the laser from its wheeled base. Sarm is thrown high and lands some distance away. She lies still.

The attackers reload and shoot at the elevator. That charge lands uncomfortably close. The whole structure shakes, causing its self-defence mechanism to bring the descending capsule to a standstill two hundred metres from the ground.

The Cult members, some of them walking bombs, use the low level cover of rocks and craters, to approach the base. One of them bursts into flame as a defender fires a pulse at him.

Jawid: Soldier of the Almighty

My recording will stop soon. But we'll move forward. One of our bomb carriers made it close to the base but they exploded him before he reached his target. We have two left. One is close to me. I instruct him to move toward the large unit I think houses their power plant. He disobeys me!

'Frack you, Mate. You've lost. I'm surrendering.'

He moves out, starts to remove his belt. I cut him down. He explodes in a ball of fire that does no harm to anything but himself and a Cusp member close by.

We are now just six. One still armed with a bomb. We will prevail. Win. We must!

Amber spots one of the terrorists moving from cover. His movements are hampered by his bulky suit stolen from MMMB1O and his explosive vest. She's never fired a pulsegun in anger. The weapons have limited effective range and shots, relying on high-capacity batteries for their charge. Only ten pulses before a recharge is required. Each colonist has a spare battery, carried in a pouch at the hip. Her short practice time makes her reluctant to fire at long range and she watches her target move clumsily from rock to rock as he approaches the base.

The whole crew are in touch with each other. They've all selected targets so that all six terrorists are covered. Most by more than one colonist.

The terrorists carry ballistic weapons that need no charge and can fire as many rounds as the man carries. Automatic weapons, they're capable of shooting many rounds per second. But they've been adapted for close range and are not accurate at a distance.

Amber, exposed in the open, seeks cover. She crouches behind the damaged laser, waiting for the terrorist to come in range.

Brigitte and six other pioneer women have moved back to the space around the airlock. They're all crouched, weapons held ready.

Maddie and Zaphod are moving their injured into the airlock one at a time. Georgiy's all but hidden in a crater not far from the fallen laser. Annie and Tu are together behind the corner of an inflatable store. They wait with their guns. Qiu recovers Sarm with the help of another pioneer woman and they carry her to Maddie and Zaphod.

Hoshiko suddenly appears behind one of the piles of rocks the mechbots left from their digging. She's very close to the approaching terrorists, who are moving slowly forward as a group. Jiang and Daiyu are a short distance from her, peering out of a crater.

A terrorist dashes across an open space and Hoshiko steps out to fire at him. She misses. He turns his weapon on her. Jiang hits him with a pulse and he goes down, spraying automatic fire wildly into the air as he falls. Hoshiko collapses.

The terrorists see the three women are isolated. They converge on them. Georgiy spots their danger and finds one of the terrorists in the open as he crosses to move closer to his comrades. A single pulse drops the terrorist. But the others are alert. They know they're outnumbered and without proper cover. Georgiy summons others of the colonists to move in, closer to the terrorist group. Hoshiko slithers forward to gather her lost gun. She has another shot. Wounds the terrorist nearest her. He falls and fires his weapon in an arc as he lies on the ground. Bullets spray everywhere and a pioneer woman falls, her leg bleeding profusely. Hoshiko lies unmoving where she last shot.

Ying dashes from cover and uses her pulse gun to finish off the terrorist. She helps the injured pioneer woman stagger to the airlock.

Two terrorists dash from cover and make for the laser and Amber. Distracted by movement, as a couple of pioneer women make for cover, she turns in time to see the terrorists approach. She raises her gun, closes her eyes, and fires. Both terrorists fall. She opens her eyes, blinks. Georgiy, his gun still aimed at the two fallen terrorists, nods at her.

Jawid: Soldier of the Almighty

I wonder. Have we been abandoned by our Almighty? Why doesn't he help in our most important mission? What has gone wrong? All about me, Cusp members die.

I am alone.

This must be the ultimate test of my faith.

I will move forward, fire my weapon as I cross the space. I think I hit one of them. A woman. Yes! She falls. I am victorious! I will finish the task and the world will know how the Cusp ended in …

His final report stops at this point, with what we now know to be a pulse hit on the terrorist leader.

Slowly, colonists emerge from various hiding places. They survey the scene.

'Tu, with me. We need to make sure none of the shits are still alive.' Georgiy moves off. Tu goes with him. They carefully approach each of the fallen in turn.

Most of the colonists make for the airlock. Two stop to pick up the pioneer woman shot by the last terrorist, take her with them. Amber stays above ground, watching Georgiy and Tu until she can be certain they're safe. Brigitte and Qiu move away to the rear of the buildings. They summon a droid to join them. We see one of the rovers driven from there to the space elevator.

Record 88: 15:32-163.01.01 Zaphod

Zaphod, gowned for surgery, is in the custom-built operating theatre with Qiu, Lin and Brigitte, also gowned and masked.

Two parallel surgical tables hold centre stage with a clear sterile screen between. He's at one with Lin. Hoshiko lies on her back, two bullet wounds ravage her abdomen. Qiu is at the other with Brigitte. They have Sarm face down on their table. Her hair has been shaved to reveal a wound at the back of her skull.

The image is silent but for soft interchanges between each surgeon and their acting nurses. Both take some time to complete their procedures, then the patients are removed by droids using stretchers.

20:17 163.01.01

Zaphod, washed clean, and weary, is standing by the consoles, his hands to his face as he tries to ward off exhaustion. He turns as Amber enters, carrying a small tray with two small glasses and a jug of ivory-toned liquid. She places the tray on the bench and then takes Zaphod by his shoulders and directs him to one of the chairs. He sits and she sits beside him. He watches her pour each a glass from the jug. They raise them rather tentatively so they clink and then down the liquid in a single gulp. She pours them another and this one they sip.

Zaphod's report:

'So, how's Katniss?'
He tilts his head to one side and considers before he answers. 'Those suits are designed for a maximum external use of eight hours, assuming life support's fully functioning. Hers was attached to the system in the capsule. Some life support was compromised following the blast. Nothing desperately serious, but temperature control was reduced and the body waste drain was kinked as she fell on top of it. Also, she was unconscious, so without fluid intake for the whole time from explosion to the point the droid reached her. About twelve hours.

'You saw she was a mess when we stripped her. Suffering hypothermia. And some back-up of bodily waste caused minor infections in bladder and bowel, not to say an unpleasant coating on her skin.

'The nanobots have sorted internals. Fuckin' brilliant invention. The rest's down to simple procedures for survival and recovery. No brain damage, and internal organs are recovering to normality. I'm keeping her in an induced coma for now, so her body can concentrate on fully repairing itself. Infection's sorted and bruising's rapidly dispersing after the jab. I've left her under mild UV with IR heating to stimulate healing and bring her slowly back to normal temperature. The cold saved her from brain damage. I'm pretty confident she'll make a full recovery.'

Amber nods. 'Kash?'

'Impossible to help. Dead seconds after the blast, judging from damage to his suit. The head injury from his fall backwards with the force of the blast would've killed him anyway, so he'll have known nothing about it. Brave man. He and Katniss undoubtedly saved us and the base from those insane criminals.'

'I saw four pioneer women brought in. How are they?'

'The tall blonde, Jenny, died from blood loss before we could save her.' He pauses and gathers himself again. 'That bubbly redhead, Mo, nearly lost her left leg, but I think I've saved it. She's otherwise fine. Jo and Helga both have residual concussion but they'll be okay. We're just keeping an eye on them. Scans show no damage.'

'How about Sarm?'

'Tell the truth, I don't know how she got up after the first time she was knocked off the laser. She's a tough one. You'd never think it to look at her, would you? Still, she had deep bruising to her back, bum and thighs. The usual jab's slowly reducing that. One of her kidneys was compromised, but the nanobots cleared the blockages caused by the trauma and signs are good. Qiu made a brilliant job of the head injury. She'll be bald for a while but there's no serious brain damage. I expect her to recover fully.'

'You're going to make me list them all?'

Zaphod shrugs. 'Rakesh had a fractured skull and broken tibia. Both are repaired and he'll only need the sling for a couple of days now the break's properly sealed. Zhen may never fully recover. I'm not convinced her problem's entirely physical. I think she's ambivalent about living now she's lost her faith completely. We need to do some serious counselling to increase her will to live. Maybe ask for Jiang's help with that. But it's a job for all of us. I've got her under obs with one of the droids.'

'Come on, Zaphod. Tell me. What's the situation with Hoshiko?'

He sinks into himself. Reaches for the glass and downs the drink. He holds it out and Amber refills it. He takes a couple of swigs and puts the glass down but picks it back up again at once. He stares into the fluid against the light from the displays. 'Touch and go. The blood loss is easy to deal with now we've got the plant working up to full speed. It's the internal damage. I sent nanobots in but one of the bullets had torn a gaping hole through one fallopian tube and shredded the cervix. I've done what I can with the nanobots but re-structuring an injury like that in such a delicate area's a nightmare. Tell the truth, I can't say yet whether she'll be able to breed.'

He turns away, uses the back of his hand to swipe under his eyes. Amber curls her arm about his shoulders, pulls him close to rest his head on her chest. He sobs silently for a short while until he recovers and sits up straight. Takes another swig and smiles gratitude at her.

'Time, then. We'll have to wait and see.' She sips her drink. 'You and Qiu have done a brilliant job. Who'd have thought she'd turn out to be so gifted? I mean, we all know you're a brilliant medic, but she was supposed to be no more than a brood mare. Damned good job we went to their rescue, eh?'

'And even better that the Chinese women kept their skills and in-telligence to themselves in front of Chang. He was the sort of monster who'd hate that superiority, the type we need to eradicate. I rarely say this, but I'm glad he's dead. He and all those terrorists who have no care for life, no concept of love, no knowledge of joy. We're better off without them.'

'What is love, Zaphod?'

He stares in silence for a moment. 'Love is delight in the joy of the loved one, I suppose.'

She considers this. 'Yes. I like that. It's especially relevant now Georgiy's told me he loves me. Come on, time you slept. Alone, I think. Rest rather than recreation for now.'

'Go to Georgiy, Amber. Enjoy. Tomorrow, we'll begin the clean-up. Tonight's a time for quiet celebration and gratitude for living through the nightmare. I'm going to spend an hour or two at Hoshiko's bedside. Keep her company and hold her hand.'

They walk out of Reppod together.

Annika's reclining on the sofa in Reppod with Jai. They appear utterly relaxed and content.

Annika's report:

'How certain?'

Anni turns to look up into his face. 'Too early for a test to confirm. But a woman knows. I'm certain, Jai.'

'Should we tell the others, or …?'

'Too late. They'll know as soon as they come in here.'

They embrace tenderly and sit up beside each other.

'The first of many. Boy or girl?'

Anni strokes her belly. 'Don't care. Healthy, clever and kind is all I want.'

'Beautiful?'

'If he or she takes after you.'

'After us.'

She stands, recovers discarded clothes from the floor and hands him his. Jai watches her dress. 'We were genetically modified for this mission, with the idea of creating superhumans. I don't think that's right. Do you?'

He follows her lead and dresses. 'We hold The Guardian in high regard. But maybe they were misguided in that respect. A race of superhumans isn't what we need. Humanity progresses and survives because we adapt. We modify our environment, by accident as much as design. Take away that spirit of adventure and the unknown and you reduce the potential for real progress.'

She sits at the consoles and Jai joins her. They link hands.

'If our brush with death means we're coming round to the idea of interbreeding with ordinary humans, that's good. We saw how the pioneer women, how Rakesh and Kash behaved. They were amazing.'

Jai nods his agreement. 'And look at what happened to the ancient Egyptians, the European royal families, when they kept their breeding to a limited gene pool. Madness.'

'If we eight interbreed exclusively, we'll soon start producing congenital idiots. No matter how much we pretend we can engineer the genes, we can't stop natural mutations. And here on Mars, we have a lot more radiation. Who knows what that might do to our DNA?'

'Do you think The Guardian confused the sociopathic nature of leaders with the reality of normal human beings, Jai?'

'Lose the influence of religion, superstition and profit and there's a good chance ordinary people will perform brilliantly.'

'Especially if they're properly educated.'

'Maybe that's our true heritage, Anni. Setting up rationally based education at Marion. A sound basis for future scientific and reasoned thinking. What do you say?'

'Let's get everyone together. Talk about forming a school to educate all the people we'll be accepting from MMMB1O, the Asteroid Belt and the Moon, shall we?'

'The eve of our second quarter. Seems like an auspicious date to begin something new and real. Won't be long before Brigitte's reunited with Buzz. Maybe they can help us fully understand how normal people think?'

They rise together and, holding hands, leave Reppod, their clothes depicting the same scene; a class full of eager students of all ages, deep in study.

Loose ends: 15:27-145.03.49 Acacia Peake

This is the end. These four hundred words are for readers who don't like loose ends. Up to you whether you read it.

First, this is my submission for my Master of Arts from the University of Mars, where I've studied for two years since my eighth birthday.

Disclaimer: if you do calculations on the dates of the reports and records you may find some don't fit exactly. A few originals were in a very poor state and recovery may have distorted dates. Also, given the nature of the recorders, certain reports probably weren't accurately dated in the first place. I've tried to put them in sensible chronological order to help readers follow events.

Info:

CUSP High Command messages were headed with the following warning, exactly as copied:

'All These Communications are
encrypTed restricted to High Command aLone. Anyone who allow it to
fall to Enemy hand will
put to tHe Death in most painful
manner is poSsible.'
(Sic)

All 'reports' from the Cult are either instructions to fighters or historical accounts apparently intended for later use by their High Command. Though what use an organisation identifying itself as a death cult would have for history is hard to imagine. I've included their less insane ramblings (truly!) to throw some light on their motives and methods. They were taken from thousands of pages of documents found via the N.U.N. back-up of the group's servers. I've presented them as found, with only the modifications or corrections needed to turn them into a form of understandable English, but keeping the original tone and carelessness.

Finally, on a personal note, I should explain I'm resident in Marion, at the university. My fantastic grandfather, Zaphod, continues as a medic. My beautiful and brilliant grandmother, Hoshiko, is Professor of Nanotech at the uni. No, there's no nepotism involved in marking my submission; that'll be done by previous students.

Both my parents have loads of half brothers and half sisters, all a mixture of Chosen and normal genes.

As to what happened to the rest of The Chosen, that's a new story. Material for a different book, which I'm going to write once I've completed my PhD. I'm thinking of giving it the title: Generation Mars: Green is the Dust.

Author's Note

If you teach English, didn't read the Intro, are a pedant, or simply feel that language shouldn't be subject to change or modification, please forgive my tampering.

There are words included in this novel that are usually presented in whole, or hyphenated, or as separate words. There are grammatical aspects, in particular 'of' for 'have', that may cause pain.

Do I have a reason, an excuse?

This is a science fiction novel, set in the future. In fact, it's set in the year 2074, a little under sixty years hence. Language is organic; it changes with time and usage and is currently changing more rapidly as a result of text speak and the internet. I've tried to reflect that in the text. But I've also tried to create a balance so readers won't be confused by these alterations to the much-loved medium we call our mother tongue.

So, if you've been offended by these changes, I'm sorry. But I considered such modifications likely over time and I want my novel to reflect as much of the future as I'm able to 'predict'.

Also by Stuart Aken

Published by Fantastic Books Publishing

The Methuselah Strain
http://getBook.at/Methuselah

A Seared Sky – Joinings
http://mybook.to/joinings

A Seared Sky – Partings
http://mybook.to/partings

A Seared Sky – Convergence
http://mybook.to/convergence

Rebirth – Invited contribution to anthology Fusion
http://www.fantasticbooksstore.com/fusion-2500.html

Hybrid Dreams – Invited contribution to anthology Synthesis
(http://www.fantasticbooksstore.com/synthesis.html

About the Author

Stuart Aken lives in the Forest of Dean, Gloucestershire, with his wife, Valerie. Their daughter, Kate, is living and working in Australia at the time of writing.

Stuart writes in multiple genres: 'The story chooses the genre, as it does the proper length. I write the tale that presents itself to me and then try to apply the appropriate label or labels to help readers decide whether or not it's for them.'

He refuses to be pigeonholed and has written a romantic thriller 'Breaking Faith', a science fiction novella 'The Methuselah Strain', an epic fantasy trilogy 'A Seared Sky', three anthologies of short stories in different genres, and has contributed to many others. This work is his latest and he threatens to extend the tale with two further episodes.

You can find his work and further details on his website at http//:stuartaken.net/

He invites you to join him on Twitter @stuartaken, and to like his Facebook Author page at http://www.facebook.com/StuartAken.

www.ingramcontent.com/pod-product-compliance
Lightning Source LLC
Chambersburg PA
CBHW051944220626
47052CB00004B/788